I0699642

Of Mages and Makers

Rel Carroll

First paperback edition July 2025
Cover and map design by My Lan Khuc @laolanart
Book design by RomanSnail LLC
Postcard design by Hannah Brimhall @hannah.b.drawing

ISBN 979-8-9862121-1-1 (ebook)
ISBN 979-8-9862121-2-8 (paperback)
ISBN 979-8-9862121-3-5 (hardback)

www.relcarroll.com

For Nat. My answer is always yes.

Disclaimers

No artificial intelligence (AI) was used in the creation of this work. This book was authored by an actual human. All art and collaborations were between actual humans. RomanSnail LLC strongly opposes loss of humanity in art, the devaluation of art and artistic skills, standardization of technological monopolies, and loss of respect for intellectual property.

This book is an adult fantasy with a mild-spice romance.
For more detailed content warnings to make informed reading choices, please visit our web page at www.relcarroll.com

Beryl Drive
Cerussite Hall
Trolleywood Park
Amphitheater
Magistry
University
Jeweled Palace
Glass District
Tourmaline
Citrine
Parure
Diadem
Jolly Cook Inn
Loupe
Luster
Calct
to Accent Territories
Gallia

They seek her near, they seek her far;
    Over sea and under star,
    They seal the gate and barricades
    To try to catch the Renegade.

They say she sails from Parure skies;
    As the Robin flies, the mage survives.
    And with this hope, the sinner prayed
    For Maker to send the Renegade.

They seek her far, they seek her wide;
    Through vale and over mountainside.
    E'en so the mages have mislaid
    Each trap made for the Renegade.

The people hail and praise her name
    While the evil search for who to blame.
    Yet with each sly disguise arrayed,
    They cannot find the Renegade.

They seek her thither, they seek her yon;
    She flies at dusk and sails at dawn,
    Every snare she will evade
    Our fearless Robin Renegade.

\- Excerpt from *The Renegade*

Chapter One

ART

I HAD ONE GOAL IN LIFE: TO BE AS USELESS AS POSSIBLE.

It was my personal philosophy, my creed, and I had too much money and too little responsibility to behave otherwise.

My father, Mr. Arthur Keays, Sr., had cultivated a vast fortune amongst the working-class merchant cogs, and in consequence, I possessed an unseemly liberal allowance (which enabled me to live near the upper echelons of society), while at the same time an apparent ineptitude (which conveniently allowed me to avoid the appearance of a permanent profession).

On the first morning of the Maker Exhibitions, I needed to be especially careful to avoid the appearance of usefulness.

I arrived at the family townhouse on the fashionable side of Beryl Drive well after breakfast. My modish suit—an emerald and beige bespoke of which I was particularly fond—was rumpled from having spent a good portion of the night in a Gallia gaming hall. I hadn't imbibed . . . much. But the smell of cigars and cheap spirits still overwhelmed my exclusive cologne. I loitered at the back door and flipped through the morning edition of *The Diamond Daily*—noting the published list of missing persons, most of whom were suspected to have conducted magic—before tucking it under my arm.

Quite theatrically, I tripped over the threshold of the servant's entrance and stumbled into the lower hall, accidentally startling one of the housemaids.

She squeaked in surprise. "Sir! It's you! Forgive me, I mean . . . I-I wasn't expecting . . ."

The young girl stammered a bit before I finally took pity on her. "Good morning, er . . . what is your name, again?"

"Martha, sir."

I monitored everyone who entered the household from servants to the members of my mother's various well-to-do-good societies. Martha was the sole caretaker of her younger sister and had come to work for the family just after her fifteenth birthday. I admired her dedication to her work and loyalty to my mum. She would never learn that of course.

I regarded her red-splotched cheeks and tightly braided hair. "Are you new?" I asked.

"No, sir. I've worked for the family near five years." At my silence, she clarified, "I am here most mornings, sir."

"Ah, that would explain it. I hate sunshine. Right then. Carry on!" I ascended the stairs to the ground floor.

Martha called up to me, sounding uncomfortable, "Sir, you might not want to disturb the Missus."

Daweson, the family butler, met me nose-to-nose at the landing. "What's all this? Ah, Mister Arthur . . . *sir*. This is a surprise."

"Morning, Daweson," I said cheerfully.

"Hence the surprise." The old fellow's disdain for me was as cold as the morning rain trickling down the back of my collar. "You certainly do love to keep the staff on our toes, sir."

I handed over the wrinkled newspaper along with my cane and bowler.

Daweson gave the hat a tight-lipped inspection. "This one is new."

"Won that off a posh gem after only two rounds of cards. But don't let me disturb you. I can show myself to the tea room."

"The Missus does not wish to be disturbed—"

"Yes, yes. So I heard." I could practically feel the old fellow's scowl as I waved my arm and sauntered through the tea room doors . . .

And stopped short.

The largest chair was stuffed with a most unusual live specimen: my mother, in a rather primitive state.

Mrs. Hatima Keays (Hattie to her friends) was well-known and well-liked in nearly every social circle from working class cogs to highbred gems. Her influence allowed me to move freely in society, conveniently abetting my reputation as an idle and useless dandy.

In preference to her private boudoir, she'd apparently ensconced herself in the family tea room. Her plump frame was propped sideways with her legs dangling over the chair arm, and her manicured toes peeked past the hem of an oversized dressing gown—a bright patchwork of sari silk. Pink curling rags threaded her dark hair, and a thick mask of something sticky and amber-colored was slathered over her face.

An equally plump pug (who answered to the unfortunate name of Sweetpea-wee) was curled into her lap, snoring loudly.

The tea room itself was bedecked with enough flowers to make even the queen's gardeners jealous. Despite my frequent objections to the design, pansy-patterned fabric attacked every inch of the sofa, and an additional horde of pastel blooms clawed their way up the floor-length window curtains. Carved vines strangled the table legs, and paper of pink and yellow rosebushes suffocated the walls.

I stole a biscuit from the sideboard, cut a path through the rain-forested furniture, and plopped into a chair shaded by a painted screen of pink camellias.

Sweetpea startled awake with a snort. The pug stretched, teetered to a standing position, and licked at the sticky substance on Mum's face.

She didn't appear to notice. She sighed over the printed pages of her latest romantic novel, and I squinted to read the title.

Robin Renegade: La Belle au bois dormant.

I popped a biscuit into my mouth and spoke through the crumbs. "Good morning, Mum. You are an absolute vision in . . . whatever you're wearing."

She slanted a look at me over the top of her novel then at the standing clock in the far corner and sprang upright like a surprise toy in a box. "Art! Why are you here so early? The Exhibitions aren't for another few hours."

Sweetpea tipped gracelessly from her lap and landed face first into the cushion beside her. The pug gave a muffled snort and, after several seconds of pawing at the cushions, eventually righted his balance.

"Were you out all night? Of course you were. And Maker only knows where you've been—airship racing and gambling and tall glass drinks. I can smell you from here. You could've at least gone home to change first."

I picked at the edge of an embroidered floret doily draped over the arm of my chair. "Technically, I'm late from when Cecily asked me to arrive. I made sure of it. I've also ordered my new suit to be sent here with scarcely enough time so I'll be fashionably late for the Exhibitions, too."

She marked her page and lowered the novel to rest on Sweetpea's wrinkled head. "My dear, it's still morning. *Early.* You have never in your life gotten an early start to anything. You were weeks overdue for your own birth. And if you were a sleep-spelled prince and Robin Renegade came to kiss you awake, you would still roll over and ask for ten more minutes! Don't pick at that."

I dropped the doily. "A reference to your latest novel, I assume?"

She sighed and hugged the book to her chest. "Robin is searching for Prince Handsome, but he is under a sleeping spell. Nothing has happened since that scandalous scene alone in the woods together, and I do wish she would get on with the rescuing because he isn't getting any younger! Although . . . I suppose because of the spell, he isn't getting any older either." She pointed an accusatory finger at me, suddenly sour. "Don't distract me. Explain yourself! And it had better be important for you to interrupt my cleanse."

"Is that what this is?"

"I intend to look my best for the Exhibitions," she said. "And I only have four more days to prepare for the Maker's Gala this weekend. You should clean up, too, if you want any pretty partners to dance with you."

"Don't be ridiculous. I always look stunning."

"Alas, we all have our burdens to bear. We are in the height of the season. You will, of course, accompany me to the Tackletons' garden party on Thursday?"

"I'm afraid I won't be able to clean up in time."

"Don't be cheeky." She reached for a bone porcelain teacup and took a sip. A large drop of the thick amber mask dripped off her face and plopped against the cup. I wasn't convinced that any partner would want to dance with someone whose face was dripping into her teacup, even someone as eccentric as my own father.

"Mum . . . what have you put on your face?"

"Honey."

"Glad we've cleared that up, then."

"It sweetens the complexion." She set down her cup and daintily patted her chin with a serviette. Sweetpea lunged for the sticky cup but, once again, tipped face first into the seat cushion. "If you won't tell me where you've been all night, you can read me the list of ladies already on your dance card—"

"You know very well I won't dance. Although I have promised to steal a glass of champagne for Cecily."

"Where *is* that girl? I haven't seen her all morning. Do you know she set the curtains on fire? Again. Last week. I'll never understand what Maker was thinking when He sent me the two of you. A good man who, for some unknown reason, misapplies sense for sarcasm. And a brilliant girl who spends the whole of her allowance on nuts and bolts and forgets to order a ballgown for the Maker's Gala. And before you ask, I've already ordered the new batiste from Madame LaMonde on her behalf."

"Art, is that you?" As if summoned, my sister leaned halfway into the doorframe at an awkward angle.

Technically, Cecily was my cousin. She'd come to live with our family as a ward. But almost immediately, I'd adopted her as my little sister. We even looked like siblings with similar chestnut hair and golden-brown skin, although her bright eyes were wide as hazelnuts while mine were more oval-shaped like almonds.

Even with her standing half-hidden by the doorframe, I caught sight of a frayed and blackened burn across the hip of her striped afternoon dress. Her hair had already escaped any attempts at captivity, and loose curls rose like a wave behind a pair of magnifying goggles strapped to her head like a band. She held a small object between an overly large pair of leather work gloves.

I might've become dependent on fashion, but Cecily couldn't care less. I'd long since stopped teasing about her *bas bleu* appearance. The game lost appeal when my target gave absolutely no reaction.

"I thought I heard your voice. You're early!"

"Why does everyone insist I'm early? I'm"—I checked the standing clock—"*at least* half an hour late! You did say half past ten, and it's after eleven."

"Yes," she said. "But, you see, I knew you would be late. So I invited you here two hours early."

"Two— A whole *two* hours? Well, that wasn't very sporting of you." I nibbled at the edge of my biscuit and sulked.

"Never mind that. I still need to clean the balance and tighten the escape wheel. Oh, and my satchel is probably on the bench in the back garden. Or the icebox. At least I don't need to worry about the blueprints—I've already turned those in. See you there?" She dashed away.

"*Where*, dear?" Mum called, but Cecily was already worlds away. "That girl is as scattered as a lost set of jacks. Do *you* know where she's gone?"

"She failed to mention that part, but I think we can safely guess."

"You don't think . . . she's not going to the Maker Exhibitions. Not dressed like *that*!"

"I'm afraid it's probably worse than that. I suspect Cecily has submitted blueprints for an invention and will publicly present her dissertation today. She's brilliant. I have no doubt she'll be awarded a title as maker . . . even dressed like that."

The Maker Exhibitions were a yearly trade fair held at Diadem University. Aspiring makers submitted blueprints before being selected to address a panel of judges with hope of receiving a makership from the queen and access to private funding. Anyone could present an invention. Thus, in theory, anyone could receive the coveted title of maker. Even my eighteen-year-old savant of a sister.

"You mentioned the Exhibitions before."

"Hm?" I glanced up from twirling the doily on one finger and was startled at the stern look Mum had leveled at me.

"You already knew," she said. "*How* did you know? Don't pick at that."

I dropped the doily. "I had my suspicions after Cecily asked me to call round today."

It wasn't an *outright* lie, but I wasn't supposed to know details of the Exhibitions. At least . . . not with any certainty. Thanks to the wide circumference of her social circle, Mum was uncommonly well-informed on social matters. But even the great Mrs. Hattie Keays lacked the vast resources at my disposal.

Two days earlier, one of my informants had stolen an early look at the list of maker-candidates and had apprised me of Cecily's application. The details were . . . concerning.

She'd registered her application without a patron.

It was rare for a gentleman maker-candidate to enter the Exhibitions without the endorsement and continued financial support of at least one patron. It was *unheard of* for a single cog girl to attempt the same feat of independence.

I couldn't interfere directly—couldn't show a deliberate interest. That would be much too useful. I could, however, muster a more indirect show of support.

"For any outcome," I said, "we might as well put in an appearance. She's not without a guardian. But with an outfit like that, the judges might very well assume Cecily is a roving orphan. She should be seen in good company."

Mum gave me a sudden, serious look. I tried not to squirm, but I'd been in forceful interrogations that made me less nervous.

"You are running out of excuses, Arthur. At some point, you're going to have to admit that you have something to care about. Whatever and whyever you play the careless rake, I know your heart. You care more than you let on."

I winced as the truth of her words pierced the center of the heart I made every effort to safeguard. Such a soft target was a liability.

"Now then." She tossed her novel onto the sofa and stood. With a startled snort, Sweetpea tipped off the sofa and waddled onto a flowered cushion near my feet. "How much time do we have? Oh, dear . . . not nearly enough. When did you say your suit is due to arrive? And have you seen Martha? Oh, never mind. I'll wind up the house chimes. Make yourself useful, dear, and have a word with Daweson? The steamcar needs to be fueled and watered as soon as possible. Otherwise, we'll certainly be late . . ."

She continued listing instructions as she bustled from the room—long, floral robe sweeping behind her. Sweetpea yipped and followed her out as fast as his stubby legs could carry him.

I pinched the floral doily and considered the effort it would take to summon Daweson and "be useful" as Mum had ordered.

I didn't consider long.

Propping my feet on Sweetpea's vacant cushion, I leaned deeper into the chair, covered my eyes with the doily, and tipped my head back for a nap.

After all, I had to keep up my useless reputation somehow.

Chapter Two

ART

The spacious, open-air amphitheater that bordered Diadem University was full to bursting, and the crowd spilled out into the surrounding streets. Every citizen in the Parure, it seemed, had congregated at the Maker Exhibitions. But only a fraction of souls were actually paying attention to the ongoing presentations.

I yawned loudly, tipped back the last of my tart cherry wine, and eyed Judge Pinefoy over the rim of my glass. He was a twitchy little man with deep-set eyes and a greasy comb-over. Despite the cool breeze, his pale skin was glossed with a sheen of sweat as he inched a hand toward the edge of the judge's table. He flicked his skeletal fingers, and a grubby rover boy darted away into the crowd. Neither one of the other judges seemed to notice.

Beside the stone and stained glass of the university lecture hall and beneath umbrella-shaped awnings, streams of people poured around showcases of make-prototypes. Along the uppermost tiers of the circular amphitheater, working-class cogs massed tightly together, children ran and shrieked, rover children wandered the crowd with trays of savory pies, and vendors peddled appliances and stemmed flowers until the smell of rich spices and spring blooms all wafted together. The next lower few tiers of stone and grass collected the wealthier cogs and gems. They sprawled on plush cushions as uniformed servants with pastel parasols provided imported wines and picnic hors d'oeuvres. We were seated beside the presentation platform on the lowermost grassy tier—curved rows of white chairs and matching round tables with silk table-cloths reserved for the wealthiest gems, close friends and family of the maker-candidates, and the patrons—a showcase for the prominent and prosperous.

In truth, the Maker Exhibitions were less an examination of maker-candidates and their prospectus inventions and more an opportunistic parade of fashion. Most of the ladies wore metallic corseted dresses, their torsos sticking up like thin taper candles out of an elaborately ruffled sconce. The more tactless gems were so laden with mechanical gadgets it was a wonder they could lift their limbs at all. One college fellow wore a brass monkey statuette perched on his shoulder. A steel clamp around his upper arm held the gaudy creature in place; however, the clamp appeared to be stuck. He strained to loosen the screws, but the fingers of his left hand were becoming notably discolored.

I, of course, was dressed to perfection. The arms and legs of my tan suit were bangled with brass gauntlets and straps, but I left the jacket unbuttoned to reveal a hand-painted leather vest depicting a rather sala-cious scene of pastoral nymphs. My cravat was pinned with a brass clip, and I twirled a polished cane with a matching brass handle. To cap it all, I'd slanted my new, rounded bowler over a pair of amber-tinted glasses.

I angled a look over the rim and winked at a nearby trio of ladies. They giggled while their elderly chaperone bristled like a bluenosed guard dog.

My reputation preceded me.

The crowd quieted as a low, mechanical thud echoed over the outdoor amphitheater. On the platform, a boyish college student wearing a baggy suit tapped the circular rim of an outspeaker device and nervously began his presentation—something about paving stones and a new formula for cement. It was a pity the crowd immediately lost interest and the hum of chatter resumed.

Again, Judge Pinefoy flicked his fingers over the edge of the table, and a nearby rover boy darted away. The judge was subtle—it'd taken me a few tries to notice the hand twitches and then to spot the rover boy. Fortunately, one of my own informants was working in the crowd as well. I trusted her to learn where the boy was headed.

The selection process for makers was confidential—the Queen's Judges intended to be impartial without exception; however, Pinefoy was clearly working out of someone's pocket.

And there was only one style of robe with pockets deep enough to buy a judge.

Beyond the merry hustle and bustle, parasols, and charcoal-steeped picnic aromas, the Magicstry was a dark smudge against the skyline like a distant steepled mountain. A perpetual haze of mist swirled between its iron spires and pooled into a courtyard with wide gates that unhinged like the jaws of a snake. The mist supposedly represented their connection to the aether—the miracles of the Great Maker. To me, it was a conspicuous reminder of the Parure's tenuous balance of power. Cogs wanted social reform. The gem wanted wealth and industry. And the Magicstry quietly siphoned away their own wealth and beneficence under the guise of piety.

"Did you hear what I said?"

I recoiled as Mum shook her printed program directly under my nose.

The morning's *cleanse* had concluded with her draped entirely in pink silks. Her feathered hat fluttered in the breeze, looking for all the aether like an enormous bird preparing to take flight, while Sweetpea was tucked under her arm like a fur accessory clutch. He was currently snoring.

"Cecily is next," she whispered loudly.

"Finally."

"There is no mention of a patron beside her entry. I assumed you would invest."

"That would suggest initiative on my part," I replied. "She didn't ask Father?"

Mum pursed her lips and fanned herself with the program. "*That girl.* Oh dear . . . but she does look nervous, doesn't she?"

Cecily did, indeed, have a distinctly green hue. She was the only woman—*girl*, really—in a long lineup of mostly college-aged men. She swayed slightly in her chair and clung to her leather satchel like a seasick woman to a life raft. Her toes tapped restlessly—flattening the grass around her. Cecily had never been one for crowds. Or people in general. Her lips were squeezed in a stubborn line of grim determination.

My heart seized with pity. I caught her eye and waved, and she quickly swung her gaze back to the grass.

"Do you know which invention she plans to present?" Mum asked. "She has quite a few to choose from."

"Haven't the foggiest. But you've done a decent job in fixing her up. At least . . . her dress is from the current decade."

"There is that. *Oh!* This is it!" Mum squealed as the boyish maker-candidate concluded his dry cement lecture to a smattering of applause.

Cecily stood and marched onto the wooden platform like a woman facing the gallows. She grimly removed a stack of papers from her leather satchel, placed them on the lectern, and gripped the sides until her knuckles turned white. However, she'd clearly rehearsed the presentational part, because her voice through the outspeaker was steady.

"Honorable Judges, Makers, colleagues, and guests. My name is Miss Cecily Keays."

She'd already drawn more attention than most of the candidates. Several people craned their heads to get a better look at the schoolgirl maker-candidate.

Judge Pinefoy was twitching with nervous energy.

"We live in a shining age of industry—the brightest the Parure has ever known. The widespread production of makes, steam-engines, and alchemical fuel has expanded our commonwealth far beyond our foundational borders and augmented our standard of living. But for all such prosperity and growth, we are far from reaching the limit of our potential. The only limit to industry lies in our own imagination as makers."

Mum led the crowd in polite applause. Cecily looked up, as if annoyed by the interruption, hastily cleared her throat to the side of the outspeaker, and continued more rapidly than before.

"Industry within the Parure is, at present, limited by a number of manufacturing pressures—inflation, supply chain disruptions, and labor shortages with the recurrent cog strikes to name a few. Above all, makers are dependent on natural resources such as our coal, iron ore, timber, and water. In view of these limitations, I began to imagine a world without temporal constraint. What if, instead, we could harness a *limitless* resource? An aetherial power?" She again cleared her throat. "I am, in fact, speaking of the conduction of magic."

The crowd took a collective intake of breath as everything inside me went numb.

"The doctrines of the Magicstry teach that mages are chosen directly by the Great Maker. Supplicants offer alms, and in turn, mages conduct miracles of healing upon the faithful. Any other purport of magic is heresy. As a result, cogs, gems, and makers alike can only philosophize in secret as to the true nature and scientific potential of magic."

"Art?" Mum asked faintly, like my name was the whole of her question. Her voice clattered loudly against the utter silence of the crowd.

"I need to sit down." I glanced at my lap. Apparently, I was already sitting.

Cecily barreled onward through her speech. "However, with dedicated research and precise experimentation, I have discovered a scientific explanation for the miracle of magic. Much like Maker Wyere's theory of conducted electricity, magic is a natural and self-sustained resource which mages have simply learned how to conduct through the instrumentality of the human body. Magic can be conducted through alternate material in like manner. Allow me to present the Conductor, a self—"

"Young lady!" the farmost judge, Maker Hayes, interrupted. His voice boomed across the lawn through a second outspeaker. Cecily jerked her head upright in surprise. The judge hunched forward and regarded her with owlish eyes. He enunciated each word. "Are you suggesting that you've somehow discovered how to make . . . *magic machines?*"

My walking cane creaked from the pressure of my grip. Anyone with a whit of sense would say her presentation was a prank. Unluckily, my sister didn't have one of those. Even a whit.

"Well . . . artificial aetheric conduction, to be precise. If you'd let me finish my dissertation you'll see that—"

I found myself standing and walking to the stage. Thousands of eyes followed me as I swung my walking cane, poking little divots into the grass, and stepped onto the wooden platform. I adjusted the outspeaker at the lectern and gave the audience a carefree smile. "Honorable Judges, gems, and all you other people . . . as Miss Keays' patron, it would be my pleasure to answer all of your questions . . . at a later time. Thank you."

Before she could say another word, I swept her papers into the leather satchel, caught Cecily by the elbow, and towed her away from the podium.

Judge Pinefoy stood and ran as the entire amphitheater ignited into chaos behind us.

Chapter Three

ART

"Art, *how could you*? You've ruined everything!"

Cecily rounded on me as soon as we passed the first white pavilion then danced sideways and continued yelling while we dashed through the crowd. If she was raging at me, at least she would keep pace. We needed to stay moving on the remote chance that we could find reinforcements before the mages located us.

Unfortunately, the Jeweled Palace was our only lifeline.

Gems and makers governed industry, holy mages conducted magic, and cogs like us were the hardworking citizens. The Parure was on the brink of civil war, and Cecily had created the make that would tip the precarious balance. To make matters worse, I was desperate enough to try to prevent the downfall. Mum had been correct—I had finally been forced to admit I cared enough about something to upend my careful life. I'd known *when* Cecily would present her make at the Exhibitions... unfortunately, I hadn't considered *what* it would be.

Shoulders aching with tension, I tucked her satchel under one arm and held my cane ahead of me like a weapon at the ready as we bobbed and weaved through displays and umbrella awnings to avoid the press of the crowd.

"This was my opportunity to *do* something with my life—to make something of myself!" she shouted. "But after your stunt, even if I become a maker, my invention will never be mass produced without a patron. The judges didn't even *look* at my blueprints!"

I tugged her arm sideways to stop her from running into an upended cart. "I'm glad we agree," I said. "The imperative in this situation is *life*. It would be a shame to watch your execution for heresy against the Magicstry. Especially because I believe executions are generally carried out at dawn, and we both know I would never wake up early enough to see you off."

She let out a winded growl of frustration. "Was that one of your jokes? At a time like this? Of course you know nothing about dreams or ambitions or goals, but did you have to turn my work into a joke, too?"

"No one there was laughing, believe me."

Anyone with the ability to conduct magic was forced to join the unbending order of the Magicstry. Those who dared refuse faced trial as heretics, accused of misusing and corrupting the sacred power of the Great Maker. Even if her magic was artificially conducted through a make, a title of Makership was Cecily's only path to safety—becoming a maker would place her directly under the queen's protection.

But first, we had to convince the queen.

I ducked behind a vendor display of woven blankets hanging on a line and emerged onto the main thoroughfare leading to the Jeweled Palace. Cecily stumbled through the blankets behind me, arms flailing. The wide, paved street was alive with color and activity—painted awnings, the glinting windows of tall buildings, and the bustle of busy people at the central-most market. A bell clanged and a green-painted tram inched forward over inlaid tracks. I tugged Cecily's hand and crossed the tracks ahead of the tram.

She continued breathlessly, "Candidates fall under the jurisdiction of the Maker Exhibitions and, therefore, the Parure. *I'm* not conducting magic. My *makes* are. The Magicstry can't do anything about that."

"Unless the Magicstry is in control of the Exhibitions," I muttered, sparing a brief glance over my shoulder. The proof was right behind us.

The lively crowd was splitting to either side of the street as quickly as a dry log beneath an axe.

The mages were coming.

We weren't going to make it.

"I know I'm not . . . I don't think the way that other people want me to," she panted. "But I thought that you of all people would be happy for me! Or at the very least relieved to have one less responsibility. I wouldn't have to be *Cecily the orphaned ward*, a cog entirely dependent on the charity of her relations. I could be *Maker Keays*, a titled gem."

Cecily was so brilliant. Sometimes I forgot how young she was or that her naive aspiration to fit into a more traditional mold was as earnest as mine—if for wildly different reasons. The only comfort I could give was the truth. "Your make is a work of genius, Gears. The queen will have no choice but to appoint you as maker . . . once we prove you're more valuable as a maker than a mage."

"Do you mean that?" She beamed. I didn't have the heart to tell her that wasn't a good thing. "But then, shouldn't we head back? Where are we going anyway?"

"We're almost there."

The palace gates were mere paces ahead.

"There is such thing as a wisdom of ignorance, yes?" I asked. "In any scientific query, it is vital to acknowledge what one doesn't know. So, in this present case, will you acknowledge my superior knowledge in matters of society and let me do the talking?"

When I looked back, she was several steps behind. She'd stopped to watch the parting crowd.

"Cecily?"

My ears popped, the air pressure changing like the sky before a storm, and air leached from my lungs. Each breath supplied less and less oxygen, like I was respiring in reverse.

Stumbling back, I shoved the leather satchel into her arms and wrested Cecily forward by the collar of her dress.

Ten steps.

Eight.

Four.

We tripped through the gates of the Jeweled Palace as the crowd parted to reveal the mages.

Mages were benevolent healers—conduits of a merciful Great Maker—generous with miracles of healing and reserved in judgment. At least, that was the character reference the Magicstry wrote on their own behalf. The two mages before us were clearly a different breed. Unlike faithful hounds, these were the guard dogs trained to kill, and they'd caught our scent.

Even worse, I recognized Master Mage Citoyen. He was a notoriously ruthless and amoral fanatic of the Gallia Magicstry. Though the Parure offered asylum to refugees, Mage Citoyen was personally responsible for the execution of dozens of purported heretics during his ministry in Gallia.

The mage beside him, a novice I'd never seen before, looked like a maltreated mutt the cruel master had trained in a dog-fighting ring. He moved with a lethal grace and loosely leashed intensity.

Long grey robes floated just above the cobbled street as the two men stalked forward. In a city of bright colors and gems, the grey robes of the mages overshadowed the scene like a full eclipse of the bright sun. The fractured crowd shied farther away from the mainstay avenue and out neighboring arteries to avoid the intake of magic that seemed to consume all oxygen.

Magic could only be conducted through physical touch. But the feeling of conduction, even nearby, was discomposing. Especially when it felt like the mages were stealing all the air.

With all that power crackling around them—Maker help us if they so much as brushed against us.

Cecily slumped in my arms, and I staggered backward. Black dots cluttered my vision.

"Halt!" The firm voice came from behind as a thick hand gripped my upper arm to steady me. "These people are civilians of the Parure. Release them and state your purpose here."

After a silence of slowing heartbeats, the pressure of magic receded, and I gasped a full breath. Cecily sank to the ground, coughing.

As my vision cleared, the hand encircling my arm loosened, and I straightened my tinted glasses and looked up into Ox's familiar face. The palace captain wore a leather coat with rank insignia, although the uniform sleeves strained against the meaty width of his shoulders. Ox was not a ready-made size. He squinted against the sun as the light soaked into the dark skin of his neatly shaved head, but his focus never wavered from the mages even as he muttered, "What grease spill have you gotten yourself into this time, Art?"

"They're not here for me," I rasped. "*Jolly* good timing seeing you here, don't you agree?"

Ox glanced down at Cecily, nodded in solemn understanding, and barked a protective order. Five nearby guards immediately surrounded us.

Cecily and I were sandwiched between a deadlock of two world powers. Was that better or worse than standing alone on the battlefield?

"I commend your discipline, Captain," Mage Citoyen called in a dried and reedy voice. "But the girl is subject to Magicstry jurisdiction. She leaves with us."

I massaged my aching throat. "Miss Cecily is here for an audience with the queen."

"We have a prior engagement," he said.

"With the queen?" I asked brightly. "My Maker, that is a curious coincidence! Why don't we all go in together? Much obliged to you for the escort, Captain."

I was acutely aware of my too-shallow breaths as Mage Citoyen cocked his head to the side, calculating.

Then, he smiled.

I could've sworn his novice winced.

"Lead the way, Captain."

Ox muttered a grim curse and something to the tune of "I hope you know what you're doing" and pivoted on his heel. I pulled Cecily to her feet, returned her fallen briefcase, and tucked her clenched fist under my arm. Her expression was tense with barely bridled rage.

"Calm down," I said. "Deep breaths. Just remember, wisdom of ignorance . . . and all that."

My walking cane clicked against stone as we ascended the staircase past a garden maze to circumvent the main hall. The mages' presence behind us felt like an itch on the back of my neck until finally we dispersed to opposite sides of the queen's receiving chamber.

The space was exquisite. Our footsteps on marble echoed from floor to vaulted ceiling, and I was briefly blinded by a brilliant ray of sunlight shining through the multicolored glass windows as I tucked my glasses into an inner pocket of my suit coat. The waft of exotic perfumes was ever-present even without gems at court. A large carved throne oppressed the room, and the throne legs were underpropped by a marble dais foiled in gold.

Within seconds of our arrival, the queen swept into the chamber through a side door. She crossed the space and regarded our impromptu party from the vantage of her throne. Notwithstanding the superiority of Gallia dressmakers, the queen wore a cheerless beige gown made exclusively in the Parure. Poor fashion choices mingled with a weak chin, watery eyes, and a profile ill-suited to a coin—Her Jeweled Majesty was almost satirically opposite in appearance to her noble station. The ring of armed guards, however, was properly imposing as was the man at her side, Maker Belwater. Publicly, Belwater was the queen's most trusted advisor. Only a teacupful of people knew that behind closed doors, he was also the Jeweled spymaster, although I'd always thought his role rather obvious. His assessing gaze darted over the room, and his skin was chalky and pale like he'd spent a lifetime hidden in shadow. The queen was indeed intimidating with the intellect of Belwater behind the throne.

"Your Jeweled Majesty, ma'am." Ox bowed low.

We followed suit.

The mages did not.

"*Well*," the queen neatly cut through the strained silence, her voice sharp and clipped. "As long as we're skipping formalities, I'll get straight to the point. Maker Belwater has appraised me of the situation. A make to conduct magic. Is it true?"

"Of course not," Mage Citoyen answered.

"And yet," I said, "you made quite a show in coming here. I rather think such dramatic fanfare would enflame, not dampen, her credibility as maker-candidate."

"And who is this person?" the queen asked.

"Mr. Keays, Your Majesty," Ox answered.

"Ah . . . I thought you looked familiar. You are the girl's guardian?"

"And patron, Your Majesty," I added.

Her eyes narrowed. "A cog as patron? How intriguing."

Mage Citoyen cut back into the conversation with a slash of his hand. "Her Exhibition lecture has already caused irreparable damage to the public mind. Conduction of magic falls under the jurisdiction of the Magicstry. Legitimate make or heresy, the outcome is the same. The girl leaves here with us."

"*Well,* we have skepticism in common, if little else," said the queen. "However, let me be perfectly clear. The Maker Exhibitions are under *my* jurisdiction. Should this make prove legitimate, the girl—Miss Cecily Keays, is it? Miss Keays will be granted a makership. In such instance, gems and mages *will* come to a compromise regarding this discovery."

I pressed a hand to my jaw to cover my relief.

Mage Citoyen clenched his jaw so tightly I heard the *pop*. The title of *maker* itself was seen as heresy—a mockery of the Great Maker— arrogant mortals attempting to claim the divine act of creation. But the mages wouldn't defy the queen and risk all-out war. At least, not openly . . . from within the Jeweled Palace itself. The number of mages was slight in comparison to gems and cogs—perhaps one in every ten thousand—which was why there remained a balance of powers. Unlike our southern neighbors, heretic mages who conducted magic outside the Magicstry were reformed rather than immediately executed. The Parure Magicstry was smart to boost their numbers by offering asylum.

Her Jeweled Majesty addressed Cecily directly. "How did you first determine this theory, young lady? I am rather curious to hear the basis of such a remarkable claim. Scientifically, is such a make even possible?"

"A simple yes or no," I muttered.

Cecily cleared her throat. "As a matter of fact, Your Majesty—"

I sighed.

"—several recent articles and innovations sparked my interest. Specifically, the writings of Mr. Walter Blacknell and, of course, Maker Gedney's contributions. The infrastructure of our industry is largely limited by two key factors: manufacturing pressures and natural resources—"

The queen's eyes glazed with disinterest.

"—Blacknell and Gedney sought to explore the potential of industry by testing the limits of each. But I sought, instead, to identify the key factors for—"

I pinched her arm.

"*Ouch!*"

"Yes, Your Majesty," I said. "The science is sound."

"Yes?" The queen pursed her lips. "*Well*, Belwater? What do you make of all this?"

The maker's assessing gaze descended upon Cecily, and I was almost surprised that such a shadow-like man could speak. "Historically, industry and magic are mutually exclusive concepts. What caused you to correlate the two?"

Cecily wrested her arm from mine, probably to avoid another pinch. "After the recent theory of electric conduction by Maker Wyere, I hypothesized aetheric conduction," she explained. "If mages are conduits to the Maker, then they are the channel through which magic flows. The *body* is a conductor, *aether* is the electric current, and *healing magic* is the energy produced. My experiments led to the theory that magic can be conducted through sources other than the human body. In point of fact, the human anatomy makes for a very poor conduit when compared with sturdier materials such as—"

"Mages are a *poor conduit*?" Citoyen snarled. "*Who has known the mind of the Maker? The sinner seeks to counsel All Creations.*"

"Belwater?" the queen interrupted.

"I would need to see the blueprints," he said. "Where are they?"

For the first time, Cecily looked unsure. "I-I submitted my blueprints with my application for the Maker Exhibitions."

A frown deepened the ridge between his eyes. "I personally searched the vault records. There were no blueprints for your conductor."

I tensed and caught Ox's eye. He shook his head in confusion. Cecily had turned in her blueprints, because Ox had seen them—which is why I'd known about her presentation.

Until the queen granted Cecily a makership, the proprietary rights of her make were directly linked to the paper records, namely the blueprints. My patronage supported her credibility. However, if someone else claimed ownership of her make, the situation between mages and makers—our situation—would become much more complicated.

"What? But . . . you must be mistaken." Cecily hugged her satchel to her middle. "I turned them in."

"Who oversaw your application?" Belwater asked.

"He was a judge."

"Yes. Which one?"

"*Pin-eh-something*? Oh, I remember! His name was Judge Pinefoy."

My heart slumped against my ribcage.

"When did you give them to Pinefoy?" Belwater asked. "Did you make a copy?"

"Um, not a full copy, no. It was the last day to turn in an application for the Exhibitions. I filled out all the paperwork at one of the Diadem University lecture halls, then turned everything into the judge on staff . . . Pinefoy."

A single day had tarnished years of my thoroughly useless reputation as, once again, I was moved to intervene. I pointed my walking stick to the mages. "Well, there you have it! What did Judge Pinefoy say when he told you about the magic machines?"

Mage Citoyen tilted his head and regarded me. I felt like a beetle on a pinboard. "I fail to understand your meaning."

"Pinefoy." I picked at an offending spot of lint on my shoulder. It was all I could do not to squirm beneath the pin of his gaze. "Isn't he an informer to the Magicstry these days? Honestly, I thought it was common knowledge at this point. I mean, the gossip is quite unanimous about the lecture bribes. So, of course, if he had access to the blueprints as— My Maker, have I said something wrong?"

The judge's treason was *not* common knowledge nor gossip, but hopefully the shock of truth about Pinefoy would distract from the lie. The queen's neck was mottled with red while Maker Belwater and Ox looked grim. Cecily gaped—for once, speechless. Surprisingly, the only favorable mien in the room belonged to the novice mage. He met my look with the barest twist of a smirk. His dark features suggested rover heritage. Why a Gio-born novice accompanied a Gallia-puritanic Master Mage was a mystery.

Mage Citoyen spoke slowly with teeth bared. "Had the Magicstry been made aware of the existence of these blueprints, we would *not* have allowed the public preaching of heresy."

That much was true. So where were Cecily's blueprints? She'd submitted her application over a week ago. Had her blueprints been missing the entire time? Was I correct and Pinefoy had something to do with it? Of course, if the judge had somehow double-crossed the mages, not even the Great Maker would save him.

The queen stood to address the full assemblage. "*Well*, this is quite the riddle. Until the blueprints are found and returned to the vault, I'm sure the young Miss Keays would much prefer to stay here at the palace under my protection."

Cecily said, "Actually—"

"You disagree?" the queen asked. "You would refuse the hospitality of your queen?"

Before Cecily could answer, I spoke low in her ear. "She's not giving you a choice, Gears. She's saying we'll stay here as guests or as prisoners."

"Oh."

Before Cecily could decide that, on principle, we'd rather be held prisoner, I replied, "We're grateful for your hospitality, Your Majesty, I'm sure."

"Oh, not you," she said with a wry smile. "Just the girl. At least until this riddle is solved." She raised her voice to address the room at large. "The particulars of this meeting do not leave this room. Do I make myself clear?"

The guards did a type of salute-click with their heels in acknowl-edgment.

"Mage Citoyen," she said. "This . . . *unfortunate* situation spells equally disastrous consequences for us both. I hope you will agree that it is in our mutual best interest to find the blueprints and negotiate a compromise. Jurisdiction between gems and mages won't matter if someone else has a magic make in their possession. Keep me informed in your search, and I will offer the Magicstry the same courtesy."

Mage Citoyen sneered in response and, without a word, turned and stalked from the room. The silent novice glanced once at Cecily and followed—a dog at his master's heel.

"*Well* . . . that was only to be expected." The queen pointed to me. "You."

I pointed to myself.

"Yes, *you* will stay. Everyone else, leave. And, Captain, please see to it that Miss Keays is escorted to our very finest guest apartment. Perhaps with space for a workshop? And send for refreshments."

Her true meaning was clear: don't let the girl out of your sight.

"Save me a biscuit, will you?" I asked.

Cecily hesitated. "But—"

"I'll see you soon. I promise."

She held my gaze, and pity welled in my chest at the terror in her eyes. I nodded, projecting calm.

"All right. Thank you, Your Majesty." She offered a rigid curtsy to the queen. Ox shot me one last look and ushered Cecily out after the guards.

Leaving me alone with the queen and her spymaster.

"*Well*, Mr. Keays," said the queen, once again settling onto her throne. "That was certainly clever of you to displace Pinefoy."

I shrugged. "I have a talent for collecting gossip, Your Majesty."

"Really? Then no doubt you've heard the rumors of . . . remind me, Belwater. What do they call the outlaw who rescues mages from the Gallia death sentence?"

"The Renegade."

"*Ah*, yes. A modern heroine . . . or hero. Like Robin Renegade of the old plays. Have you heard talk of this person?"

"And little else," I said. "Gems search every concert hall and dance floor hoping to catch a glimpse of a mysterious stranger, and my tailor is unnaturally enamored by the idea of sweeping capes and full-grain leather masks. I'm quite jealous of the rogue for stealing all the attention."

"Are you?" she mused. "I knew your name was familiar to me. You see, I have a talent for hearing things, too. Like news of frequent travel to and from Gallia. A man who spends an exorbitant amount of notes on foreign tailors. Or a wealthy cog without any apparent profession."

My palms began to sweat. I schooled my expression into my usual smirk and gave a sweeping bow. "I live for vanity, Your Majesty."

"*Well*, allow me to indulge your egotism. I am entrusting you with this assignment. *You*, Mr. Keays, will find and return my blueprints."

I laughed. "Wait . . . you're serious?"

"Quite."

Belwater frowned.

"I'm not sure I understand, Your Majesty," I said.

"As patron to your own sister, you have more invested in this make than anyone. Miss Keays isn't the first person with a desire to unlock the secrets of the Magicstry. She is, however, the first to survive the attempt. Am I correct in assuming you brought the girl here to keep her safe from the Magicstry? *Well* . . . without those blueprints, how are you planning to keep her safe from *me*?"

The sweat on my palms chilled as everything inside me went numb.

"That make belongs to the Parure. And unless you locate and return my blueprints before the mages intervene, your sister carries the obligation to compensate for my loss. I *want* those magic machines, and she *will* make them for me. The comfort of her little holiday here at the palace is entirely dependent on your cooperation."

"Your Majesty." Belwater advanced to her side. "Is this really necessary? There is no need to involve a cog. I have my own men who—"

"Who failed to secure the blueprints in the first place. No, I want to ensure that Mr. Keays is advocating for our interests as well as his own. Do I make myself clear?"

I nodded tightly.

"The ring." The queen gestured Belwater forward. He grunted, slipped a gold ring from his finger, and descended the stairs to place it directly in my hand. His eyes were hard as they stared into mine.

Warily, I inspected the gold band and ruby set in a pointed crown.

"Congratulations on your *promotion*, Mr. Keays," said the queen. "You are holding the seal ring of a Ruby Agent. Every resource of the Parure is at your disposal. I trust you will use it wisely? Maker Belwater will oversee your activities."

He looked about as thrilled as I felt.

I swallowed the knot in my throat and swept a low bow. "I'm honored, Your Majesty."

"Good." The queen rose. "You have until, let's say . . . the night of the Maker's Gala to bring me those blueprints. Otherwise, Miss Keays will not receive a makership. I eagerly await your return. As does your sister." With the last word, she exited the way she had come.

Belwater frowned. "Report back regularly." He, too, strode from the room.

Alone, I stared down at the ring. The warm metal stuck to my clammy palm. Thanks to me, Cecily has become a prisoner of war. Was that better or worse than involuntarily joining the Magicstry without any natural ability to conduct magic?

Of course, without a makership, Cecily would be tried by the Magicstry as a heretic and killed.

Then there was the more selfish fear that I wouldn't be seen as useless anymore.

Not only was the careful balance of my useless life upended, but the full weight of the Parure had somehow landed entirely on my shoulders. If I wasn't as strong as a mythical telamon god, Cecily would be crushed . . . along with everyone else.

I felt the full weight of the ring as I slid the band onto my finger and twisted the ruby to face my palm. Finally, I forced my legs to move my feet. The tap of my walking cane on marble echoed loudly through the empty space. Thankfully, my careless character was still strapped to me like armor, because as soon as I exited the chamber, I was no longer alone.

The Magicstry had left their guard dog behind.

As soon as he saw me, the novice mage pushed himself off the wall where he'd been leaning and came to meet me. His grey robes clung inelegantly against his calves when before they'd seemed to float above the ground. His face was sharp and stony, and when he spoke for the first time, his voice was like a sack of rocks grating together. But he had a Parure accent, not Gio as I'd supposed.

"They already took your sister away."

"Without biscuits?" I scoffed. "The palace certainly has lost altitude if they're too cheap for a tea service."

I trusted Ox to look after her. He'd never failed before, and he was the one who'd alerted me to her maker application in the first place. I doubted her anger toward me would cool anytime soon, but Ox might at least manage to convince Cecily my intentions were pure.

"At least she's not in prison," said the mage.

"For the present."

"Still," he said, "you were smart to bring her here."

I raised a brow. "Funny . . . I usually enjoy compliments . . . when they're free. However, yours feel like there's a price attached. To what do I owe the honor of your company?"

He didn't hesitate. "I'm here to help you."

I barked a laugh. "Why would the Magicstry be interested in helping me?"

"The *Magicstry* is not. Mage Citoyen believes that keeping an eye on you would be a waste of time and resources while your sister remains in custody. You care too much to abandon her here."

I suppressed a wince.

"However, I personally believe you are my best chance at finding those blueprints," he said. "And I am *your* best chance at keeping your sister safe from the Magicstry."

"Is that right?"

"Mage Citoyen is a single-minded man," he rasped. "He will stop at nothing to destroy every threat to his beliefs. A magic make is a threat to the very existence of mages. He would never think to use the blueprints as a tool. He will burn the blueprints, Pinefoy will be dead before anyone else can question him, and as long as your sister is alive, he considers her to be a threat as well."

I hid the feeling of dread from my expression and rolled my tongue inside my cheek. "But you *don't* represent the Magicstry?" I asked.

"Not without my conduit's blessing."

"Ah yes, because I'm a waste of time. You're quite right, there. So, Mage Citoyen wants to destroy the blueprints, and you want them for . . . yourself?"

"I believe they can be used."

"Why do you think I could or *would* help you find them?"

"Why did the queen assign you to the task?" he asked.

"You were listening." Exactly how much had the mage heard?

"The clouds parted and the Great Maker spoke to me in a vision. And I was listening."

I squinted at him. "My word . . . was that . . . was that a *joke*? I can't tell. Everything about you is so . . . grey." I rubbed the back of my neck. "What happens if I fail to find the blueprints?"

"Like the queen said, jurisdiction won't matter if someone else has them."

I stared him down. "And what happens *when* I find the blueprints? If you were listening, then you know the blueprints are crucial to me as well."

His sharp features twisted into a smile—the first real expression I'd seen from him. "Then, we'll *compromise*."

Find the blueprints. Deliver them to the queen. Save Cecily. All under the watchful gaze of a mage. Plain sailing. I could probably eat a piece of cake, too.

I compartmented the deep twist of fear in my gut for later and pretended not to care.

The mage held out his hand. "Harland."

"Given name only? Art." We shook once. I looked him up and down. "Our first order of business is to find you a change of clothes. Then we're going after Pinefoy . . . if he's still alive. You can tell me everything you know about him on the way."

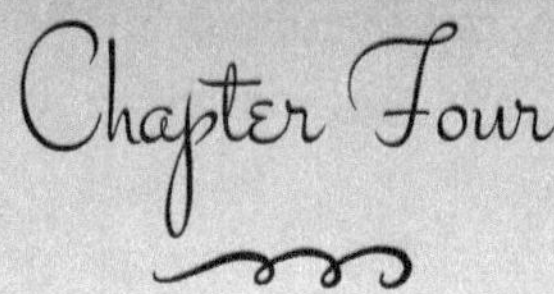

Chapter Four

Audrey

All the air seemed to be on the other side of the glass.

A summer breeze whispered through the glossy green leaves, and high above, a solitary ship with billowing sails floated among the white cotton clouds. Some fortunate aeronaut was currently looking down on hunting avians—master of the skies. How would it feel to fly higher than the birds?

Faut y aller.

"Audrey, are you even listening?"

At the sound of my name, my elbow plunked against a random cluster of piano keys. Guiltily, I swiveled on the bench with my back to the window and the distant promise of fresh air. Grandmother's eastern parlor was stiflingly warm (with a constant fire even in summer) and smelled overwhelmingly of floor polish and musty furniture.

The Diadem Museum of Antiquities had a similar smell.

Grandmother and Maker Malowney regarded me expectantly.

Apparently, I'd missed a part of their conversation that required a response.

"Forgive me," I said, putting on a contrite smile. "My head was in the clouds. Did you ask something?"

Grandmother frowned, her powdered wrinkles deepening with disapproval. Propriety left no room for inattention, even when the carriage was already waiting for me at the end of the drive. I was still expected to play a dutiful role—the tragic character I most often performed at Grandmother's behest.

Maker Malowney seemed to take pity on me. "I was just about to change topics," he said. "I've been remonstrating about my patrons for some time. But I believe you are interested in hearing more about the latest Maker Exhibitions, are you not, Miss Clune?"

I straightened in my seat. "Yes, of course. Tell me everything!"

"*Audrey!*" Grandmother visibly flinched. "A gem of the right set does not make demands. It's vulgar. You will apologize this instant."

Even though Grandmother gave orders like a seasoned general, I was rarely permitted statements or opinions. I inhaled deeply and remembered to act dutiful. "I apologize, Maker Malowney. Would you *please* tell me? Was anyone new granted a makership?"

Grandmother sniffed at my curiosity but otherwise made no further comment. She resented such signs of cog growth. (Uppish middle-class merchants and old-money gems seated at the same dinner party table—positively immoral!) But as the age of industry advanced and the title of maker became more coveted than a barony, even Grandmother couldn't afford to ignore progress. Quite literally. Her gem name would have tarnished in obscure poverty if not for recent financial guidance from Maker Malowney. Our business alliance with him was more profitable than past grudges.

Of course, as both gem and maker, old and new money, industry and tradition, Grandmother had deemed Andrew Malowney doubly qualified as a suitable match for me.

I wasn't so certain.

He smiled blandly and swiped a hand along his neatly slicked hair. "I'm gratified to hear you take such an interest in my work. Unfortunately, my stay here in the country prevented me from attending the

Exhibitions in person. But from what I read in my correspondences, yesterday's Exhibition was quite the scandal. Something to do with a new cog candidate. Apparently, her make was extraordinary, but she disappeared before finishing her presentation."

I tilted my head, surprised any cogborn woman would practically turn down a title. "Has that ever been done?"

"Not to my knowledge."

"Who is she?" I asked.

"*That* is the scandalous part." He leaned closer to me as if to share a secret. The sharp scent of tobacco and mint briefly overpowered the stale floor polish. "Mind you, I don't wish to spread gossip. But from what I hear, she is the young ward of a wealthy patron. But the Magicstry—a Master Mage and his novice—also claim authority. They even stormed the Jeweled Palace to find her. So, perhaps she comes recommended from an even higher source." He tapped his forehead in silent salute to the Great Maker.

He was about to say more when Grandmother cleared her throat and gave me a meaningful glance. "At least the cog girl had enough sense to refuse a makership. The chit ought to avoid trouble and focus on marrying into a lustrous family, if anyone will have her. After all, a Jeweled title supersedes that of maker. You are from the right set of people, Mr. Malowney. No earthly appellation takes precedence over that fact. The same is true for Audrey," she said. "Despite her . . . *uncon-ventional* upbringing, a polished pedigree will always shine."

A compliment to herself and a slight to my mother all in the same breath.

The piano bench scraped against the floor as I abruptly stood and moved to the window. Outside, John attempted to soothe the impatient horses. "It's getting late," I said. "I really should set out."

Maker Malowney looked unsure as to whether he should stand on ceremony.

Grandmother regarded me with pursed lips. "Still insistent on this wild holiday, are you? Why don't you play something first?"

"I already have. Forgive me, Maker Malowney. Aunt Emma expects my arrival before sundown, and I wouldn't want her to worry. If I leave now, I should still be able to reach Diadem before dark."

Grandmother narrowed her eyes at me and turned to Maker Malowney with an overdramatic shrug. "Naturally, we must do what we can to help our poorer relations."

He nodded solemnly. "*Naturally*."

Of course, I'd been the one to beg an allowance for Aunt Emma. Grandmother had eventually ceded a recurrent transfer of funds from my dowry—the one left to me by my mother. And Maker Malowney had promised that, should we marry, my aunt would continue to be cared for.

"I hope you won't mind," he said hesitantly, "but I've ordered my own jarvey, Ivo, to accompany you. I do worry about you traveling alone."

"I—"

"Well, that is *very* kind, isn't it, Audrey?" Grandmother offered Maker Malowney a grey-toothed smile. "Now, why don't you walk out together?"

"It would be my pleasure." With her permission, Maker Malowney stood smoothly from the low settee.

Stifling a sigh, I gave my thanks, collected my effects, and hurried to the door as fast as I could without actually sprinting. A dutiful grand-daughter would never run to escape her home.

"And Audrey . . ."

I froze with one gloved hand on the doorframe. "Yes, Grandmother?"

"We will see you at the Maker's Gala."

Her threat chased me the rest of the way out the door.

Once free of the overhanging eaves, I exhaled the musty manor air, tilted my face to the warm sunshine, and filled my lungs to capacity with sweet scents of summer. John gave me a deeply creased smile and friendly wave from beside the carriage while another jarvey, presumably Ivo, was busy loading the luggage. Spotting me, he jogged up the path.

"Allow me, Miss," he offered.

"Thank you." I handed him my carpetbag. The backs of his knuckles were scarred as was the side of his shaved head, and I wondered how Maker Malowney had come to hire him. Maker Malowney was generally quite particular about appearances.

"Shall we?"

I startled as Maker Malowney appeared at my side and offered me an arm, even though his cherry-red steam auto glinted at the opposite side of the drive. As both maker and patron in auto and armament manufacture, he owned only the best. The expensive make was as luxurious as a Jeweled Palace barouche. A four-wheeled frame supported the large, open cabin lined with furs and leather, and a tall, black smokestack stood between the covered boiler and bumper like a cigarette between the brightly painted lips of a revue girl.

Our horse-drawn carriage looked positively antiquated alongside such a modern make. Even compared with the rest of the rural county of Luster, Grandmother was terribly old-fashioned.

Maker Malowney donned a pair of soft deerskin gloves and handed me into the carriage. But he didn't let go of my hand. "It seems an *age* till I shall see you again."

I frowned, confused by the sudden change in his demeanor. "Sorry?"

"Won't you postpone your journey, my dove?" He pouted.

"My . . . *dove*? You know very well that another delay is not possible. My aunt requested a visit months ago, and I cannot deny her. She and I will have so little time together before the gala."

He pouted again. "You know what a jealous man I am. Yet you'd leave me here? *Alone*?"

"I'll see you again in two days at the gala."

"But—"

"I really must be off," I said with what I hoped was a note of finality and not annoyance. "My aunt wouldn't want me traveling after dark."

"Then allow me to ask you just one more question before you go."

Oh, mon Dieu.

"Miss Clune . . . *Audrey*." He paused meaningfully and tossed a slice of hair from his forehead.

I glanced back at the house. Was Grandmother watching from the windows? No? Then who was he playing to? Our conversation was like a poorly performed scene from *La Inamorato*, the dramatic opera, with two uncomfortable jarveys as our audience. Our marriage was already arranged, and I understood the reasons both as a matter of practicality and preservation. Given my unpredictable bouts of pain and fragile social standing, I doubted anyone else would accept me as I was. He needn't attempt to reassure me with overtures of romance.

"You *must* know how I feel about you," he said.

Of course I knew. He felt nothing for me. He did, however, feel a great deal for my dowry—wealth earned by my mother that transferred directly to his investment balances. On cue, Maker Malowney rubbed my gloved hand between his, like rubbing two banknotes together.

"Maker Malowney—"

"Please . . . call me *Andrew*."

"*Maker Malowney*. I have no doubt of your feelings for me."

"Then you cannot be in any doubt of my intentions?"

I'd resolved to accept Maker Malowney should he offer marriage, but I had hoped for more time. The holiday with Aunt Emma would be my last visit alone and unchaperoned. If I accepted his proposal now, it would not be proper for the fiancé of Maker Andrew McDevitt Malowney to dance at the Queen's Gala. I would spend my final days of freedom leaning against the wallpaper. And the garden party would be even worse—all wedding plans and trite tittle-tattle.

I took a deep breath through my nose, and something like fortitude flooded through me until my ribs ached from the pressure.

"Make—*Andrew*. I really must go. This is such a significant topic, and I'm sure you'll agree that here and now, in a soon-to-be moving carriage, is not the proper place or time to discuss it. However, I would be happy to hear everything you have to say upon my return."

He paused. A smooth smile spread across his face until his dark mustache stretched thin over his upper lip. "I see the game we're playing. Very well, little minx."

"I'm not a dove anymore?" I asked flatly.

"I suppose I must let you fly free," he said. "I have some business to attend to, but there is a particular question I should very much like to ask you upon your return. I will see you at the Maker's Gala, though the minutes will feel like hours and the hours will feel like years!"

Without warning, he pressed his lips roughly against my glove in his most dedicated imitation of passion yet. I could almost feel the mustache wax seeping through the material to my skin.

I was tired of the scene—the character I was forced to play. If I couldn't act my way through five minutes of conversation with him, how was I ever going to perform a lifelong role as his leading lady?

Partnership would run much smoother if we could both simply tell the truth.

After what felt like minutes turned to hours and hours turned to years, he let go and stepped back. "Farewell. Until our next meeting."

John moved to the door and kindly handed in the rest of my skirts while Ivo quickly took his seat in the box.

"Thank you, Mr. John," I said through the window.

"Let's get you on your way," he answered in a kind voice that only tightened the ache in my ribs. I stared straight ahead at the seat in front of me. I didn't dare look back at my future as the carriage lurched free of the gravel drive and onto the open country road beyond.

Chapter Five

Audrey

Ordinarily, I was not permitted to leave the manor without a travel companion.

My maid, Pauline, was a vinegary woman who pulled my laces and hair too tight. But like everyone else in the household, she'd been hired by Grandmother. I had little say in her employment and whether she accompanied me on excursions. My city visits with Aunt Emma were the rare exception. The supply of two coachmen was sufficient to see me to Diadem, and Grandmother grudgingly agreed it would be discourteous to burden my poor aunt with more than one guest after she'd fallen on such hard times. The solitary journey was far more pleasant without Pauline acting the role of my sharp-tongued shadow.

As soon as the carriage pulled free of the drive and the scrape of hooves on rock changed to the dampened thumps on dirt roads, I hauled over my carpetbag—an eastern rug design of gold and blue—opened the brass clasp and rummaged deep inside. Most of my belongings were packed in a large trunk strapped securely to the roof of the carriage. Even so, I had to dig around a folded shawl, small money purse, stack of letters from my aunt, and a bag of roasted nuts before my fingers found the rolled pages of my playscript. It was the kind of play my mother had loved and my governess (hired by my Grandmother) had thoroughly disapproved—full of adventure, intrigue, romance, and all sorts of words that a true gem would never find appealing.

But Mother hadn't raised me like a gem. She'd taught me how to pretend instead.

So, for the next two hours, I lounged across the bench—my gloves and shoes abandoned and stockinged feet curled up beneath my full skirts—and I pretended.

I read my lines aloud as Robin Renegade, a self-assured heroine of mystery. I lived outside the constraints of society. I laughed at danger while handsome men (who looked nothing at all like Maker Malowney) fought and died by my side. And I almost didn't notice when the carriage slowed and came to a late-afternoon stop.

It took some scrambling, but I managed to hide my dog-eared script, sweep the bag of nutshells under a cushion, and replace my shoes (unlaced) just before Ivo, a gangly opposite of Mr. John, popped open the carriage door and unfolded the steps.

The wayside town was little more than a small cluster of buildings, a hitching post, and a modest inn where travelers could rest for the night, although the inn looked as though it'd been refurbished since the last time I'd passed through. The shutters were a brighter shade of green, and a newly painted wooden sign swung in the light breeze: *The Jolly Cook,* with a comical, painted caricature of a portly man wearing a white apron. I caught a whiff of something savory and seasoned.

"Don't worry about me, Mr. Ivo," I said. "Both of you come inside once you're finished, and I'll have food waiting."

"But Miss—"

I waved away his protests. "You've both been driving for hours. I can certainly manage to order us some food."

He smiled boyishly, dipped his head, and left to help John water the horses.

I subtly stretched my cramped legs and back as I made for the door but slowed my pace as the untied boot laces flapped loosely against my ankles. I was a lady again. And a lady certainly couldn't be seen tripping over her own feet.

The savory smell of food increased as I carefully stepped inside, and my stomach rumbled in response. I'd foregone afternoon teatime in my hasty escape to freedom—the small bag of nuts a poor substitute for three-course sandwiches and savories.

The inn had indeed changed since my last visit, but the overall structure was the same. A generous cluster of tables filled the center of a spacious, two-story dining hall. Adjacent archways led to a series of private sitting rooms, and a cornered staircase led to several boarding rooms above. Along the far wall, plush armchairs were arranged opposite a large fireplace. Two of the chairs were occupied by a pair of gentlemen conversing quietly together. Neither of them looked my way when I entered, but a portly man bustled out from behind the bar. I immediately recognized him as the Jolly Cook from the painted sign—complete with a clean, white apron and a kind, ageless face.

"Hallo, hallo there, young miss!" he greeted warmly. His rural accent was thick—hailing from the Parure side of the Gallia border. If the round proprietor was shocked by a lady entering his inn unescorted, it didn't show. He hollered over his shoulder at a swinging kitchen door. "Mae, come out here!" He turned back to me with a wide grin. "What can I do fer yeh?"

"What smells so delicious?" I asked.

"That would be the pork pies if my daughter don't burn 'em."

"I'd love a table and a full meal, please. And my coachman and groom will require something to eat as well."

"Would you like a private room, Miss er . . ."

"Clune."

"Clune, you say?" He looked thoughtful, scrutinizing my face.

I tried my best not to notice. "No, thank you. I prefer to eat out here."

"Well, Miss Clune. Yeh can have yer pick of any of the tables—'tis a bit early for the supper crowd. And what'll yeh have to drink? We have tea, wine, or somethin' stronger, though yeh hardly look to be the type fer ale in the afternoon."

"Tea would be perfect, thank you. And what may I call you, sir?"

"Oh, Merciful Maker! Forgive my head. It forgets things. I'm Mr. Jolly, the proprietor."

"You really are the Jolly Cook," I said.

His jowls shook as he nodded proudly.

"I knew Mr. Kessler," I said. "He ran this inn for such a long time, but I like the changes you've made." The clean space and newer furnishings beside the fire felt roomy but comfortable.

Mr. Jolly followed my gaze to the first-floor railing. "Well, thank yeh, miss. I always loved this old place. And Mr. Kessler, Maker rest his soul, passed away nearly a year ago. My daughter and I bought the inn and have been runnin' it ever since. Speaking of which—" He hollered toward the kitchen a second time. "Mae!"

Shaking his head, he turned back to me. But once again, his eyes took on an inquisitive look. "We'd be happy to cater to such fine company as yehrself. Pardon me for saying so, but yeh look an awful lot like . . . well, like an actress. Er . . . I mean no disrespect!" He backtracked quickly, probably afraid to associate me with someone below my Jeweled station. "She were the most beautiful thing I ever seen. Or heard. Yeh could surely be her twin."

I sighed. "Are you referring to the actress Dame Gemma?"

His chins bobbed eagerly. "That's her! The very Dame!"

"Yes . . . She was my mother."

Her real name was Amalie Toussaint, a farmer's daughter from Gallia. But after she left Gallia, the public knew her as Dame Gemma, celebrated actress and *diamond of the Parure*. But to me, she was much more.

My mother made faces behind the backs of visiting dignitaries during dinner parties then snuck away to eat dessert with me in the kitchen. She sang *aria di bravuras* each morning and (when she wasn't at the theatre) lullabies in the evening. She wrapped my toes after dance lessons and showed me her own feet, each worn callus a requital of hard work. She taught me how to curve my fingers over the piano keys and how to breathe music into my voice. Even after her illness, she was the most beautiful woman—beyond compare.

She was a perfect memory.

Impossible to live up to.

"Yer mother, was she?" Mr. Jolly exhaled and placed a hand over the heart of his apron pocket. "I only saw her perform once, but once was enough to remember her fer a lifetime. Yeh look just like her," he repeated with a soft expression.

I curled my toes inside my unlaced boots, reconsidering a private room.

Mr. Jolly added, "I don't mean to overstep, but it must be hard for yeh to live without her while trying to live up to her name."

My ankle buckled to the side, and I gripped the edge of a nearby table to steady myself. "I . . . thank you."

He was right. It *was* difficult to live up to the name of a legend without her there to guide me. After a moment's thought, I returned the compliment in kind. "It must be difficult for you to adopt this inn after Mr. Kessler owned it for so long."

"Well, now . . ." He hummed thoughtfully. "We all have names to live up to, I suppose. But it's the names we choose that matter."

If only life were that simple.

I smiled—a real smile—and the poor man blushed a deep cherry red. He rubbed a hand over the bald pate of his head, but we were both saved further embarrassment when a girl, only a few years younger than me, charged through the swinging kitchen door into the main room. Her hair frizzed around her wide-cheeked face like a halo of red curls. But it was her eyes that most caught my attention—keen and observant.

"I'm here, Da. Whatcha want?"

"The best of everything. And extra portions, if yeh please."

The girl looked me over critically—noting my unlaced boots—and plodded back into the kitchen. I seated myself at one of the outer tables with a full view of the bright room while Mr. Jolly brought over a self-heating teapot—an inventive model from the capital I'd only seen once before—with a full tea service including sugars, honey, and sweetened cream. I poured myself a fresh cup and took a sip. The tea was strongly steeped, but the bright, lemony flavor was delicious. I added only a touch of sweet cream to the brew.

After a few minutes, John and Ivo entered the hall, nodded politely, and took up seats at a raised counter near the kitchen. Mr. Jolly immediately brought them drinks (something stronger than tea), and they chatted amiably until Mae bustled back in with a lunch service large enough to feed a small army: a bowl of meat swimming in thick gravy, a large loaf of freshly baked bread with creamed butter, cheese, a collection of preserves, boiled eggs, a mix of root vegetables, a small bowl of caramelized pearl onions, and a tray of pastries all marked with different patterns of golden crusts. Mr. Jolly chuckled at the stunned look on my face as he helped Mae unload tray after tray onto my table.

"I didn't know the Queen's Guard was encamped here," I said. "Will an entire regiment be joining me for dinner?"

Mr. Jolly's chuckle turned into a startled laugh, and he glanced over his shoulder toward the two men seated beside the fireplace. For a moment, I worried they'd overheard our interaction and would recognize me as well. "No, Miss. No handsome queen's men here."

"Only handsome cooks?"

He boomed an even heartier laugh and pointed to each of the pastries in turn. "There's venison, pork, and vegetable. Don't bother with anything yeh don't like, but eat up."

While Mr. Jolly continued to point out dishes, I obediently filled my plate. The heaping portions weren't very ladylike. But once again, I couldn't resist that hungry feeling of freedom. The same feeling that caused me to slip off my boots and read romantic plays in my road-carriage also claimed that a hearty portion of rich foods was good thinking.

Rubbing the top of his head, Mr. Jolly glanced around the room again. "Well, Miss, yeh'll need the sustenance, so I hear. Your men tell me that yeh've come from Luster County and are bound fer Diadem tonight?"

"*Mm*. To Tourmaline." I pulled the bread and block of cheese closer to my plate.

"That's quite a long journey ter make alone," he said. "Most of the country gems are already in the city, what with the Maker Exhibitions and Queen's Gala. If I may ask, why the delay? What brings yeh to the city now?"

"I'm visiting my aunt."

"Any special reason?"

I hesitated and fidgeted with a cloth serviette. It felt odd for someone to show such an interest in my life. Grandmother never did. How could I explain my last week of freedom?

"I haven't seen my aunt for months, and there are . . . emergent circumstances that will likely limit my future visits as well. But Aunt Emma is the only relative I have left. At least on my mother's side. The longer I stay away, the more I miss her. The more I miss . . . them."

"*I see.*" Mr. Jolly nodded solemnly. The sympathy in his gaze was too much. No stranger had a right to be so kind.

Feeling self-conscious, I flourished the serviette like a white flag and tucked it onto my lap. "I expect plenty of mollycoddling. Aunt Emma likes to fuss over my hair while I read aloud from the most recent maker prospectus. We wander the Glass District except on rainy days when we drink chocolate by the fire, and we take streetcar rides at the garden parties. It will be the perfect holiday!" I tried not to let the excitement in my voice slump as I added, "I return to the country immediately after the gala. So you can be sure I'll be back for more pastries. Of course, with the size of *this* meal, I won't need to eat again until then!"

He chuckled softly, but the solemnity of his gaze didn't waver. "My doors will always be open to yeh, Miss Clune."

"Thank you."

Mr. Jolly glanced over his shoulder as the two gentlemen rose from their chairs beside the fireplace. I'd almost forgotten the men were there. They donned their hats—a fashionable bowler and a thin, cloth cap—but didn't acknowledge us as they left the inn through a side door.

Mr. Jolly cleared his throat and moved to pour more tea. "May I offer yeh a piece of advice?"

"Of course."

"Don't travel after dark."

"I'm . . . not sure I understand."

"The roads aren't safe," he said simply.

"Are they in disrepair? I realize a steamcar would be more effective, but I've traveled by carriage many times before without any trouble."

"Oh, I'll bet yeh are more than a match fer any trouble that comes yer way," he said with a round-cheeked grin. But he quickly sobered again. "The Parure is changing. And after the recent Maker Exhibitions . . . frankly, Miss, it's not safe fer a lady—or *anyone*—to travel alone. Places that may have been friendly in the past are becoming more, er . . . well, my advice would be to either eat your meal quickly and set out, or stay and rest fer the evening. Otherwise, yeh'll be traveling after dark before safely reaching yer aunt."

The advice was sound, even if his delivery felt a bit dramatic. "Thank you, Mr. Jolly. I will hurry. Would you kindly ask my coachmen to do the same? As much as I would love to further enjoy your hospitality, that pleasure will have to wait for our return journey. My aunt is expecting me for supper."

He looked genuinely relieved by my answer. "Very good, Miss."

But even though I quickly devoured my meal and the summer sun was late to dip below the horizon, a tide of clouds rolled in and an early darkness swallowed the carriage long before we reached our destination.

Chapter Six

AUDREY

WITH ONLY A HANDFUL OF SCENES LEFT IN MY PLAYSCRIPT and a burning desire to see the corrupt lawman brought to justice, I conceded victory to the darkness. *The Blithe Adventures of Robin Renegade* would have to wait until daylight. I bookmarked the page with a letter from my aunt and felt around the dark cabin for my carpetbag. I fumbled with the clasp and safely stowed the script inside. After tucking my bag against the cushion beside me as a makeshift pillow, I turned my attention to the darkened windows.

I could barely see the road by the light of the lanterns swinging from the antiquated carriage. What inhabited the space beyond our lone circle of light? A chill ran down my spine as I remembered Mr. Jolly's warning. *After the recent Maker Exhibitions . . . frankly, Miss, it's not safe to travel alone.* Why wouldn't travel be safe after the Exhibitions? What monstrous thing lurked in the foggy night?

Despite my overactive imagination, I eventually grew tired of staring out at the empty darkness. By my estimation, we were still a solid hour from our destination—just enough time to rumple my dress and hair if I fell asleep. I fought the rhythmic creak, the soothing lull, and the familiar sway of the carriage, but my eyes grew heavy.

A loud crack broke the spell of the carriage, and I jolted upright. My first thought was that a monster had found us.

A second crack. And that time, fully awake, I recognized the sound.

I'd heard gunshots only once before on a hunting expedition, but it was the same: a loud crack of ignition followed by reverberating echoes.

The horses whinnied, and I lurched against the door as the horses' panic jostled the carriage. Ivo and John shouted frantically, but the scrape of grinding metal drowned out their words. I braced my feet against the opposite seat as the carriage skidded sideways.

A shadowy figure fleeted past my window, and my breath caught in my chest as I put the pieces together.

Highwaymen were attacking from the skies.

I knew about highwaymen, of course. I'd read a great many novels and plays that featured appearances by the rough, uncultured rogues. According to the stories, the highwaymen would anchor onto our carriage and demand our possessions—namely our jewelry and gold. But if they were particularly vile, they might demand another *valuable* from me as well.

I continued to brace against the opposite seat and gripped the door latch tightly as the shadowy figure flanked our position, suspended from a rope ladder. As if holding the door closed would do any good. I had nowhere to go and nothing to do but wait for the airship above to overtake us.

Soon, the villains would force open the door and drag the trembling damsel by the hair into the road. Disheveled and muddy, she would cry out, but her desperate pleas would only be met with amusement. Satisfaction even. She would put a cold hand to her forehead and swoon, except . . .

Except this wasn't some scripted scene waiting to play out.

I had a choice in which part to act.

So why would I *ever* choose to play the hysterical damsel?

My mother was the finest actress the Parure had ever known. Draped in glittering costumes and illuminated beneath the bright lights, Dame Gemma could move an audience of thousands to tears with her soliloquies. She could roll them in the aisles with her jokes and enchant them into silence with the passion of her arias.

The real woman behind the actress was no different. My mother had never limited her acting skills to the stage. All the world was her stage. She transformed herself anywhere into any sort of person. She could converse easily with cogs, but she'd also loved my father enough to play his idea of a proper gem. She'd smiled at the backbiting gossips of society, gained a proper understanding of muslin, and graciously hosted elegant dinner parties . . . until, of course, she and I climbed out the back window to escape the aspic course.

My mother was anyone she chose to be, and right then, I needed to make a choice, too.

In my role as ingenue—the dutiful granddaughter—I smiled and batted my eyelashes at Maker Malowney to lenify Grandmother and protect myself against the advances of more disagreeable suitors. My beauty, elegance, and ability to follow the rules kept me safe while, at the same time, diverting my audience.

But that same character would not protect me here on the road . . .

In the dark . . .

Against savage aeronauts with guns.

I was in a very different sort of story now. When it came to confronting highwaymen, my beauty was not an asset. If I wanted to survive, I needed to be more than a Jeweled lady with a pretty smile.

I needed to be smart.

Even as so many memories crowded my thoughts, I chose my new role within seconds. I did not smooth my hair or adjust my wrinkled skirts. Instead, I slapped my cheeks and forced myself to focus on calming my frantic pulse with deep, even breaths. Like preparing for a play, I imagined I was someone else—someone who wasn't terrified by the prospect of savage highwaymen. Someone who wasn't merely a pretty decoration that was dusted off and set on the piano bench for her grandmother's dinner parties.

Someone like Robin Renegade.

As the carriage slid to a shaky stop, a second manrope ladder unfurled from above. The aggravated snorts and whinnies from the horses interrupted the thrumming chug of a steam engine overhead. A debate between muffled voices and the box rocked as John and Ivo hastily descended from their post. I sat up straight but couldn't see far beyond the humid condensation on the window, across the dark and foggy landscape—only the faint outline of a small frigate hovering above. I was hardly even performing as I leaned closer and peered outside. The carriage lanterns swung and clanked against their chains, and even from behind the glass pane, the air smelled like sulfur. Soon, the horses calmed and muffled voices faded until the only sound was the soft mechanical thrum and a hiss of steam above.

A large figure suddenly eclipsed the window. I lurched back in surprise, and the door flew open. The figure retreated until he—clearly a man—was only a tall silhouette in the dark.

A silhouette with a pistol pointed directly at me.

His long shadow shifted across the ground in time with the swinging lantern like a bare, winter tree branch swaying in the wind.

"Surrender your belongings!" he demanded in a deep voice. "Money, jewelry, luggage . . . all of it!"

"You'll allow me to stay inside the carriage?" I asked, relieved to hear that my voice wasn't shaking. Robin Renegade would never have shown fear.

"If you surrender your belongings," he repeated.

I hesitated.

"Now!" he demanded.

"Well . . . I imagine your tactic would be more effective if you followed the traditional highwaymen script of 'stand and deliver.' It's much more concise. And that way, by having me leave the carriage, you can be sure there is no possibility of me concealing a weapon."

"You . . ." The silhouette scratched at the back of his neck. "Are you concealing a weapon?"

My only weapon was my intellect. Was that sharp enough? Robin Renegade's certainly was. "Yes, in fact, I am."

"Then show me your hands. And step outside where we can see you!"

Or else . . . ? I waited, but only silence followed. The man didn't seem to be good at making direct threats. What would he do if I chose *not* to comply? Aside from the warning shots, the highwaymen hadn't used their weapons. But would he shoot now?

Before I could wield my next response, a second man stepped into the edge of the lantern light. "They're tied down," he said. His voice rasped like thick boots shuffling against gravel.

The practical Robin character inside me felt reassured. Dead men didn't need to be tied.

"What's taking so long?" he asked.

Light glinted off the triple barrels of his pistol as he gestured toward the carriage. I'd never seen such a weapon. It was likely one of the newer makes from the capital (or even a weapon designed by Maker Malowney). Then, as the lantern shadows stilled and my eyes adjusted to the darkness outside, I noticed something even more interesting: I knew these men. The highwaymen—the taller one with the bowler hat beside his companion with the strange gun and flat wool cap—were an unmistakable pair, even with their faces shrouded in darkness.

Straightaway, I recognized them as the men from the inn.

"Step out of the carriage," said Bowler Hat. "This is your last warning."

"No, thank you!" I called back pleasantly.

He fell back a step as if I had pushed him. "Excuse me?"

"No, thank you. I'd rather stay here. The seats are quite comfortable." To emphasize my point, I propped my feet directly on the seat across from me, ankles covered by my full skirts.

Flat Cap shifted his weight and hefted his gun into both hands. "Maybe we didn't make ourselves clear—"

"True. You have *not* made yourselves clear," I said. "You are very insistent, but I have yet to hear any *real* threats. Let me lay out the facts for you, gentlemen. There are only two options here: either I am in danger or I am not in danger." I pointed one finger out the open door. "One. If I am *not* in any danger, what exactly is the incentive for me to leave my cushion? Or two"—I held up a second finger—"if I *am* in danger, my best option is also to stay put. Leaving the safety of the carriage not only robs me of my comfortable shelter but also neither of you is wearing a mask. I would be able to identify you. And, I imagine, that would only make my situation even *more* precarious. Either way,

I'm staying here." I wiggled my fingers at them in a small wave and quickly withdrew my hand into the carriage.

Seconds passed in heavy silence.

Finally, the tall man tipped back his bowler hat and laughed. His laughter echoed over the landscape, over the soft stamp of the horse hooves and punctuative hiss of steam from the airship above. He held up his hands in defeat. "I surrender! I'm coming in to talk. Please, don't shoot." He passed his weapon to the flat-cap man who shrugged, shouldered both guns, and sauntered away toward his previous post.

Bowler Hat closed the distance in three large strides, grasped the sides of the carriage, and climbed in without lowering the steps. I swung my feet off the seat in time to avoid a collision as he thumped down on the bench. The carriage rocked under his weight.

His genuine smile glinted in the lantern light. "Dear lady, please forgive me . . . forgive *our* disgraceful manners."

"Your *manners*?" I asked. "Not your method of operation?"

"That, too." He removed his hat, and several brown curls fell loose, making him look younger than I'd supposed—more boyish. "Your forgiveness?"

"That depends . . . I will not forgive any injury to myself nor my coachmen."

"Your men are unharmed, though a great deal more frightened than you seem to be."

Contrary to his coarse tone, his smart-set accent was pure; however, I did not fail to notice the highwayman had not made any direct promises for our *continued* safety. He folded his arms over his dark vest, appraising me. So, with the confidence of Robin Renegade, I returned his bold appraisal in kind and positioned myself in a way that put me closer to the door—closer to escape.

He certainly didn't *look* like a highwayman. He looked the same as he had at the inn—like a gentleman. Though why any true gem would resort to carriage robbing was beyond me. I'd never imagined a highwayman removing his hat for a lady. (Of course, even without the hat, his head nearly brushed the carriage hood. So perhaps the gesture was simply out of necessity.) His hair was dark, and the wind-tousled curls draped partially over his eyes, which were the shape and warm color of toasted almonds. I couldn't see any weapons on his person, but that didn't mean there weren't any hidden beneath the thick folds of his leather flight jacket or layered within the wide-shouldered cut of his blanche shirt and brocade double-buttoned vest. He wore no visible jewelry apart from a single round ruby in a gold ring setting.

The overall image was a little rough but, I had to admit, very handsome.

"What, no more clever quips?" he asked with a smirk. "Are you finally frightened of me or simply admiring the view?"

He'd caught me dead to rights. I raised my chin and met his eyes. "You are about as frightening as my cousin's lapdog, Sissy. True, she nips and bares her teeth, but it's all for show."

"Are you implying that I'm all bark and no bite? Would you rather I use *real* threats?"

"I'd rather you use honesty."

"Hm. An intriguing demand, but quite a high asking price. The honest truth is a precious commodity these days." He rolled his bottom lip between his teeth. "Very well. If you refuse to let me steal from you, I'm willing to make a fair trade instead: my honesty for yours."

I narrowed my eyes at him. "All right." I held out my hand the same way Maker Malowney concluded investment meetings. I hoped my gesture looked like something Robin Renegade would do or, at the very least, *confident*. "We have a deal."

He glanced at my outstretched hand and lightly folded it within his. "Honest truth?"

"Honest truth," I repeated.

We shook once.

He didn't let go, and I was suddenly conscious of the bare skin of my palm against his. "You never answered my question," he said. "Now that you've made your appraisal, what do you make of me? Do you admire the view?"

"Yes."

He blinked, noticeably surprised, and I suppressed a smile. He wasn't the only one who could play a rogue.

"My turn," I said. "Why the—"

"Yes. You are quite captivating."

"That . . . wasn't my question." I cleared my throat and gestured to the airship above. "Obviously, this is not your chosen career path. And *that*"—I turned his hand over, revealing his ruby ring—"is probably worth more than this entire carriage. So, why the highwayman act? Why thievery?"

He hastily withdrew his hand and twisted the ring on his finger until the ruby faced inward. If I didn't know any better, I'd have thought he looked self-conscious. But the expression was fleeting. "The situation is difficult to explain."

"Perhaps you see yourself as a noble hero? 'Steal from the greedy to give to the needy,'" I quoted *The Renegade*.

He huffed and mumbled, "More like rob the cog to reward the rich."

"That hardly sounds like a noble cause. Or a catching adage."

"It depends on who you ask," he said, leaning forward onto his elbows. "The gems seem to like it."

My carriage was roomy, but *roomy* wasn't enough to keep a comfortable distance from such a large man. His knees brushed mine. And when he looked over at me, I could see light flecks of gold around the irises of his eyes. My breath caught, but I fought the urge to lean back. I would *not* give him the satisfaction of backing down. Unfortunately, he seemed to notice my discomposure because he grinned wickedly and did not correct the proximate posture.

"We're looking for something," he said. "Something that would be dangerous if it fell into the wrong hands."

"That is . . . vague."

"Then perhaps you'd care to tell me more about it?"

"I'm not sure—wait, you don't think that *I* have this . . . *whatever* dangerous thing you are chasing?" I almost laughed in relief. "Well, you won't find anything out of the ordinary here apart from a woman traveling to visit her aunt, I assure you. I am sorry your search has been in vain. No, truly. Why are you looking at me like that? I haven't the least idea what you're talking about."

"We were led to believe that *something* would be transported outside the capital in a unique manner. With all respect, your carriage is a bit . . ."

"Outdated?"

"Medieval. And what is more unique than a woman traveling alone? On the week of the Queen's Gala, no less. Wouldn't the lady already be in town for the social season?"

"Wouldn't a gentleman mind his own business instead of assaulting the lady's *medieval* carriage?"

He snorted lightly and gave me a suggestive smile. "I'll admit . . . it is difficult to feel like a gentleman in your presence." But, like a gentleman, he righted his posture and once again folded his arms loosely over his wide chest.

I exhaled, relaxing slightly. I hadn't realized I'd been holding my breath, but I felt much safer knowing I didn't seem to have anything he wanted enough to take.

"Let me assure you, Mister . . .?" I paused, waiting for him to supply me with a name.

He smirked and shook his head.

"Let me assure you that the only *somethings* I have in this carriage are an insignificant collection of petty change, some personal letters, a pair of gloves, a hideously orange shawl, and a small box of pastries from The Jolly Cook Inn." I intentionally did *not* mention my romantic play. No need to give the dramatic rogue any more ideas.

"What, no concealed weapon?"

I hesitated. "Nothing too dangerous."

"Oh, I disagree." He eyed me meaningfully. "But I accept the 'honest truth' of your inventory. And so I must depart and leave you to the rest of your journey."

He reached out across the carriage, so I sat forward and took his hand in another firm, businesslike shake. Once again, he did not pull away. Keeping his gaze on my face, he bent forward until his hair fell across his eyes and tickled my wrist. Then he kissed my hand—a very slow, very deliberate kiss.

I couldn't look away. Couldn't breathe. Or think.

Every thought absorbed into the smile of his lips as they pressed against my skin and the feel of his fingers as they traced light circles against my inner palm. His soft breaths warmed the back of my hand.

I didn't have the faintest idea what Robin Renegade would do in my situation, let alone what *I* should do. His kiss was nothing like a kiss from Maker Malowney. This man—this kiss—was deep, passionate, and the suggestion in his touch made my skin ignite with heated implications. The feeling shivered down my spine all the way to my toes.

"One more question," I whispered.

He raised a brow.

"What does it feel like to fly?"

He smiled against my skin. "Enjoy your stay in Tourmaline," he said, voice low. "I hope to have the pleasure of seeing you again soon."

"Thank you, I—wait! I never told you my destination. Were you listening to my conversation with Mr. Jolly?"

He winked and dropped my hand. Then he swung through the door and strode out into the night. Within seconds, the manropes were raised and the faint silhouette of the airship disappeared against the dark sky. The highwaymen were gone as quickly as they had come.

John and Ivo rushed to my foggy carriage window. Evidently, they'd been set free. Once assured that I was unharmed, they leapt back into the driver's box and urged the horses forward. It wasn't until the carriage was moving again and I collapsed limply into my seat, every muscle aching, that I realized my carpetbag was missing.

Chapter Seven

ART

T HAT HAD NOT GONE TO PLAN.

My airship bobbed slightly as Harland and I climbed back aboard.

An earlier search of Pinefoy's estate held no clues. In fact, it was suspicious how ordinary the judge's home had seemed until Harland tapped his boot at a single, red speck on a wooden floorboard.

"Mage Citoyen has already been here."

"How do you know?" I asked.

The mage merely gave me a dead stare. "We're not going to find Pinefoy. Or anything else pertinent for that matter."

Instead, we'd looked into his connections. Pinefoy had only one living heir, Andrew McDevitt Malowney. I knew of him—a greasy man with unnervingly straight teeth who, undeterred by a clear deficit in personality, somehow managed to be popular with the ladies. Evidently, nepotism ran through the Pinefoy veins, because Malowney also happened to be a prominent maker. He'd doubtless inherited the title and stood to inherit everything else from the judge as well. Depending on how much he'd loved his great-uncle, it was his lucky day. (Of course, it could take years before Pinefoy was legally presumed dead and the estate passed on after him.)

When questioning the staff, we'd learned Malowney had recently visited the manor. But despite the height of the social season and the Maker Exhibitions, he'd unexpectedly left Diadem for the country. The timing was suspicious, even if his bride-to-be lived in Luster County. Which, with a few pence from heaven, meant he'd likely stopped to refuel one of his expensive steam autos in Loupe at The Jolly Cook Inn.

Beyond asking Mae a few questions, I didn't share my connection to the inn with Harland. He already knew or could easily guess my secrets. He didn't need to know about my close relationship with the Jollys as well.

Eventually, we'd located the estate of Lady Clune and her grand-daughter, Miss Audrey Clune. But before we could make berth and pay a call, the young Miss Clune set off in her antiquated carriage (with at least one bodyguard posing as a jarvey) while Malowney stayed behind.

We had a choice to make: stay and question Malowney or follow the curious woman and carriage headed toward Diadem. The woman in the carriage—fiancée to the sole heir of Judge Pinefoy and his entire estate—was, at a minimum, privy to important information.

She also happened to be the most delightful obstacle I'd ever come across.

"What are you smiling about?" Harland knocked into my shoulder as the ship rocked against an air current.

I quickly amended my expression. "I didn't realize I was."

"Did you find something?"

I pulled a folded box out of the carpetbag and offered it up to him. "Care for a pastry? I know from experience these don't travel well. We'll have to eat them now."

He responded with the usual dead stare.

"Suit yourself." I untied the string, opened the box, and took a large bite out of one of Jolly's famous confections. I frequented The Jolly Cook Inn for more than one reason. The first because the inn was located halfway between Diadem and the Gallia border. A close second was the food.

Harland removed a small envelope from his inner pocket. "While you were flirting, I nicked this off the jarvey. The ugly one. There was nothing in the luggage."

Licking my fingers, I held a lantern higher. The envelope looked like a formal invitation with scrawling calligraphy along the front. It was addressed to *Lord-Maker Tackleton of Cerussite Hall*.

I groaned, and Harland ticked a brow.

"I have a feeling I'm not going to like this," I answered.

The wax seal was red—indicating the invitation had been sent by a man—and stamped with three gears winding together. Harland ran a finger underneath, and the seal cracked open. The thick card read:

My Dear Lord-Maker,

Thank you for your generous donation. In accordance with our agreement, the designs will be delivered tomorrow morning. You have until seven o'clock the night of Our Lustrous Majesty's Gala to present the remainder of your investment at the Maker's Club. I'm sure I don't need to emphasize the need for confidentiality or the consequences for your failure to comply with the aforementioned conditions.

I look forward to our rewarding partnership.

Sincerely,
M.

"You were right," Harland said. "Malowney had the blueprints."

"And it looks as though he's sold them to *Tackleton*."

"You know him?"

"Only by obligation," I replied. "Why? Did my tone give it away?" I sighed and ran a hand over my face. "Tomorrow is the annual Tackleton garden party. Assuming this letter was meant to be delivered tonight and the blueprints are delivered tomorrow morning, our opportune window to steal them back is while Tackleton is busy entertaining. Which means . . . I'm going to a family party. At least Mum will be happy."

"My condolences." Harland leaned against the taffrail and crossed his arms. "So, Pinefoy stole the blueprints. Malowney was in on it, fled to the country, and sold the blueprints to Tackleton. We're still working with assumptions. We need more information."

"I agree, but every clue leads us here. At least we know Tackleton is a major player."

"Any news from Belwater?" he asked.

"Not yet."

"*Hm*. Let me know if you find anything useful," he said, jutting his chin to the carpetbag. He turned and ascended the stairs to the bridge.

Harland had leastwise proved himself a capable partner in crime—I'd give him that much. He'd followed my navigational flight instructions without question and hadn't interfered with the woman in the carriage. Also, he seemed about as interested in crossing paths with the Magicstry as I was. There was a reason he was working outside the Magicstry, even if he kept that reason to himself. He hadn't shared *why* he wanted the blueprints. But for all other questions, I trusted our compromise while it lasted.

Still, I wouldn't share any intimate details of my work with him. I had no way of knowing how much of my conversation with the queen he'd overheard, and I wasn't about to give him any more information unless absolutely necessary.

I wiped my fingers on a handkerchief and sat cross-legged on the deck to rummage through the carpetbag. There had to be something else . . .

I chuckled as I withdrew a rolled-up play script about Robin Renegade. Flipping through the pages, I discovered the play was a farce similar to the novels Mum liked to read with a plenitude of venturous plots and impractical heroics.

Setting the script aside, I removed a truly hideous shawl and found a stack of letters. Every letter was written from "Aunt Emma" (no formal name). I shuffled the stack twice but found no letters from her betrothed.

I found nothing else in the bag I did not expect. Miss Clune had told the honest truth, which presented another problem—I was sorely tempted to read her private correspondence. Not because I expected to find more information. I simply wanted to learn more about Miss Clune. Rummaging through her personal effects only made me like her more.

I *shouldn't*. Miss Clune was an affianced woman. Of course, something as trifling as a betrothal hadn't stopped Art Keays, the useless flirt, before. But for the first time in recent memory, I'd been entirely myself. I hadn't needed to pretend. Ironic, considering I'd posed as a useless dandy posing as a Ruby Agent posing as a highwayman. The layers of disguise were stifling. It was a relief to be myself with someone I could almost guarantee I'd never see again. Clearly, Miss Clune and I did not run in the same social circles. No one in gem or wealthy cog society would voluntarily travel in that paperboard box on wheels, and according to the return address on her letters, her aunt resided in one of the shabbier districts in Tourmaline.

Clune was one of the older gem names. Malowney must be looking for a better title. But why in all aether would a woman like that ever agree to marry an oil spill like Malowney? Was it for his connections?

At any other time, such questions might matter. The only reason I would see her again was for a reason I invented.

Unless . . . was she involved in the theft?

I spun the ruby ring on my finger and got to my feet. With Harland at the helm, I adjusted the sheets to better angle our sails and fired up the boiler to gain lift. "We're going to Cerussite Hall, but first, I need you to make a stop."

Chapter Eight

Audrey

Even though it was late by the time I arrived, my aunt's cramped townhouse on the outskirts of the residential suburb of Tourmaline was lit from every window to welcome me. My tension instantly dissolved at the sight.

I was finally home.

The foggy air smelled a bit like cabbage from the corner café coupled with residual puddles of rainwater—definitely a contrast from the musty scents of Grandmother's sprawling country manor. But I could breathe deeply in the city.

As soon as the carriage stopped beside the narrow curb, Aunt Emma rushed outside to greet me. Before I could reach for the latch, she popped open the door, kicked down the folding step over a cloudy puddle of water, and unceremoniously hauled me out of the carriage by my shoulders. I laughed and fell into her open arms. Threading my arms through hers, I pulled back and studied her face. Her cheeks had thinned since I'd last seen her, and silvery streaks of grey wove through her light hair. Barely into her forties, she already looked like a much older woman.

My mother had kept a portrait of my aunt from younger days. The artist had portrayed Aunt Emma as full of life—vibrant and wild. The woman before me was like a poorly rendered copy of that painting, as if the Great Maker had chosen to picture her true face with less color and shape. She was too thin. Too sedate. Instead of a portrait, she was a still life.

Aunt Emma rarely spoke about her past, especially her childhood in Gallia. But I frequently wondered what sorts of heartbreak haunted her memories. Something tragic had dimmed that spark of wildfire in her eyes. She looked so pale under the light of the thin moon—a dim shade of her former self. But she was smiling, and I smiled brightly back at her.

"*Exactement!* You are right on time!" she said. Unlike my mother, Aunt Emma purposefully held onto her melodious Gallia accent.

I laughed. "What do you mean? We're hours late!"

"Well, on time from when the letter arrived." Keeping one arm through mine, she steered me toward the house.

"What letter?"

"The letter from your gentleman. He mentioned your stopover in Loupe."

I stopped walking. "My . . . gentleman? In Loupe?"

"You're repeating everything I say, *mon cœur.*"

"My gent—*a* gentleman was here?"

She shot me a look of poorly suppressed mischief. "Whatever is the matter? A courier arrived with a letter which explained that you were detained but safe, and I should expect your arrival within the hour, and — Are your ears turning pink?"

I knocked her hand away and surely failed to sound casual as I asked, "By any chance, was this *courier* wearing a bowler hat. Or a cloth hat?"

"*Oui*, I believe he was wearing a cloth cap."

I swallowed. "May I see the letter?"

Her lips quirked. But she released my arm, pulled a thick folded paper from the pocket of her old-fashioned skirts, and handed it to me. I turned it over and examined the red wax seal embossed with gold and instantly recognized the imprint—a large circle surrounded by points like a crown. It was the same pattern and design as the ruby and setting of the highwayman's ring.

I hastily unfolded the letter and read:

My Dear Lady,

I write to inform you that your niece is well and you may expect her arrival within the hour. I had the immense pleasure of encountering Miss Clune during her stopover at The Jolly Cook in Loupe, although I am afraid I unnecessarily delayed her journey. Please forgive me for any worry I may have inadvertently caused. Her company was difficult to resist.

On a second point, please inform Miss Clune that I am in possession of her missing luggage, and I would be most delighted to call in person to return said belongings at your earliest convenience. You may address your response to Cerussite Hall, care of

Your Honest Servant,
A. K.

HONEST SERVANT INDEED!

The specific wording of his missive might have been truthful, but it lacked a full signature. No formal title before the initials. Nothing that might give any further clues as to his identity. Whereas *he* had obviously discovered my name and where to find Aunt Emma.

Had the rogue read my letters?

More importantly, exactly what motive could he have for treating my stolen carpetbag like a wayward puppy? It wasn't as if my bag had casually wandered off! Did he mean to leverage my belongings? That bag contained nothing I could not bear to part with. Granted, the thought of him discovering my silly playscript was enough of an embarrassment to make my ears burn again with shame. The bag itself had been a gift from my favorite governess before she'd been dismissed by Grandmother. Oh—and the pastries! I'd been looking forward to sampling more of Mr. Jolly's delicious cooking.

One thing was clear. The *gentleman* in question expected me to keep the true details of our meeting a secret. I hummed through my nose in frustration and glanced up to find Aunt Emma monitoring my reaction with an amused expression.

"That letter was obviously meant more for you than for me," she said. "What happened to your luggage?"

In defiance of the letter, I saw no reason to keep secrets from dear Aunt Emma. I was about to launch into the full story when she added, "And how did you get mixed up with a Ruby Guard?"

"A *what*?" I took a deep breath to formulate a coherent question. "How do you know that he is an officer of the queen?"

"I recognize the seal, *mon cœur*. You didn't know? Well, I suppose there aren't many who would." She tapped the indented red and gold wax on the letter and paused long enough that I flicked her arm. "*Juste ciel!* I saw that same seal on a ring several years ago. When Amalie was at the height of her fame, thousands of people would travel to Diadem to attend a single performance. The Jeweled Palace was practically overrun. So the queen assigned a handful of guards to protect Amalie during her stay. There were military soldiers, and then there were . . . well, we never officially learned who they were. Some sort of defense or intelligence officers. Two men who wore no military attire and no insignia apart from a ruby signet ring. From what I could tell, they followed only direct orders from the queen herself."

"And you're sure *this* is the same signet . . . or the same seal?"

"*J'en suis sûr.*" She nodded and tilted her head to the side. "Is this the man you wrote to me about? The one your grandmother wants you to marry? She would like a royalist gem, wouldn't she? But here—" She tapped the letter again. "He seems very different from what you've written to me in your letters."

"No. That is Maker Malowney. I've never met this man until today."

"*Ah bon*? How intriguing."

"Indeed." What reason would an officer of the queen have for concealing his identity? More importantly, why would he rob my carriage? The highwayman had said he was looking for something that could be dangerous if it fell into the wrong hands. The idea of an unknown threat coming anywhere near Aunt Emma . . .

Until I knew what game I'd inadvertently joined, I decided to hold onto my cards before laying them out on the table.

"Intriguing enough to tell me more?" she asked.

"Not really, no," I said with a shrug.

"I see." She sighed noisily. "Well, Mr. Nothing has a very elegant way of writing. And he must have been handsome to delay your journey for so long."

"What? No, that's not—"

"Too bad that letter is addressed to me and not to you. Otherwise, I might let you keep it."

I quickly refolded the letter and thrust it out to her. "I don't want it."

"Of course, *mon cœur*," she said with a grave nod. "But aren't you going to write him back?"

"I most certainly am not." He could choke on those pastries for all I cared.

"Well, I suppose that makes sense," she said. "If he is a guest at the Hall, you won't have to write. We should see him in person at the garden party tomorrow."

That brought me up short. I'd almost forgotten about the garden party. Every year, Lady Tackleton of Cerussite Hall received practically every gem in the city for a garden party the week of the Queen's Gala. Lord-Maker Tackleton displayed the working models of his most modern airship designs, and all sorts of games and recreations were spaced throughout the surrounding Trolleywood Park.

I'd only attended once, the year before. The weather had been miserably hot—too hot even for Lord Tackleton to inflate the airships for guest use. I was devastated I'd lost the opportunity to fly. Then I'd stubbed my toe during the first game and was unable to dance or hike the forest paths to the lake for boating. Freshly churned ice cream was the one pleasance I remembered with fondness, but even the lure of a second taste was not enough to tempt me into another meeting with the highway-intelligence-officer.

Especially not if Aunt Emma kept teasing me.

Besides, the highwayman had referenced Cerussite Hall, but that did not automatically signify we occupied similar social circles. He couldn't be well-known in society—not if he was drifting around robbing carriages. Perhaps he was visiting one of the lower halls?

"Do we really need to go?" I asked. "We barely have time alone together, and even less time to prepare for the gala. We could spend the day walking the Glass District. You promised to trade the latest town news for my country gossip while we eat boxed chocolates. Oh! And I brought a bundle of ribbons we can stitch for our dresses."

"Stitching ribbons? Oh dear. You must really want to avoid Mr. Nothing if you're begging to sew."

I grimaced. Aunt Emma knew me too well.

"But the point is moot," she said. "I have already written to Lady Tackleton to accept our invitation. Besides, why would you want to give up the *immense pleasure* of seeing your officer again?"

"It was *his* immense pleasure, not mine," I grumbled.

Aunt Emma laughed and waved at someone over my shoulder. I turned and saw John making his way down the narrow steps from the townhouse. "Thank you for delivering my niece safely."

If only she knew how difficult *that* task had been.

"You know where to find the stables?" she asked. "Just two blocks north past the costermongers square. I need to check on the linens, Audrey, *mon cœur*. But I've already made up your room and left out a late supper in the kitchen. Join me there?" Without waiting for an answer from either of us, she waved once more and ducked inside.

John met me under the dim streetlamp. At the sight of his face, I let out a small cry of alarm. He had a bandaged cut above his left eye.

"Mr. John. What happened? *When* did that happen?"

He dug a toe against the pavement. "The carriage, Miss."

"You never said a word!"

"Nothin' to fret." He tugged back his hat and scratched at a spot of thinning white hair. "I hit my head on the box railing when the horses spooked. I'm just glad you're all right, Miss."

"Why didn't you tell me?" I fussed and tilted his head farther into the light shining from the cottage windows, and I inspected his blood-stained livery and scabbed cut. "So much blood! This cut must have been deep, but I'm glad you were able to stop the bleeding. I—I haven't exactly told my Aunt the whole of what happened . . . not yet. But I'll ask her how to clean your tunic. *Hm.* The scab looks thin and clean, and this bandage is tidy work. Good work there."

"Oh, it weren't me, Miss," he said. "The man on the road took care of it."

"Sorry?"

"Right nice pair of rascals if you ask me, though I heard you givin' em the what fer. The sullen one apologized when he saw my head, an' offered to bandage me back together. Stopped the bleedin' straight 'way."

"You mean . . . he helped bandage your head while you were tied up?" I asked.

John frowned quizzically. "I'm not sure as I understand, Miss. Once he reached the ground, the fellow waved us down, calmed the horses, and set me under a tree just as soon as he seen me head. I don't know naught about being tied up."

They're tied down, he'd said.

I'd assumed the highwayman had meant the coachmen. But he'd simply tethered the spooked horses. What else had I *assumed*? Or what else had that man led me to believe simply by playing the part of mysterious highwayman? My curiosity piqued.

"Miss?"

"Oh, forgive me," I said, shaking myself back to the present. "Do you need anything? I could make an offering to the local Magicstry and petition them to heal you," I said, even though I shivered at the thought of braving those hard eyes and dark robes.

Thankfully, he was shaking his head before I'd finished. "No, thank you. That won't be necessary. I only come to tell you that Ivo and me—

we delivered your trunk upstairs. Will you be needing anything else before we retire for the night?"

"No, thank you, John."

"Right, then. We'll be at the Bearing Street boarding house. Just send a runner when you need me to collect you. Goodnight, Miss." He tipped his hat and headed back to the carriage at an easy pace.

I turned for the door but stopped when I remembered the sealed letter in my hand—the same hand the highwayman had kissed. I glanced to make sure Aunt Emma was still inside and opened it and reread its contents, suppressing a smile.

Difficult to resist, hmm? Perhaps I would attend the garden party. Then that highway-officer-rogue would learn just how irresistible I could be with a head full of questions and a mystery to solve.

Chapter Nine

Audrey

Aunt Emma made me feel like the gravity of her world. She asked me constant questions, fussed over my hair, and selected my afternoon dress for our excursion into the city. Grandmother might not welcome my foreign heritage, but even she had to admit that Gallia fashion was the best. The crème silk fabric wouldn't look half so elegant without the expert cut and copper stitching.

Then it was my turn to pamper Aunt Emma. She resisted, of course, but I knew exactly where to push and prod her into surrender. In the end, she allowed me to plait her hair into a more intricate style, and I selected a rose-pink dress and teardrop hat—only a few years out of date—that brought out a little more color in her drawn cheeks. She even accepted, albeit reluctantly, a mauve wrap I'd brought for her to wear.

Meanwhile, we discussed who she'd seen in town for the social season, the latest plays each of us had read, and my laughable attempts at lawn tennis. And somehow, as we huddled together in my cramped but cozy room, I breathed easier than I had in months.

After sharing a box of Dominica's Fine Chocolates in lieu of teatime, we set out.

Rather than suffer the embarrassment of driving horses along the neatly paved city streets, Aunt Emma and I opted to ride the city streetcar uptown to the Glass District before taking the carriage the rest of the way to Cerussite Hall.

Diadem City was truly the centerpiece of the Parure. Even in the cog neighborhoods, most homes were designed with at least one multicolored stained glass window and iron settings of intricate latticework. Owing to a popular architectural trend from a handful of decades earlier, tenement buildings also included a knobby observatory tower veined with clear glass like a *croquembouche* held together with spun sugar.

Soon, the residential neighborhoods gave way to more shops and restaurants, and the innermost city streets were a riot of color and sound. Merchant cogs strung patterned awnings between brightly painted rooftops and displayed their wares in every available cranny of space between eye-catching window displays. And everywhere, amid the to-ing and fro-ing of modern living, steam rose in puffs from auto engines, water pumps, and factory turbines to fly with the freedom of downy clouds.

I leaned out the open window of the streetcar and inhaled the humidity, the sweet scent of plantains and cream overlapped with fried cakes, and honey-grilled vegetables over smokey fires. But I plopped back onto my seat cushion as the streetcar hit a bump in the road. Aunt Emma smoothed my hair back into place.

"Will Lady Tackleton have strawberries and ice cream this year?" I asked.

"But of course—*bon ton!* Now, before we arrive . . . tell me about the handsome man! At least, I assume Mr. Nothing is handsome. You haven't told me anything about him."

I groaned. "Can't we be free of men a little while longer? Why ruin the conversation?"

"I want to hear about this Ruby Agent of yours before I meet him."

"He . . ." I still had no idea what to say. I was nervous to involve Aunt Emma in something I didn't fully understand. And in the light of day, I was rather embarrassed to tell my aunt the whole story. If I did, I would have to admit that the Ruby Agent and I had not been formally introduced, the majority of our conversation had taken place alone in a dark carriage, and his intentions (like his name) were a complete mystery to me. What would happen when we met at the garden party and Aunt Emma expected me to lead introductions?

A Robin Renegade character did not easily coincide with my role as a doting niece.

It was clear the highwayman planned to keep his secrets. But he owed me an explanation—several explanations, in fact.

His search for something potentially dangerous.

My missing bag.

That kiss . . .

All of it.

I rubbed the back of my hand and held onto the bench in front of me as the streetcar hit a bump. I would not lie to Aunt Emma, but I also worded my response carefully. "I can truthfully say that he is a complete mystery to me." *First of which is his name.* "We saw each other at The Jolly Cook Inn. He later came into possession of my carpetbag and wishes to return it."

"What was the 'delay' he mentioned?"

"I had some trouble with my carriage, that's all. No, don't look at me like that. Truly, that is all I can tell you."

"Hm. Then tell me about your Mr. Malowney."

"Maker Malowney," I corrected automatically.

"*Maker* Malowney, is he?" she asked. "Well, your letters were unnecessarily vague about him, too. Have things progressed with him?"

"My letters are hardly censored. You know I tell you everything."

She gestured for me to elaborate. "What is he like?"

What could I say? *By marrying him, I'll be able to access my inheritance left by my mother. He's rich enough that we'll both be provided for.*

I could never abandon Aunt Emma, not when she depended on me for her living. I'd been too selfish. I'd dodged Maker Malowney's proposal simply to postpone the obligation, and I hadn't even considered how my delay might affect Aunt Emma. The passing buildings rose and flattened like waves on a stone sea even as a tight knot of shame surged around my stomach like *mal de mer*. But I mustered a cheerful response.

"Maker Malowney occupies the most modern social circles of technological advancement. His makes—mostly steamcars and weapons manufacturing—have been featured at the Jeweled Palace. And in addition to his work as maker, he is also a patron for several new inventions. About two years ago, he started managing Grandmother's business investments in her attempt to bring the household into a more modern era. He is also closely related to Judge Vincent Pinefoy. Have you heard of him?"

"A judge for the Maker Exhibitions? Clearly he is very impressive. But I asked about your man. What is he, *Malowney*, like? Give me his personal character, not a social resume. I don't need his pedigree."

"Well . . ." I picked at a frayed edge of the seat upholstery. "He has been invited to dine with us quite often and fills our evenings with plenty of conversation."

The corner of her mouth twitched with a smile. "You mean he's a windbag."

"I didn't say that."

"Pompous then."

"*No*, at least . . . he's very educated," I said. "And handsome."

"Handsome how?"

"Classically handsome. He has very straight teeth and—"

"Oh, for Maker's sake!" She threw up her hands.

"It's the truth!"

She gave me a flat stare. "That may be the truth. Now, tell me something *real*."

"I *am*."

"*Audrey*." She waited until I met her gaze. "The only *real* information I've learned from our last few minutes of conversation is that your grandmother continues to control your life, you think that Mr.— *Maker* Malowney is boring and self-centered, but you are completely captivated by this mystery officer of yours."

"I never said any of that."

"Not with words." She winked.

I held in my rebut with pinched lips as the streetcar stopped and a pair of older women took the seats across from us. But perhaps Aunt Emma was right. Perhaps I was captivated. Not by the highwayman himself. (How could I be captivated after only five minutes of conversation with the man?) But rather by the freedom he represented. I was more likely smitten with Robin Renegade and the notion of a new character for myself. She was a person who sailed the skies, demanded honesty, and trailblazed her own future, while Audrey Clune saw only one path before her.

As the streetcar resumed our journey, I leaned my forehead against the open window frame and peeked up at the alleyway of open sky between buildings. "I'm determined to see the airships," I said resolutely.

Aunt Emma playfully bumped my shoulder with hers. "Stay away from lawn tennis, then. You'll stub your toe and miss the air tour."

"Oh, don't tease! But you are right, I'd better not hazard the lawn games. In fact, I may never touch ground again once I finally reach the skies."

"*Never* again? Not even to join me in the picnic tent?"

I clutched her arm and pretended to swoon. "Not without dessert! And never without you, dear aunt, of course. Oh, look!" We passed the purple-trimmed windows of a music box shop. The boxes were an ingenious invention of music with dancers that twirled on top. Even in passing, I recognized some as popular figures from classic opera and ballet while other miniature statuettes represented familiar fairytales and folklore. A music box played and dancers twirled with a lamp behind them; their shadows danced across a white screen like a puppet show, acting the allegorical tale of a boy and his pet bullfrog.

"What a clever window display!" I marveled. "Have you seen it? You're not becoming a hermitess, are you? You're leaving the house? You're getting fresh air?"

"I open the window at least once a month," Aunt Emma replied dryly.

"Thankfully, I know you're teasing. You have more friends here than the entire population of Luster County."

"Ah, yes. That miserable place. I suppose it would be rude of me never to ask . . . how is Her Majesty of Luster?"

"Grandmother is *quite well*. As always. She sends her regards."

Aunt Emma gave an indelicate guffaw and received an indignant look from the two matronly women seated on the bench across from us. "Dishonesty is never civil, *mon cœur*. I know very well Eugenia sends me anything but her regards. A snake in a box, maybe."

No love was lost between my grandmother and Aunt Emma. Grandmother made her opinions quite clear—and loudly—about what she thought of my father marrying not only a Gallia immigrant but an actress as well. The Toussaint family was the single unkempt branch on her otherwise perfectly cultivated family tree.

Aunt Emma noticed my fallen expression. "I apologize. That was unkind of me. I don't wish to come between you and your grandmother. She and I have converse opinions, especially concerning your upbringing . . . but I respect the care she's taken to raise you."

"No, that's not it. Do you ever wish . . ." I bit my lip.

"Hm?"

I shook my head. "I shouldn't have said anything."

"Please. I wish to hear."

I turned away as a light trill of music drifted through the open window. A group of children were dancing beside a street performer. The younger ones shouted and rang imaginary bells as our streetcar passed.

"Do you ever wonder if things could've been different?" I asked quietly. "What life would be like if I'd come to live with you after Mother died?" I quickly backtracked. "I realize that wasn't possible. But I miss you when we're apart."

"Not possible?"

"I'm happiest when I'm here with you. In Luster, I'm obligated to playact . . . to *become* someone else. But here, I'm closer to the person I want to be." I hesitated. How could I put things delicately? "I've always known that your . . . *circumstances* prevent me from coming to live with you. At least until I'm financially independent. But Mother's bequest is held in trust until my twenty-first birthday. Until then, Grandmother is my ruler in judgment, and I would never wish to risk your future by upsetting her—"

Aunt Emma put a hand to her temple. She was shaking her head, blinking rapidly. "Audrey. What exactly has your grandmother told you about my situation? For that matter, what has she told you about *your* situation? About your inheritance?"

I stuttered, unsure how to answer.

"*Cette femme est—*" She glanced around the streetcar—at the matronly women who shot her another affronted look at the sudden outburst—and pinched the bridge of her nose. After several deep breaths, she faced me and clasped my hands tightly in hers. "*Mon cœur* . . . you *always* have a home with me."

"But—" My lungs felt constricted by the sudden swelling of my heart. "How?" I rasped.

"You were *so* young when Amalie died," she said. "Barely sixteen. I tried to take you in, but your grandmother insisted she could offer you so much more in life. A familiar environment. Gem society. Education. We both eventually agreed that considering your— We agreed that the country is safer than Diadem. I thought I was making the right choice for you at the time. I thought . . . I *assumed* you were happy and safe in Luster." She tipped my chin and looked directly into my eyes. "But if you are unhappy, *none* of that matters."

I blinked back sudden tears.

"Clearly, I was mistaken to wait. I should have shared more with you. I should have—" She glanced over her shoulder. "You deserve so much more. Tonight, after the party, will you have a cup of chocolate with me? I promise to share everything. Then you may decide whether to forgive me for waiting so long."

"Of course I'll forgive you!"

"I hope so. Every choice I've made has been in an effort to allow yours, even though I failed to see how miserable you've been."

"I never said I was miserable."

"Not with words." She brushed a stray tear from my cheek. "Now, ring the bell. This is our stop."

Chapter Ten

Audrey

Aunt Emma's promise filled me with hope, yet I was ravenous for more answers. Was there truly another choice—another future—open to me?

A tingling tension bubbled beneath my skin—a blend of excitement and nervous energy. Life in Diadem was nothing like the quiet isolation of my country upbringing. The city streets were alive with music, like hearing a symphony after years of little more than whispers.

John met us at the streetcar stop, and we left our bench seats behind for the cushioned comfort of my carriage box. As we drove, the bustling shops gave way to the trees and winding streams of Trolleywood Park, the city symphony dimming as we turned onto a private drive.

At last, we arrived at Cerussite Hall.

A long queue of steam autos wound around the impressive drive of the manor—including some unique designs I'd only heard described in conversations with Maker Malowney or seen in penciled blueprint drawings in the *Illustrated Journal of Manufacture and Build*. I observed each with interest. One was an open-topped rig shaped like a serving dish with a steam-stack ladle. Another was built more like a suit of armor with plated metal flaps shielding the bonnet and sturdy boiler. The occupants were equally modernized with belt corsets, tall boots, and brass pins. I scanned the crowd for a bowler hat.

"As a guest of the Hall," Aunt Emma said, "I expect he's already inside."

I snapped my attention back to the steam autos without comment.

Ours was the only horse-drawn carriage—a method of transportation so obscure it had even attracted the attention of highwaymen. It was better than a hired hackney—but not by much. We were certainly attracting attention at the Hall. (No one else left droppings along the pristine pavement.)

Aunt Emma either didn't mind the ignominy or simply ignored the stares, and she sustained our conversation with anecdotes about her longtime friendship with Lady Tackleton, the mistress of Cerussite Hall.

We edged forward in line. Our horses stomped and huffed impatiently until we pulled up alongside the staircase and arched double doors of Cerussite Hall. Every angle and detail of the vast manor had been constructed with extreme precision. Carved pillars as thick as oak tree trunks supported a curved balcony which gracefully shadowed the main entrance. Detailed metal railings lined the balcony and lower levels like an elegant lace trim, and slender gas lantern posts were interspersed around the entire foundation. As the mineral name suggested, the whitewashed exterior of Cerussite Hall framed tall sloping windows that brightly refracted rainbows of light and color.

John handed us out of the box, and a smartly dressed servant escorted us directly up the wide steps and into the Hall, the inside of which was even grander than the exterior. Elaborately framed paintings of pastoral fields and shepherdesses hung above impeccable furnishings, and the reflective windows cast dancing rainbows along the lush Eastern rugs. Even more fantastical than the windows were the miniature tram tracks laid directly into the wood floors. I watched, fascinated, as a mechanized trolley carrying a full silver tea service and biscuits chugged past my toes and into the next room.

The servant ushered us upstairs to a private dressing room where we deposited our wraps and reticules into the growing collection of finery. Aunt Emma insisted on dusting me off and rearranging my copper derby in front of the full-length mirror before making our appearance on the lawn. She also insisted on brushing a bit of metallic creme on my lips to match the copper wire stitched though my bodice. I didn't protest too much. The highwaymen had seen me on a dark road in a rumpled travel dress. But the society garden party was an entirely different setting, and I was a Jeweled lady with a stunning costume to match. With my fair hair pinned to cascade over one shoulder beneath my slanted hat, a dress of crème silk, and boned bodice with filigreed copper stitching along the waist and neckline, I looked like a classical statue marbled with veins of copper—a pagan goddess of romance.

Grandmother allowed me to manage my own wardrobe. In that, at least, I was *au fait*.

Once Aunt Emma had finished her inspection of me, I pulled her in front of the mirror, smoothed her skirts, and pinned an errant curl. Once again, I was struck by how much Aunt Emma had changed. She was unquestionably beautiful, but her prematurely greying hair only seemed to emphasize the small, downturned lines crinkling around her eyes and mouth, and her rose-pink dress was plain and the cut outdated. What had caused such a downturn in her fortunes? She'd never lacked friends or social connection. Still, I thought of how lonely her life must be without a husband or children and no money to travel.

"What is that look for?" she asked, meeting my gaze in the mirror.

"I've missed you, Aunt Emma. I can't think of a single place I'd rather be than here with you."

"*Quelle absurdité.*" But she pulled me into a tight embrace. "We will talk more tonight. Oh, I've wrinkled your dress!" She repeated the smoothing process over again.

The same servant was waiting for us outside the dressing room door when we emerged. He bowed and led the way downstairs, past the tea trollies, and out onto the back terrace. From there, we had a full view of the grounds.

And the sky.

Moored but five yards above the garden gazebo was the most beautiful airship I'd ever seen. Her build was like a miniature frigate, named after the red-bellied frigatebird from the tropics, with a single decked gondola and maneuverable sails around three partially inflated swells. She looked graceful, fast, and utterly perfect. I barely noticed the three additional airships anchored throughout the gardens.

Unlike the year before which had been stiflingly hot, the weather was idyllic. Puffy white clouds dotted the sky with no sign of rain until later in the evening. I inhaled deeply and imagined the slight breeze trickling through the park, along the lawn, and through the sails of the airship before gently brushing my face and the ends of my hair with smells of budding summer flowers and clean canvas.

What would Cerussite Hall and the trees look like from the sky? How long would it take to reach the Jeweled Palace? How long before I saw frigatebirds and tropicbirds on the southern coast? Would I even miss the doves?

Aunt Emma was tugging at my hand. "Come along, *mon cœur*. Lady Tackleton is waiting."

Reluctantly, I dropped my gaze from the sky and descended the terrace steps.

A large white pavilion stood in the center of the meticulously manicured lawn. Servants toted baskets of china between tables loaded with artfully stacked food and drinks. Farther down, clusters of armchairs, lounges, and a thick, vast carpeting of imported blankets were arranged in neat semicircles under the shade while a string quartet played beautiful, lulling music. On the far side of the lawn, I spotted several ongoing sporting activities including archery, croquet, and my least favorite, lawn tennis. A thick line of trees marked the edge of Trolleywood Park. The trollies chugged to and from the lakeshore at the center of the park where boats and boatmen provided tours. Beyond the Trolleywood, the multicolored spires of the city peeked above even the tallest trees.

The party was well underway—ladies dressed in wide bonnets and pastel gowns flitted from one circle of gossip to the next like butterflies searching for nectar, a group of children ran beside a foxhound, and gentlemen milled together or clumped near the sporting stations. Every Jeweled family, it seemed, had turned up for the event. I wouldn't have been surprised if the queen herself floated in on her air yacht.

So, where would I find a rogue highwayman with a stolen carpetbag?

Aunt Emma led us directly to a pair of women standing beneath the shade of the white pavilion. The first was Lady Tackleton. She was a pillar of ageless elegance dressed in silks of soft gold, and her light brown hair was arranged gracefully beneath a wide sunbonnet. The second woman wore a fabulously embroidered saree. But in place of a reticule, she carried a stubby dog.

Lady Tackleton smiled as we approached. "Emmaline, I'm so glad you've come! And I see you've brought your niece, Miss Clune. You are both very welcome!" She and Aunt Emma embraced in a warm greeting. "Have you met Mrs. Keays?"

"Please, call me Hattie!" The plump woman flapped a hand as she spoke. "Emmaline speaks so highly of you."

"I'm very pleased to meet you," I said with a curtsy. "And thank you for extending your invitation to include me, Lady Tackleton. Your home is even more exquisite than I remember."

"We've made a few additions since last year, including a pianoforte on the lawn, but my . . . you are stunning. I daresay you've grown even prettier than the last time I saw you. As pretty as your mother, Maker rest her soul, and just as accomplished or so I hear! You must agree to play for us, Miss Clune."

"I doubt my performance will live up to your expectations if I'm measured against my mother, but I'm afraid I've only ever played for dinner parties. I didn't prepare—"

"Don't let her feign modesty," interrupted Aunt Emma. "Audrey is just as pretty, just as talented, and just as willing to perform in company as my dear sister ever was."

"Aunt Emma!" My mother had not been known for her modesty. "Grandmother wouldn't approve. She doesn't like me to play outside of her private parties."

Aunt Emma stared me down. "Your grandmother isn't here."

"Yes, but—"

"Audrey, *mon cœur*. What do *you* want to do?"

What did I want? I hardly ever answered that question. Lady Tackleton watched me with a hopeful smile, but Aunt Emma waited for my genuine answer. Tentatively, I nodded. "I would love to play."

"Then it's settled," Lady Tackleton said with a glittering laugh. "I will make the announcement myself."

"Allow me!" A gentleman spoke behind me. "I have no idea what I'm supposed to announce, but everyone knows I'm the best at getting attention."

I stepped aside to make room for the newcomer.

And froze.

He was as handsome as I remembered with tousled hair and almond eyes, but the highwayman had changed costumes. The leather flight jacket and vest were gone, replaced by a full suit in varying shades of tan with a burgundy waistcoat. Not a speck of lint flawed the expensive fabric. Gold chains were strung between buttonholes like stage curtains, and a series of gold cuffs curved around the shell of his ear. His curly hair was neatly combed beneath a tan bowler, and his eyes were lined with kajal.

He looked like a complete rake.

I clamped my jaw closed and glanced at his hand. He wore the gold ring, but the ruby seal was turned in toward his palm.

Also, he hadn't yet seemed to notice me. Did he not recognize me?

"There you are, my dear boy!" Hattie Keays exclaimed. "I wondered where you'd gone."

Lady Tackleton motioned for him to join our circle. "Allow me to introduce Miss Toussaint and her lovely niece, Miss Audrey Clune."

His startled gaze snapped to mine—eyes comically wide.

I'd already found my footing, so it was gratifying to watch him teeter so far off-balance.

Hattie Keays proudly patted the highwayman's elbow with her free hand. "This is my son, Mr. Arthur Keays."

"Your . . . *son*?" The smile I leveled at him could have deflated an entire airship ballonet. "Pleasure to see you again, *Mr. Keays*."

"Oh!" Hattie Keays glanced between us with apparent interest. "Have you already been introduced?"

He made a choking sound covered by a cough.

"We have already met, yes." I hoped no one noticed the distinction between 'met' and 'introduced.' But I was grateful I'd been spared the embarrassment of introducing my aunt to a man with no name.

"What a splendid coincidence!" She beamed, clearly overlooking the tension between us. "Did you hear, Art? Miss Clune has just agreed to honor us with a piano performance."

However disconcerting a meeting with the mother of my highway robber might be for me, *he* looked positively mortified. But then, like the moon eclipsing the sun, the highwayman obscured himself behind his new character once more, adopting a lax posture and lazy smirk. "I can think of nothing I'd rather hear, including the sound of my own voice."

I blinked at the glaring change, trying and failing to make some sense of the situation. I couldn't very well call him out in front of his mother and aunt, peers of Parure society, could I? Not to mention their close friendship with Aunt Emma. Who was this man, really?

So much for the 'honest truth.'

"Mrs—Hattie is your mother. And you are also Lady Tackleton's nephew?" I hedged.

"The *favorite* nephew, naturally," he corrected. "We are not blood relatives, though she has been kind enough to adopt me as such."

"Lady Tackleton is the sister to my sister-in-law," said Hattie Keays.

Mr. Keays gave a languid bow to Aunt Emma and glanced between us. "It is a pleasure to make your acquaintance, Miss Toussaint. I see the family resemblance. And Miss Clune . . ." He took my hand—the same hand he'd kissed the night before. "You look positively radiant in the sunlight."

He must have guessed my retort about highway robbers at night. Because before I could speak, his eyes crinkled at the corners with mischief, and he pinned my hand firmly under his arm. "There are some very fine refreshments across the lawn. Miss Clune, you *must* allow me to escort you. With you on my arm, no one will be able to withstand our combined beauty."

"How chivalrous. There wouldn't happen to be any *pastries*"—I grunted, attempting to free my hand—"would there?"

He held fast. "Pastries? Are they your favorite?"

"They *were*."

That mischievous look again. "What a coincidence! I recently obtained a box of the most delicious pastries from The Jolly Cook Inn. Alas, I ate them all. If only I'd known sooner, I could've shared."

Insufferable!

Unfortunately for me, Aunt Emma joined in. "Don't let her mislead you, Mr. Keays. I have it on good authority that my niece very much prefers strawberries and ice cream."

"Does she now? And what other advice can you offer me about Miss Clune on 'good authority'?"

"Oh, 'good authority' can't tell you everything, I'm afraid. You'll have to find out the rest for yourself. And now, if you'll excuse me, I should go and say hello to Mrs. Darbansville."

"We don't know a Mrs. Darbansville," I said.

"Then I should go and meet her."

"I'll come with you," said Hattie Keays. "As long as you promise not to mention the Exhibitions. Honestly, each rumor is sillier than the last."

Aunt Emma kissed cheeks with Lady Tackleton. "Have a lovely time. Good day, Mr. Keays!"

"But—"

They promptly set off across the lawn toward Trolleywood, and Lady Tackleton greeted a new cluster of guests.

I tried not to feel abandoned. After all, I had a growing collection of questions that needed answering. Where was my carpetbag? Who was the real highway-robber-Mr.-Keays? And why was he staring down at me with that tilted smile?

"I like your aunt," he said. "Luckily she gave me the advantage. I don't know what I would have done if the both of you had joined forces against me. You make quite a formidable pair. Shall we begin our afternoon with strawberries and cream, then?" Without waiting for an answer, he led me toward the refreshment pavilion.

"*Our* afternoon? You are very forward, sir, to assume my particular company. I am not in the habit of spending my afternoons with strangers."

"Would you prefer to spend another evening together instead?"

I wanted to pinch that drowsy smirk off his face. But if Robin Renegade could keep her calm, then so would I. "Let's start with the basics, shall we? Who are you?"

"I should think my mum and aunt covered that topic significantly well."

"I was referring to your character, *Mr. Keays.* Were you playing at being a highwayman last evening, or is this dandified version of you the real pretense?"

"I assure you, I am quite sincere in my pretenses."

I scoffed. "As I recall, we made an agreement in respect of the *honest truth.*"

For the first time, his lazy smile tightened at the edges. "Yes . . . we did."

"Then what is your rank?"

"Beg pardon?"

"Lieutenant, perhaps?" I mused. "Or are you Sergeant Keays? I am unfamiliar with the terms. What rank is one required to earn to become a Ruby Agent?"

He stumbled slightly on the downward slope of grass. "Why would you think—"

"The seal on your letter," I said. Because truthfully, I had not recognized his ring until Aunt Emma identified the seal.

"Don't tell me that you read your aunt's *private* letter?" Once again, he turned the smirk up full-steam. He tapped the brim of his hat as a couple strolled past us in the opposite direction. "If I'd known you were so eager to hear from me, I could have written a letter for you, too. Something much more . . . personal."

I certainly would *not* mention that his letter to my aunt was currently tucked inside my reticule nor that I had read its contents.

Several times.

Or that I also found his company difficult to resist. I refused to let him redirect the conversation. "Why did you accost my carriage?" I asked.

"Technically we—"

"Why not command us to stop in the name of the queen?"

"Well, Miss Clu—"

"Why did you conceal your identity?"

"I—"

And why—"

"For Maker's sake, lower your voice!" he hissed.

"*Aha!*"

He pivoted and faced me directly. "*Please*, Miss Clune. No one can know."

"About your moonlighting as a thief?"

He frowned and pointedly fiddled with his ring.

"Or do you mean . . . does no one here know about your . . . *career*?" I asked.

He shook his head.

"Not even your mother?"

"The ring is . . . a recent promotion." The anxiety in his voice did not match his posture. He was still an actor playing a part. But the flaws in his performance were easy for me to spot now that I knew which part he was playing.

The rake was the pretense. The highwayman, the man I met the night previous, was real. Did that mean the depth—that passion—was real, too? Why would he maintain such a pretense even in the company of family?

He cast a harried look around the lawn. Even with no one nearby, his next words were spoken low. "Any exposure could jeopardize my . . . *assignment* and compromise my safety, not to mention the safety of everyone involved, including you, Miss Clune."

"Is that a threat?"

"What? No! Of course not. Well, technically I shouldn't allow—but, no! You are not in any danger from me, Miss Clune. The fault is mine. And you . . . you're teasing me, aren't you?"

I grinned. "You're not very good at making direct threats, you know."

He sighed heavily. "I underestimated you. A mistake I seem to have made more than once, first in attempting to waylay your carriage and second in my failure to conceal my . . . interests. I would hate for my error to put you at risk."

I hummed, considering. "Am I to understand that the details of our meeting last night, if revealed, would put anyone involved, directly or indirectly, in danger?"

He nodded, and I immediately resolved to speak with Aunt Emma. Was she in danger now, too? I doubted she would mention the royal seal or the letter, but I needed to be sure.

"Please, Miss Clune," he murmured. "What will it take for you to promise me your silence?"

I considered him—his earnest gaze beneath the thick kajal eyeliner. Despite the unorthodox manner of our meeting, his behavior in the carriage had been gentlemanly. His travel companion had apologized and dressed the cut on John's head. Hattie Keays and Lady Tackleton, close relatives and prominent members of society, had personally vouched for his character with our introduction. Even the letter to Aunt Emma had been carefully worded so as not to betray the danger of our first meeting. I believed Mr. Keays because, well, because I couldn't imagine him lying. He frequently left out information, but everything he *did* say felt like the honest truth.

I believed him.

But he didn't know that.

I gleefully considered my options. I could demand anything. I *should* demand the return of my carpetbag and be done with the matter entirely. But as the quiet hum of voices and peaceful pluck of strings filled the warm air, my blood thrummed a contrary song. Each heartbeat felt like the pounding of a drum. Every shallow breath crashed through my lungs like a cymbal. How could I silence that beckoning song of adventure? Why should I sit in the shade and wait for the denouement of my life to play out?

Mr. Keays was on a secret assignment from the queen in pursuit of something dangerous. He was a major player on a royal stage. Meanwhile, I felt like the understudy to my own life. I practiced and prepared for a chance to sing in the spotlight but waited in the wings. I'd tried my best to live up to my mother's name after she died. All the while, I waited to be noticed for my own accomplishments. I waited for the day when I could finally meet my grandmother's approval. I waited every year for those precious few weeks of freedom. Aunt Emma made a promise but left me waiting for answers.

I waited, and waited.

But waiting wasn't enough. I needed to act.

My mother had never accepted anything less than a leading role, both onstage and in life. Why couldn't I play a bigger role in my own life?

"Let me help." The words left my mouth before I fully realized what I'd said, and I winced.

A gem of the right set does not make demands.

"Help with what?"

"I, uh . . ." I cleared my throat. "I want to help with your assignment. Wait! Hear me out—"

A cluster of young jacks passed, and I drew him behind a ring of wooden chairs facing the string quartet until we were isolated with no one to overhear our conversation.

"You apprehended the wrong carriage, so unless you intercepted the transportation of '*something potentially dangerous*' between last night and this afternoon, your assignment is, as of yet, unfulfilled. You asked for my silence, Mr. Keays? Well, I want the honest truth from you, and I don't mean in pieces like in your letter to my aunt."

"*Ah*, so you did read my letter!"

I fought the urge to duck my head. "Answer all of my questions with the honest truth, let me help with your assignment, and in return, I guarantee my complete discretion."

The corner of his mouth twitched upward. "You have more questions?"

"You didn't think I would stop at your name and rank, did you?"

"I had hoped." He hummed a frustrated sigh through his nose. "What if I promise to answer your questions with as much truth as possible? I cannot betray confidences."

"All right . . . that is fair. And?"

He folded his arms.

I folded mine. "Do not make the mistake of underestimating me a third time."

"Is that a threat?" he asked.

"*No! Of course not.*"

He shook his head and chuckled. "I certainly wouldn't want to stand on the opposite side of a battlefield from you, Miss Clune. But I mean what I say. I do not want to put you at risk. Greater involvement also means greater endangerment. Are you truly willing to help without knowing the full circumstances? Clearly, you're a gem. But there are other parties, other loyalties to consider."

I raised my chin and met his gaze.

Mr. Keays regarded me with those almond eyes, and for a moment I was convinced that he would refuse. But he held out his hand to me. "Honest truth?"

I took it. "Honest truth."

"Despite my better judgment, I do have an idea how you might provide assistance . . ." He trailed off as a pair of ladies seated themselves in two of the closest wooden chairs. "But might I suggest we move our conversation somewhere less populated to plot our alliance?"

"What do you have in mind?"

He lowered our hands but not his direct gaze. "How do you feel about courtship?"

"Court—I beg your pardon?"

He smirked. "My airship . . . the *Courtship*. I could bring you aboard. Escort a tour."

"The frigate?" I couldn't curb my wide smile. "She's yours, isn't she?"

"Mm. I remember your interest."

I turned on the spot and took off toward the garden of airships. Behind me, Mr. Keays laughed and lengthened his stride to keep up.

Chapter Eleven

Art

Courtship was a sleek yet sturdy ship built for speed and elegance. The light, wind-beaten sails fluttered loosely around slender masts, giving the look of a vessel that was made to outrun both clouds and trouble.

The passenger airship moored beside her looked about as elegant as a white bathtub hanging from a balloon. "That one is my uncle's latest investment," I said, jutting my chin toward the ship, pristinely clean from disuse. "What do you think? Do I have a rival villain of the skies?"

Miss Clune paused her sprint to consider the wide hull where the name "Miss Conduct" was written in looping cursive alongside a needlessly detailed painting of a woman wearing a loosely draped opera dress. The handle of a lorgnette was wedged between her considerable assets, and her pink heart-lips were pursed in a suggestive smile. She was exactly the sort of *sophistication* my uncle imputed to.

"She's hardly a proper ship," Miss Clune scoffed. "For decorative purposes only. Miss Conduct, however, appears to be a rather skillful women, doesn't she?"

Of course that would be her observation. Miss Clune continued to surprise me. An unexpected pang of loss for my sister caught me off guard. Still, a slow grin crept across my face. "You should meet Cecily."

"Who?"

"My sister. I think you'd like her."

"First an aunt, then a mother, and now a sister? You're surrounded by women. How in all aether are you excused from acting like a complete *rake*?"

Her inflection made "rake" sound like another word entirely.

I shrugged away my unease. "They've never seen anything different."

"You mean you've never shown them anything different? Yet you acted out of character for me. Or rather you quit acting." She challenged me with her stare. "Why?"

I'd earned quite a collection of dangerous enemies over the years, but Miss Clune was undoubtably the most dangerous threat of all.

I was intrigued.

And that meant some part of me cared.

It was only one chance encounter, yet I'd felt relieved to betray those parts of me that had been walled away for so long. Her carriage was an antique. Her destination was a West Tourmaline address—the shabby side of town that generally housed factory cogs and the more humble immigrants. I'd never expected to see Miss Clune in gem society—not outside the company of her fiancé.

Obviously, I'd been wrong.

And with the honest truth between us, she knew that anything different was a lie. Miss Clune jeopardized everything I'd worked for.

My work depended on secrecy. Every life I saved hinged on my ability to wear the right mask, say the right thing, and never let the seams of my disguise show. If too many people suspected the truth, everything would surely collapse.

"Are you coming?" she asked.

I met her at the spiral staircase in the center of the vine-covered gazebo which led onto the slanted roof. There, a partition of ropes connected to a removable rope ladder. The rungs had been retrofitted for easy-access as the party guests were hardly dressed for an athletic climb.

Miss Clune practically danced onto the deck. I followed and leaned against the taffrail to watch her reaction. What did she see? Unlike my uncle's passenger airships, *Courtship* was weathered with regular use. We bobbed near eye-level with Trolleywood Park where the trees wound round the hills like a choppy green stream. But all that landscape faded into my periphery as Miss Clune clutched her hat, tipped her face to the sun, and inhaled deeply. Shadows from the rippling sails and swells fluttered over her flushed skin.

Maker, she was marvelous. I'd never met a woman with such presence. Miss Clune danced as though everyone in the world was watching and she didn't care one whit.

I hadn't realized I'd been holding my breath until my voice came out hoarse. "Have you flown before?"

She started as if she'd forgotten I was there. "Never. When do we set sail? Could we fly over the park? I'd love to see the boats out on the lake."

We could leave right now. Would stealing her away get us the blueprints? If she was in league with Malowney, he'd come for her—and fast. If she wasn't, their connection would still make her useful. Could I afford to ignore Miss Clune as possible leverage?

"While I admire your confidence," I said, "I doubt your very *formidable* aunt would consider a solo flight appropriate without a chaperone."

"Oh . . . of course." She failed to hide the disappointment in her voice. "But where is the rest of your crew?"

"Not aboard at present."

"I see."

I gestured for her to join me at the taffrail. "But now we can have a private conversation in plain sight where I promise not to be tempted to do anything truly wicked."

She actually snorted.

"*Besides*," I continued, "there are regulations to follow and harness trainings even for passengers. See here—" I flipped open the latch and lid on the nearest gearbox, reached inside, and brought out a harness. "This is worn over a *blouson* and ties off here to the railing. As you can imagine, a tumble overboard is not quite the same from the air as it is over water." I carefully folded and replaced the bundle of straps and buckles. "She's a racing ship. And, in my experience, the fastest working model thanks to a lightened boiler design. The blueprints were evaluated and patented at the Exhibitions last year. But even with a prototype, patrons have shown little interest in development apart from maybe funding a racing team. So she truly is one of a kind."

"But she's beautiful! Why won't anyone invest?"

I rubbed the back of my neck. "Most gems see airships, or makes in general, as a status symbol. So even a small vessel like this would never be made accessible to the public. Or at least never mass produced for affordability even with all the good it might do. Country doctors would have a faster way to reach their patients. Farmers could transport their goods to multiple cities before they spoil. But as long as the Maker Exhibitions continue the way they are, there will continue to be a phenomenal concentration of power in the hands of very few. Vessels like that" —I jutted my chin at the *Miss Conduct*—"are nothing more than puffed pleasure yachts for holidays and sporting events. Our society, the elites like makers and gems, simply reinforce repressive economic institutions in power. And the rest—"

She was watching me with a bemused smile.

I cleared my throat. "Forgive me. I'm rather passionate about the topic."

"If I didn't know any better, I might assume you were a revolutionary highwayman." She tugged at my coat sleeve playfully but quickly turned contemplative. "But that is not at all the character you play in society. Why are you here, Mr. Keays?"

Honest truth? "I enjoy your company."

"No, why are you here at Cerussite Hall? And *no*, I'm not asking about any social obligation. What does the garden party have to do with your assignment?"

"We're back to business, then? Very well." I thought a moment. "What do you know about the most recent Maker Exhibitions?"

"Well, Mr. Jolly warned me about a change in the political climate, and a maker in Luster shared the hearsay—"

I glanced up sharply at the mention of, I assumed, Malowney.

"—but I'm afraid I didn't learn much. There was a scandal

involving one of the candidates . . . a cog who turned down a maker-ship? Or she left the Exhibitions before she could receive a makership? She might also have something to do with the Magicstry? I'm unaware of the particulars." She shrugged sadly. "Luster is somewhat isolating. What do I need to know?"

The real question was what information *could* she know? The Magicstry had suppressed open discussion of magic machines, and the queen forbade us from sharing the particulars of our meeting. No one could learn about the missing blueprints or that we were even aware of their disappearance. Most importantly, I couldn't endanger Cecily. Whoever held the blueprints could claim the make as their own, blocking Cecily from formal recognition as Maker and leaving her at the mercy of the Magicstry. The only reason she remained safe from the Magicstry was because she was prisoner to the Parure.

Miss Clune was fiancée to Maker Malowney, the nephew of Judge Pinefoy and my leading suspect in the theft of Cecily's blueprints. Even if Miss Clune was unaware of the theft, could I trust her not to reveal information to Malowney, deliberately or no?

Regardless, I did believe she could be of assistance—with or without knowledge of the particulars.

I hedged my reply. "Three major interest groups are at play here. First, the gems and makers who, of course, govern both the state and industry. Second, the Magicstry claims religious jurisdiction over the conduction of magic. And then there are the cogs, our hardworking citizens, whose only means of influence is now characterized by conflict. You've heard of the Homestead Strike? The balance of power between interests has been tenuous at best, but the Maker Exhibitions just adjusted the scales."

"And where does a highwayman Ruby Agent fit in?"

There were too many cares pulling me in different directions. Too many lies. "I can only say that I am here in an attempt to realign our center of gravity."

"Here?" She gazed out across the park. "You alone can shoulder the weight of the entire Parure? My, you really are full of yourself, aren't you?"

I smirked without any real humor. "Who else? In my experience, no one else cares."

"Of course they care," she said softly. "Everyone wishes to be free. They're just too isolated to lift the weight together and too weak to bear it alone. And so gravity most often wins." A sudden breeze whipped against us. She clutched the railing and closed her eyes—not out of fear, I realized, but to savor the feeling.

"It's a pity we cannot fly," I murmured. She opened her eyes, unsurprised to find me watching. "But I suppose it's for the best. You're already looking a bit wind-tossed." A golden strand of hair tangled against her lips. On impulse, I reached to brush it back but caught myself. The feel of her lips against my fingers was one honest truth I shouldn't wish to learn. I backed away and gestured to the lawn instead. "You wouldn't want to look too disarranged before your performance."

"My—" She blinked and tucked the stray curl beneath her hat. "I'd almost forgotten. I should persuade Lady Tackleton a different way. I'm afraid Aunt Emma may have presented my musical ability with a little too much vainglory."

"I thought you wanted to help with my assignment."

"Yes. Of course, I do."

"Then your performance is exactly what we need."

She eyed me skeptically. "And how *exactly* does a music performance help balance an entire country?"

A curl of her hair drifted free once more. Mercifully, she caught it before I did. After one last wistful look over the railing, she ducked beneath the shrouds and out of the wind.

I followed but quickly realized my mistake.

Nestled together beneath the weblike ropes, we were no longer in view of the park. No one else was there to watch as Miss Clune draped the loose curls of her hair over one shoulder and smoothed a finger across her lips. No one else was there to notice the quickening of my breath or how the deck suddenly tilted beneath my feet.

"Mr. Keays?"

I swallowed and averted my gaze from the graceful arch of her neck. "Erm—what was the question?"

"How does my music—"

"Ah, yes. I need you to create a . . . feminine distraction. Your performance is the perfect opportunity."

"This distraction requires a specific gender?"

"The person I need to distract is, well, let's just say he's a relatively easy mark if you have a pretty face. And unfortunately, my pretty face won't do." I gave her a sideways smile.

"Not pretty enough?"

"We're relatives."

"Hm." She narrowed her eyes. "Music is not what I expected when I asked to help you."

"Asked? Don't you mean blackmailed?"

She shrugged, unperturbed. "What is the purpose of this distraction?" At my hesitation, she folded her arms. "Do you forget the terms of our bargain?"

"I'm well aware. Your discretion in exchange for my honest truth. Help me in this, and *then* I will answer more of your questions."

"I can't help you with ignorance."

I folded my arms, mirroring her stance.

"You do know that my acting skills extend beyond the role of the innocent ingénue, don't you?" she asked.

"Oh, no one would believe you are entirely innocent."

She gaped. "Of all the ill-mannered, *lusterless* . . . wait, you still don't believe me, do you? Is that why you stole my bag? Which, by the way, you have yet to *return*."

"Did you still want it back? I'm afraid it's too late now," I teased. "You failed to mention the bag in our terms."

"But—"

"You can hardly blame me for stealing it in the first place. You admitted to carrying a concealed weapon, and it was my duty to investigate. Besides . . ." I took a step closer. "How else was I supposed to learn your name? I needed a calling card."

She took a step closer, too. "You stole my bag for a calling card?"

"The letter in your playscript served well enough. Interesting choice of reading material."

A flush bloomed across her cheeks. "Of all the—"

"Would you have given me your name if I'd asked?"

"Certainly not!" She roughly gathered the folds of her skirts, preparing to descend the ladder. "Even so, that was a terrible thing to do. Admit it! You distracted me with a kiss while you stole my bag."

I couldn't suppress the wide grin that spread across my face. "I took your bag long before the kiss."

She paused. "You did? When—*how* did you take it?"

Teasing her was too much fun. "You are quite correct," I said seriously. "Stealing is about distraction."

Beckoning her to the ladder, I held out a hand. With a *tsk* click of her tongue, she slapped her palm into mine. Of course, for both of us to reach the narrow rungs, we'd angled our bodies closer together. Close enough that when she glanced up, her nose skimmed the edge of my collar. Our hats brushed, and she tilted her head to adjust her brim.

Her lips were breaths away from mine.

"Like this," I murmured. "While you were watching my hand, you weren't watching for what I actually wish to steal."

I let my gaze slide down along her jaw . . . her chin . . . her lips . . .

"In your carriage, you were distracted because you were watching the door and window. All I had to do was lean forward—"

I leaned slightly forward.

"—and take it."

Our eyes locked. The barest ring of sapphire blue encircled a dilation of black in her eyes.

Only then did I realize my mistake.

Because I'd started the teasing, I foolishly assumed I stood at the helm, so I was free to fly. But it turned out my ship was built in a bottle. Because with that one look, I wasn't alone in my desire. Miss Clune trapped me within the intensity of her gaze. Her soft sigh was like a fever against my skin.

She has a fiancé.

She could be a thief.

She already knows too much.

You're not supposed to care.

With each objection, I forced my retreat. I needed to put distance between us. "I had your bag long before the kiss. *That* distraction was for fun."

"You—" She rocked back on her heels. "I never would have allowed such an intimacy if you haven't acted so—"

"Yes?"

"So intimidating!" she shot back and instantly bit her lip.

"You found me intimidating? I was beginning to think that nothing could unsettle you."

She glared, and I hoped the only heat left in her gaze was outrage. "I won't make the same mistake twice. My first impression was correct, it seems. There is nothing intimidating about you, Mr. Keays. You may have respectable relations, and you may wear the ring of a Ruby Agent, but I see who you truly are. A *gem* would never take advantage of such distractions. You are nothing more than a spineless thief!"

"Would a *lady* blackmail an agent of the queen?" I asked. "Still, it's pleasing to know that a kiss on the hand was enough to drive you to distraction."

Her hand balled into a fist. I wondered if I should duck or stand still. Miss Clune was right—no man of honor would have backed her into such a compromising position. Thankfully, we were high enough in the air behind the shrouds, no one would have seen the bit of our conversation that took place beneath my hat; otherwise, we could easily become the gossip of the entire city.

You're not supposed to care.

Without waiting for her to follow, I grasped the railing, descended the ladder, and chased the spiral of stairs back to solid ground.

Chapter Twelve

AUDREY

I TURNED FROM THE WIND AND COVERED MY FLUSHED FACE with my hands.

Frustration . . . lust . . . embarrassment . . . it was all the same tangled knot of emotion in my chest. My toes curled inside my boots when I thought about how close I'd come to kissing Mr. Keays. Of course, I'd known the rake was mocking me. I'd all but admitted I couldn't stop thinking about one kiss on my hand. But that knowledge hadn't curbed the urge to raise up on my toes and capture his lips against mine . . . to inhale the rich coffee of his breath . . . to weave my fingers through the thick curls of his hair then drag our bodies together as—

I slapped my cheeks.

Miss Conduct seemed to chide me from across the garden—her silly pink lips pursed mid-giggle. I was almost, very nearly, as good as engaged. Yet I hadn't once considered Maker Malowney in this story.

My selfishness was sobering.

By the time I left the sky for solid ground, my passion had cooled enough to consider the greater implications of our conversation. Mr. Keays *had* (on purpose or by chance) given me another answer.

Stealing was about distraction.

The purpose of my performance was to distract a gentleman relation.

And if my performance was a distraction . . . then what else was Mr. Keays planning to steal?

I joined him beside a patch of wildflowers. "Very well, I accept. I'll be your *distraction*."

"Indeed?"

"But I expect answers."

"And you will get them," he promised with a hand over his heart. "I give you my honest truth. Until then, I'm sure that— *Ah*, there you are!" He broke off mid-sentence. Once again, as completely as the moon eclipsing the sun, the dandy character returned, although this time, I easily caught brief glimpses of the real man glinting from behind the mask.

"Just the man we were discussing!" Mr. Keays gave a significant glance meant only for me. Taking my cue, I turned my curiosity toward a tall, starched gem approaching the gazebo.

Lord-Maker Tackleton.

Lord Tackleton had earned the coveted title of Maker after investing in his own inventions. But where his lustrous wife was hospitable, he was equivalently disinterested—just the sort of person my grandmother would befriend.

He was a head taller than most men and lean. A large nose was his leading feature which was only overshadowed by grey, heavyset eyebrows. His pressed suit was decorated with miniature gadgets and inventions like military epaulets—a collapsible monocular, a miniature songbird that quietly whistled from a delicately jeweled beak, a silver pocket chain—and his hat and cuffs were banded with copper. Such brassy, city fashion looked out of place against the bright greens and light blues of the pastoral park scenery.

Lord-Maker Tackleton marched toward us with rigid posture and an even more rigid air of pomposity. He greeted Mr. Keays with a frown. "Nephew."

"Uncle Elias. May I present your guest from Luster, Miss Audrey Clune. Miss Clune . . . *this* is Lord-Maker Tackleton," he said with weighted importance, as if I'd anxiously waited for a chance to meet the man.

I did not know what part the Lord of Cerussite Hall played in the assignment of a Ruby Agent, but I dutifully accepted my role as The Distraction. At least . . . I knew how self-important men like Maker Malowney and Lord-Maker Tackleton expected to be distracted.

I curtsied deeply, gave a (slightly shy) smile, and peeked up through my thick lashes at the maker. "It is *such* a pleasure to meet our distinguished host. I've seen your photographs in the paper, but you're even taller in person."

Lord-Maker Tackleton's reaction was almost disappointingly predictable. I supplied him with his own expectations, and like most men with a title, land, and an assumption of control over the women around him, his hardened expression softened.

"Pleasure." He gestured to the lawn and stage before us. "My wife tells me that you have agreed to favor us with your musical talents. I wonder, Miss Clune, would you permit me to announce your intended selection this afternoon?"

Never mind that Mr. Keays had already offered.

"I would be *honored*, Your Makership!" I cooed.

Mr. Keays coughed and covered his mouth.

"Oh, Mr. Keays, my throat feels a tad irritated as well," I said. "Perhaps the breeze is picking up? Please, find yourself a drink, and would you be so kind as to bring me a glass of water? He's been so attentive to my needs," I explained to Lord-Maker Tackleton before tapping my throat. "A drink would be so helpful before my performance, and I will be well cared for until your return. You see? I'm sure that Lord-Maker Tackleton and I will keep fine company together."

"Freshen mine while you're at it," the Lord-Maker demanded and passed him an empty snifter. "Brandy."

The dandy Mr. Keays sketched a complacent bow, but I sensed disapproval as he eyed Lord-Maker Tackleton from beneath lowered lids. Specifically, the outer pocket of his suit coat. I could only guess why. He retreated to the refreshment pavilion, and I hoped the errand would buy him time to do . . . whatever he needed to do. Meanwhile, I could easily sustain conversation as we wandered in the direction of the stage.

"Your pianoforte," I began, "isn't some sort of modern invention, is it? Not a new instrument with automated strings and hammers? I don't think my skill extends to anything quite so out of the ordinary."

I think Lord Tackleton meant for his smile to be reassuring. Mostly, I felt like I'd accidentally brushed my arm against a smear of engine grease. "Just an ordinary pianoforte, my gel, but of the finest quality, I assure you. It was manufactured by Dill and Sons."

"A fine instrument," I agreed, but the praise was only half-false. Dill and Sons was a quality manufacturer, although the tone of their instruments was generally too bright for my liking. I preferred a richer sound —deep and resonant. "Cerussite Hall has so many grand inventions from the capital, Lord-Maker. Are any of them your designs?"

His posture straightened even taller. "A fair share."

"This one?" I asked, gently tapping the bird on his shoulder.

"The whistle? Maker, no! Nothing so ornamental as this. My work has real, vendible value."

"*Oh*, forgive me. I didn't mean to cause offense."

"Quite so. *I* specialize in the design of airships for Her Jeweled Majesty's armada."

"Like this one?" From our vantage point, Miss Conduct seemed to be leering down at us.

"Ah, *Miss Conduct*? My lady is the latest from my private manufactory! One of a kind, not unlike yourself."

Of all the comparisons! At least my anger would produce a flattering blush. "How clever."

"It's all rather complicated, but my patented design is buoyant even in high-aether. In fact, I returned only late yesterday afternoon after a field test in the country."

My interest instantly piqued. "Last afternoon?"

"Indeed."

"Did you really? What part of the country? Perhaps we were near each other!"

"Hm. I don't recall. Why do you ask?"

Fearing I'd sounded too curious for my character, I added, "I think I should be scared to fly so high. Do you fly often, then?"

"I'm well accustomed."

"What an extraordinary way to travel." And on the very same day two highwaymen failed to intercept the transportation of something potentially dangerous. Mr. Keays waylaid my carriage, and after failing to locate anything more interesting than my carpetbag, he'd gone on to Cerussite Hall. Even if the garden party happened to be held at the home of one of his relatives, it couldn't be coincidence.

He was The Thief.

I was The Distraction.

What part did the Lord-Maker play? The Villain?

With a steadying breath, I steered him to the platform stage and steered our conversation in an equally intentional direction. "Are you working on anything new?"

"As a matter of fact," he said, "an opportunity just came to me." He patted his left pocket.

"Really? Do tell!"

It was impolite of me to pry, like listening in on the practice before an original piano composition was performance-ready. As expected, Lord-Maker Tackleton tsked. "You should know, my gel, I can't say more."

"No?"

"Not until the blueprints are officially patented by the queen's judges. And then there is the process of choosing investors to fund the production. I could easily fund the invention myself, you know. But the Maker Exhibitions are designed to keep things . . . *private*. So, of course, until such a time as my *findings* are published, I should keep silent on the matter."

"Of course."

"Disappointed?" he asked.

"I understand . . . but you needn't exaggerate to impress me."

"Exaggerate? I—"

"So much secrecy over this week's doodad, soon-to-be next week's thingamabob . . . a storm in a teacup, no doubt."

"Now see here!" He leaned in. His breath smelled like bitters and brandy and stale cigar smoke. "I have access to an invention that could change the future of makes. The Parure, even. Wars have been fought over less!"

I gripped his arm. "Is your work truly that *dangerous?*"

He sniffed, somewhat mollified. "All in the line of duty."

"I see. I mean . . . I didn't *realize.*"

"Quite right." He was patting the breast pocket of his suit coat like a man feeling for his wallet in a pickpocket neighborhood. He tipped his head uncomfortably close (with another waft of the brandy on his breath.) "I'm nothing if not a hospitable man. Have you never been up in an airship before today, Miss Clune? It's an exhilarating feeling."

My attention caught on his pocket. Mr. Keays had glanced at the very same pocket just before he left.

The invention is here. In his pocket.

And it was my fault that Mr. Keays wasn't there to retrieve it.

Of course, how could I have known what Mr. Keays meant to steal? He hadn't exactly been generous with information. Regardless, I had to make things right.

Following an impulse, I tripped.

Lord-Maker Tackleton caught me by the arm.

I collided gracelessly into his side.

And slipped my hand into the left pocket of his coat.

"*Oh*, I beg your pardon!" I hastily withdrew my hand but did not look at my fist clenched around a small, hard object. A locket? A metal chain?

"How clumsy of me! I shall be the shame of the party!"

Only then did I consider exactly what I'd done, and fear nearly overtook my senses. Surely, my pathetic attempt at petty theft would be noticed. The Lord-Maker would see through such an obvious distraction. He'd notice the absent weight against the seams of his left pocket. Or someone else had spotted the slip of my hand. Any moment they would cry *foul* and *shame.* Aunt Emma would be humiliated. The Tackletons would, of course, inform my grandmother. The punishment of her displeasure would be far worse than any public disgrace.

I braced for the consequences . . . but nothing happened.

Lord-Maker Tackleton didn't even notice my mortified expression.

Only my close proximity. His glazed eyes slithered along my neckline. I cringed but didn't dare correct my balance lest he notice my fist pressed against the folds of my skirts. Eventually, his roaming eyes found my face again. A smooth smile snaked across his jaw. "A divot in the lawn, no doubt. No harm done, Miss Clune."

My sigh of relief was genuine. "You are too generous, Lord-Maker. Please, forget this ever happened."

He nodded, and his thoughts seemed to alight on something new. "Now I remember. Miss *Clune*. You are Andrew's gel?"

I very nearly tripped again. "I am acquainted with Maker Malowney, yes, but I am not *his*. That is . . . there is no understanding between us."

"No, indeed?"

"Not at all. At least, not at this time. But if you'll excuse me—" I gestured to the platform stage. "I ought to take my place. I believe your guests are growing restless under the gathering clouds."

"Quite." He didn't move. Something about his pointed attention was making me nervous, and not because of the small object gripped tightly within my sweaty palm. I should have chosen a different character. I very much disliked feeling like a cowering creature beneath his predatory gaze.

"Miss Clune?" asked a familiar voice. "Are you well?"

"Mr. Keays! There you are!" I announced with a little too much enthusiasm. He appeared at my side holding a tall glass of water and a short glass barely lined with a dark brown liquid.

Once again, fear seized me. What if Mr. Keays tried to hand me the glass? Could I first hide the stolen object? I did not have my reticule. My dress, despite the many layers and folds, had not been fashioned with a single pocket, and I was not wearing gloves. But I couldn't keep my hand balled into a fist forever. Even a blind woman would notice when I started playing a piano solo with only my left hand.

On another impulse, I pivoted toward Mr. Keays and placed my hand over my chest. The warmed metal object slipped down my bodice and settled with an uncomfortable pinch between my breasts.

"You've arrived just in time, Mr. Keays," I said, feeling a little breathless. My corset was too tight. My ribs and hands ached. "I ought to warm my voice and hands before my performance."

"Chivalry is one of my many fine qualities, yes." His easy tone turned dark. "I've freshened your drink, Uncle. But it looks as though you've had enough already."

With a glare, Lord-Maker Tackleton seized the snifter and knocked back the dark shot of liquid in one gulp. With bitter breath reinforced with brandy, he leaned over me. "It was a great pleasure to meet you, Miss Clune. I look forward to more such *pleasures* in the future." He shoved the glass back at Mr. Keays and marched beneath the trellis proscenium arch and across the stage.

Mr. Keays sucked in a sharp breath through his nose. "I should not have left you."

"I'm sorry I sent you away. I didn't realize . . . But don't worry," I whispered. "I have it."

He dragged his gaze from the stage. "What do you have?"

"What was in his Lordship's left suit pocket? La, that sounds like some sort of riddle, doesn't it?"

Mr. Keays stared at me long enough that I wondered if I'd been wrong. Had I acted on a false instinct?

"That is what you need, isn't it?" I asked. "The thing you're here to steal?"

"You . . ." Mr. Keays worked his jaw with a few nameless sounds. "You stole the key?"

A key! "That's right. You *were* planning to steal it, weren't you?"

"Yes, but—"

"So, the dangerous invention is here!" I whispered, triumphant. I shot him a satisfied smile. "And judging by your expression, you seem to have made the mistake of underestimating me a third time. Did you think I wouldn't figure it out?"

"I was only gone for a few minutes! How—"

"Like you said. I was the distraction."

His voice went startlingly cold. "You should not have done that."

"I'm sorry?" I asked.

"Of all the senseless—" He pinched the bridge of his nose and inhaled once, deeply, and held out a hand. "Give it to me. *Now,* Miss Clune. Before the performance."

At my hesitation, he thunked both the empty snifter and full water glass onto the edge of the stage and again held out a hand at waist level. With his body angled toward the proscenium, a garden trellis covered in blooming vines, our exchange would be blocked from the view of most onlookers. But I couldn't give him the key even if I should wish to. Currently pressed between the privacy of my stays and skin, there was no conceivable method to fish it out of the deep and still remain a lady. How could I possibly explain *that* without embarrassment? My temper—ordinarily kept on a tight rein—rose in defense.

"Absolutely not!" I snapped. "You accosted my carriage, stole my property, then gratified yourself by using me as a target for your *distraction*. You have no right to object to my involvement now."

"My only objection is that you are keeping the key from me. Don't you realize? Your *performance* was the distraction, not that shameless bit of flirting."

"*My* flirting? Your scales of judgment are out of balance, sir!"

"I needed enough time to steal the key *and* search the Hall," he hissed. "Now he could discover the key missing at any moment."

"I . . . *oh.*" I rubbed the palms of my hands. "Perhaps if you'd shared your plans sooner, I could have helped you. But I'm afraid the *item* in question is, uh, inaccessible at the moment."

"Where?" he ground out through gritted teeth.

I glanced meaningfully down the front of my dress and back up to him. "*Inaccessible.*"

The rogue finally proved to be a gem, because his cheeks colored a deep crimson-red and his gaze snapped up from where it had followed mine. Unfortunately, the brief flash of heat in his eyes only seemed to fan the flame of his temper. "*That* is the first place my uncle would care to look, or couldn't you guess?"

"How dare y—"

He held up a hand. "I apologize. That was out of line. I am angry with myself for encouraging you to distract a man like my *uncle*." He said the word like a curse and sighed and ran a hand against the side of his hat. "This is not your fault. However, I must insist that you excuse yourself to the lounge. Meet me on the first landing with the key."

"You may insist all you like, but my absence would arouse even more suspicion. Look now, the musicians are leaving the stage. I'm expected to perform any minute."

"That wasn't a request."

"I am not a soldier for you to order about."

"This is *exactly* why I did not want you involved."

"Because I won't take orders?"

Mr. Keays drew himself up to his considerably full height, but whatever he was about to say next was interrupted as Aunt Emma swept between us. "There you are, *mon cœur*!"

I fell back a step. I hadn't realized how close we were standing, or that my aching hands were—not for the first time that afternoon—balled into fists.

"Is something amiss?" she asked cheerfully, but her eyes slid sideways indicating the gathering crowd. "You look as though you're having some sort of disagreement."

We stood behind the trellis proscenium but not hidden from the audience members seated on the ends of the first several rows. Hattie Keays fanned herself with a clutch of feathers and gleefully whispered to the finely clad woman seated beside her. Not for the first time, my cheeks and ears felt hot. Our fight had drawn too much attention. I should have known better. Wherever there were people, there would always be an audience.

With a deep, cooling breath, I rolled my tense shoulders to a level posture—the confident poise of Robin Renegade. I shouldn't have acted any other part. I shouldn't have let my guard down around Mr. Keays, or Mr. Highwayman, or whoever else he pretended to be.

"Thank you, Aunt Emma. I didn't realize the time. I must've been *distracted*. Mr. Keays, I am grateful for the water, but you must excuse me. We may continue our discussion after my performance."

And with the final word, I swept onto the stage.

Chapter Thirteen

ART

I FORCED MYSELF TO TURN AWAY FROM THE STAGE. WHAT else could I do with the key out of reach?

Or . . . beyond my grasp? No, that wasn't right either.

And why had I cared more about how Miss Clune obtained the key than one failed opportunity to search the study safe box for the blueprints?

What would Cecily make of the situation? She always had an answer —usually an impractical one. Still, she'd have solved this mystery far faster than I was managing to.

"Arthur, my dear!" Mum beckoned me closer. The seat beside her (clearly reserved for me) was already taken up by Sweetpea—belly-up and snoring. Mum and dog were completely encircled by finely clad women, all of whom batted various fans and frills at me like overstated eyelashes. After Cecily's Exhibition, there seemed to be even more of them surrounding Mum than usual. They'd chosen the seats closest to the pianoforte—directly at eye-level with Miss Clune. She was rotating her wrists and quietly humming some sort of vocal exercise. Her slender fingers moved as if on invisible keys. With her sharp mind, she probably had stacks of memorized music to choose from. I was curious to hear her singing voice when her speaking voice was already so melodic. She took a sip of water and—

Devil take me, I was staring again.

I turned on my heel, attempted an impish grin as I tipped my hat to Mum and her coterie, and retreated to the house. I had a meeting scheduled with Belwater, but I'd hoped to make a report *after* I'd searched the safe. He could help me smuggle the blueprints out of the Hall without Harland—and by extension, the Magicstry—looking over my shoulder. But the timing was too close, and I was anxious to hear news of Cecily. I'd have to meet Belwater first, return and retrieve the key from Miss Clune, and pray to all aether that Tackleton was too tipsy to notice anything amiss.

I dammed my mind against a conflicting surge of emotion.

I hadn't expected Miss Clune to possess such skill in acting. She'd never been anything other than herself—all confidence and intellect. It was disconcerting to watch her transform before my eyes. She'd become exactly the sort of woman Tackleton would take an interest in—a simpering ninny.

Then again, I'd asked her to.

She was the perfect distraction, and I rather hated myself for it.

Tackleton concluded his—slightly slurred—introduction speech to polite applause, my aunt smiled at her husband with an elegance that belittled the man even more than his own inebriation, and with a gracious curtsy, Miss Clune swept back her full skirts and took her place behind the piano.

I turned away and ascended the stairs to the veranda to enter the lower Hall.

Until Miss Clune began to play, and then, I couldn't take another step.

The melody was haunting—not the usual cadence for an outdoor performance. She portioned out the first few lines of music with care, savoring the sweeter notes, but eventually increased the tempo into a recognizable tune. The composition, I knew, was a foreign poem set to music entitled "Le Voleur Voyage"—"The Traveling Thief"—the story of a mysterious highway thief who traveled remote roads with only his horse and a magical map to guide him to the world's most precious treasures.

Miss Clune glanced up from the keys and met my gaze long enough to smile at her own joke: *Le Voleur Voyage*. Had she guessed I spoke Gallia, or was the language coincidence? However educated the gems of the Parure might be, I very much doubted the *lustrée monde* was wholly fluent.

The haunting melody swelled into something richer until she paused. Her hands hovered over the black and white keys for one . . . two . . . three breaths of silence. She held me against the tips of her fingers.

Then I was lost to her song.

The traveling thief had a lonely life, and the hooves of his horse were sore. But a magical map guided him to the most beautiful treasures that mortals ever beheld. From the carriage of a young lord, he stole a ruby the size of an eagle's nest egg. The map told him where to steal the sword of a soldier which was forged with perfect balance from the lightest and strongest alloy of metal. The thief robbed the Old Queen herself who wore a crown of pure gold upon her head. But none of these great treasures brought the thief happiness. No amount of wealth could cure loneliness, and golden horseshoes could not cure sore hooves. The rider's wanderlust only grew, and his desire for treasure increased. And so, his loneliness grew, and his horse continued to have sore hooves.

THE ACCOMPANIMENT SWELLED, WEAVING IMAGES OF LONG roads and glittering treasures between each line of music. I was wholly absorbed in the darkness of the roads, the thudding hooves of galloping horses, and the gradually dulling gleam of treasure.

Finally, the thief grew angry. With disappointment as his only lasting reward for endless wandering, the thief commanded the map to show him the greatest treasure in all the world. Perhaps then, with the greatest treasure in his possession, he would be content to end his search. The map agreed but feared the thief would not appreciate the true value of owning such a priceless treasure.

MISS CLUNE GLANCED UP FROM THE KEYS, AND HER EYES were like a mirror to my own emotions, reflecting the promise of lyrics to come. I knew the ending of the poem, but I hadn't prepared for the way my heart sang in response.

The map guided the thief to a little carriage on a small, dusty road. The carriage was old, the wheels rusted, but inside the thief found the most beautiful woman he had ever beheld. Her long hair was more golden than the crown of the queen, her full lips redder than rubies, and her keen eyes sharper than folded steel.

The thief was confused. 'I am here for the greatest treasure,' said he.

The beautiful woman untied a locket from around her neck. He eagerly snatched it from her slender hand. But when he looked closer, the thief discovered that the locket was worthlessly plain. It was made of cheap metal and tied around her neck by a simple ribbon.

'What is this?' he asked with disdain. 'I seek the greatest treasure. You have given me a street market trinket!'

'It is willingly given,' said she. 'Is my heart really worth so little to you?'

The thief carefully opened the locket, and inside was the brightest jewel he had ever seen, the color and cut indescribable. It pulsed against his hand like the beat of his own heart. The thief fell to his knees and bowed his head in shame. 'Forgive me, lady. I will cherish your heart as the greatest treasure.'

'Then I will let you keep it.'

Thereafter, the thief no longer wandered, the horse was content to pull the old carriage for his mistress for his hooves were no longer sore, and the magical map forever pointed to the greatest treasure: the heart that belonged only to the thief.

HER VOICE SAILED AWAY ON THE WIND, AND THE MUSIC slowed until the last notes faded into silence. In the heartbeats that followed, she slowly raised her eyes to mine once more—the honest truth laid bare between us.

Elsewhere, the audience was standing. Mum joined the boisterous applause. The coterie of ladies dabbed their misty eyes with lace hand-kerchiefs, and my aunt rushed onstage.

Miss Clune blinked and rose from the bench and curtsied beside the piano. But I still felt the anchor of her gaze, the cool breeze of a dark night, the soft press of her hand against my upturned lips, and a new truth between us like the pulse of my own heart.

I wasn't supposed to care.

~

"IS THAT THE FIANCÉE?"

I hadn't realized the mage was standing at my shoulder. The crea-ture was so demmed quiet. Breaking free of the trance, I tore my gaze away from Miss Clune only to realize I'd attached myself to one of the Hall pillars like a welded statue. I straightened and turned toward Harland but immediately recoiled at his appearance. He'd changed clothes; however, his new attire was somehow worse than the drab grey of the Magicstry robes. He'd donned the loose coat of a house servant, but it bagged around his shoulders and waist as if his very skeletal struc-ture were ill-fitted to ordinary human proportions.

"Off reporting to your master, I assume?" I asked blandly. "How is Mage Citoyen?"

"He sends his regards."

"Was that . . . a joke?"

"As I said before, Mage Citoyen isn't interested in you. It's odd. He seems to think he already has everything, but he won't act before the queen announces the makership titles. Gems and mages are too busy watching each other."

I frowned. "He doesn't want the blueprints anymore?"

"He might be waiting to see who gets the official credit before the Magicstry publicly makes a move. If Cecily isn't named Maker, he can take her designs without a challenge."

His words hung heavily between us. "Or?"

"Or he might already have them. Either way, we're behind in the race." He glanced toward my uncle in the crowd below. "Did you get the key?"

"I—*uh*." I pinched a cuff on the shell of my ear. "I've enlisted the help of a third party. But once we have the key, the lockbox is in the upstairs study. As a guest of my aunt, I have more freedom to wander the Hall, but it's best to leave as little connection between us and the blueprints as possible. Plausible deniability and all that. Do you think you can manage to clear the main staircase? There's at least one guard posted inside the Hall."

"Where will you be?"

"I have one more thing to attend to."

"Anything I should know about?" he asked.

"I'd better see what the gems are up to. Is there anything else I should know after your meeting with Citoyen?"

He shrugged.

I hoped that meant no.

His expression turned contemplative. "The fiancée . . . did you know she would be here?"

I glanced at Miss Clune. She was very nearly buried beneath a mountain of admirers. "No, her presence here is merely happy coincidence. We can return her carpetbag now and save the trip to Tourmaline."

"Did she see you?"

"Don't worry. She knows I'm a Ruby Agent on a mission for the queen. She won't say anything to jeopardize our plan."

His dark brow furrowed. "You seemed quite enraptured by her performance."

My heart hammered inside my chest. "I'm beginning to see why a prick like Malowney would endeavor to marry a gem like her." I sidestepped around him. "Come in through the house. I'll take you to the library. No one is going to believe you're my servant, not with such an ill-fitted uniform. What happened to the suit I bought you?"

The mage tugged at the long sleeves of his coat. He looked almost uncomfortable. "No one was going to believe I was a gem either."

I eyed him as he held open the door, but I didn't comment further.

Either the servants were fully occupied in the kitchens or out savoring the final few rays of sunshine with the guests, because after leaving Harland, I slipped unnoticed through a fresh-smelling laundry room, out a side door, and onto a narrow path that wound through the Trolleywood. To my left, the path led in the direction of the front drive, but a westerly wind steered me deeper into the park. Above the tree line, my lady *Courtship* bobbed a polite greeting.

Eventually, I stopped where tram tracks crossed a small clearing, and roughly two minutes later, I bounded aboard the moving tram and caught a lift out of the park to the main city street.

Belwater was waiting for me beneath the sunshade of the first station. The ghostly informer wore a flat expression and nondescript coat that paired perfectly with the grimy paint of the streetcar stop.

However, he wasn't alone.

Ox was there, too. The burly man had changed out of uniform and into a casual waistcoat and sleeveless shirt. His crossed arms looked like two tree trunks had fallen across his chest.

My nerves immediately stood on end. Had Belwater guessed our connection? Ox had never broken the law, but his off-duty alliances weren't exactly innocent either. He had a family—a wife and son. Were they in danger now, too? Ox didn't *look* concerned, but that didn't stop me from feeling racked with guilt even as I saluted a bored greeting, disembarked and circumvented a small crowd of passengers waiting to board, then spoke without preamble. "I don't have much time."

"And I have another appointment. Walk with me." Belwater set off at a sprightly pace. "You remember Captain Williams, I presume? He is in charge of looking after your sister. I thought you'd like to hear a report from him directly."

My tension lessened slightly, and I tipped my hat. "Captain. Do you have news? Is Cecily safe?"

Ox snorted and ducked beneath the low branch of a tree shading the pavement. "You should be asking if the palace is safe after she set fire to the curtains."

"*Ah*. That does occasionally happen, yes. I suggest removing all flammables."

"The staff already stripped the workshop bare."

"But she is well?"

Ox's smile was full of kindness. "She is well."

A phantom pain I hadn't known I'd been holding eased from my chest. I masked my relief by facing the street of terraced houses with polychrome brickwork and tall, pitched roofs. So close to Trolleywood Park, the industrious neighborhood had clearly tried its best to mimic the classic architectural styles of some of the more popular ancestral estates but with a colorful flare.

"I'm afraid the Magicstry, however, has painted your sister in a poor light," said Belwater with a glance over his shoulder. "You've likely heard, Mage Citoyen has publicly renounced her as a heretic attempting to stir up trouble with a fraudulent make. I hope, for her sake, her make proves otherwise."

"And Pinefoy?" I asked.

"We don't know anything for sure. He could've gone into hiding, but with no sign of him after forty-eight hours, well . . ." Belwater frowned, solemn.

"What about his nephew, Malowney?" I asked.

"Do you mean Maker Malowney?" He hummed in consideration. "I'm not sure what you think he has to do with this. We're keeping an eye on all of Pinefoy's connections. As far as I'm aware, Maker Malowney has been staying at some country estate. He wasn't in the city when any of this happened."

"Is he marrying Miss Clune or the grandmother?" I muttered under my breath. Lengthening my stride to meet Belwater at a busy street corner, I added, "Still, Pinefoy left a few more leads for me to follow."

"Yes, about that." Belwater broke off and addressed Ox. "Thank you for your report, Captain. You're free to go." Ox nodded and marched back the way we came.

Belwater led me across the opposite intersection. "Rest assured, every Ruby Agent in Diadem is searching for the blueprints. They will find them, and your sister will be safe . . . with or without your assistance. *You* are inessential."

I smoothed a hand over my jaw. The queen had set the stage—and me—as the perfect scapegoat if things went sideways. The more they pushed me aside, the tighter the noose felt. Yet still, I forced a smile while suffocating.

"*Inessential*," I said. "Is that a reassurance or an insult?"

"It's a warning. While I have no doubt you're an adept when it comes to evading the Magicstry," he said wryly, "I question the practicability of your involvement here."

I huffed a laugh. "As do I. But my *involvement* wasn't exactly voluntary, was it?"

"Precisely. What's the phrase? 'Alliances are built on the burial ground of common enemies?' The queen seems to think you and I have a common enemy. After all, we're both out to catch a thief. But I know better than to trust an unaligned renegade." His voice hardened. "I am a gem, Mr. Keays. My loyalty is and always will be to the Parure. Whereas blackmail is short-changed loyalty. A cog like you will never add up."

A hackney pulled up beside the curb without being hailed. Belwater seemed to expect the steam auto's arrival because he opened the door and slid smoothly inside. "Do what you will to find the blueprints, but heed my warning, Mr. Keays. My loyalty is to something greater than self-interest. I won't stop until every enemy of the Parure is buried."

With a signal for the driver, the hackney eased back into the street, turned the corner, and was gone.

I stared numbly ahead. The feeling of uselessness wasn't nearly as gratifying as in the past. Belwater trusted the Renegade about as much as I trusted nationalist fanatics. What would happen when I returned the blueprints? Or worse, what if Belwater somehow secured the blueprints first? In either case, the queen would claim everything. Cecily would not only lose ownership of her own make but also her leverage. I believed Belwater when he promised that Cecily would be safe. But she would never be free.

And it would be all my fault.

Of course, things could be worse. The Magicstry could steal the blueprints first. Then Cecily would be a hostage until her inevitable execution as a heretic.

The weight of my task settled even more heavily onto my shoulders. Not only did I need to find the blueprints first, but I needed a safer way to make the exchange: the blueprints for Cecily and her deserved title as maker.

Belwater had an entire network of covert Ruby Agents. I had a few friends . . . and Harland—a mage I barely trusted. Then there was Miss Clune—a woman I *shouldn't* trust. At least I hadn't given Belwater any information about Malowney's secret messages and item smuggled away in Cerussite Hall.

I needed to get back. I'd be even more *useless* if I stood slumped against the corner light post all day. I dodged between steam autos as I crossed the street and jogged back to the station.

Ox was there waiting for me. He'd somehow squeezed himself onto a narrow metalwork bench. I took the seat opposite him.

"You're still here?" I asked.

"Thought you might want me to relay a message."

"Two, in fact."

"Hm?"

"Tell Cecily I don't expect her to forgive me, but I do ask her to hear me out before carrying out whatever plan she has to murder me."

Ox grunted. "You'll be dead before setting foot in the same room as her. You know. . ." He ran a meaty hand over the side his shaved head. "It's not my place to say, but there was another reason I warned you about her application to the Exhibitions. The next time you see her, if you survive, you need to ask her *why* she didn't list a patron. You saved her life, I'm sure of that. But when it comes to that make of hers, Cecily knows what she's doing. At least, more than you give her credit for."

"Why, Ox . . . I'm stunned. I think that's the most I've ever heard you say in one sitting."

He grunted.

"Thank you for looking after her," I said seriously.

"Mmhm."

Right on time, the bell signaled an approaching tram. I'd be in and out of Trolleywood Park within exactly fifteen minutes. Hopefully, Harland had already taken care of the Hall. Miss Clune had the key. All I needed were the blueprints. And a better plan.

"What was the second message?" Ox asked as I stepped up a low curb and onto the station platform.

"Ah, yes." I grinned. "Please tell Mae to prepare the *Courtship* for launch. I may need to make a quick exit."

Chapter Fourteen

IT WAS SOME TIME BEFORE I BROKE FREE OF THE CROWD.

I was stunned by the adoration. A handful of guests mentioned my mother, but a majority asked about me directly. How long had I been playing? Did I often perform in company? Where would my next performance be held? I'd never received so much personal attention.

I'd performed dozens of musical recitals before the age of sixteen. That was when my mother had died. Without her there to occupy the spotlight, I'd been asked to play what felt like hundreds more. I was a second-rate understudy to her memory—a slightly shorter copy of golden hair, bright eyes, and slender fingers.

Ordinarily, my choice of music depended on the audience or, more often, Grandmother's expectations. For dinners or house parties, I almost always played a lighthearted piece by Poquelin. Smaller groups of businessmen or Maker Malowney's patrons generally appreciated something more refined. And a restless audience enjoyed lively cantatas by Byrdell.

I fit the role that was required.

I met expectations.

I chose my music, my words, the very nature of my character—all of it for them.

Lady Tackleton expected my performance to complement her party.

Hattie Keays expected an even better show than the fight she'd witnessed between me and Mr. Keays.

Even my aunt—tender-hearted Aunt Emma—expected a memory. Aunt Emma saw my true character, but her perception of me was tinted with memories of my mother. How could she ever see me otherwise?

I was reminded of Mr. Jolly's words. *It must be hard for you to live without her while still trying to live up to her name. But it's what we do with our own life that matters.*

And that was why I wouldn't feel embarrassed for stealing the key.

Of course, I *had* acted rather impulsively.

But he—

No. I'd tasted adventure like tart pastries or pollen on the spring wind. Was it any wonder, then, why I'd so desperately seized the opportunity to perform a leading role?

Each reaction to my performance only seemed to underscore this newfound perspective. Thankfully, Lord-Maker Tackleton was similarly detained by the attentions of his guests and was, I hoped, too busy to notice an empty left pocket. I peered through the press of shoulders. The hidden key pinched my skin, and my hands ached more than usual after my performance. I rubbed my palms together and grasped Aunt Emma's arm and leaned toward her ear. "I need to go up to the lounge."

She looked between me and the manor with a faint smile. "*Va le trouver.* Left your locket inside, did you?"

Outright denial would only encourage her. When I'd chosen "Le Voleur Voyage," I'd meant to sing about a highway rogue who still hadn't returned my carpetbag. But in my haste, I hadn't considered the ending of the song. I *shouldn't* consider that last look that had passed between us.

"I'd like to freshen up," I said. "Something inside my bodice is pinching."

She nodded and glanced up at the sky. Only a few small patches of blue peeked between marshaling clouds. "You can gather our things while I give our final regards to Lady Tackleton."

"We're leaving? But . . . so soon?"

She held me by the arms to study my face. "Your performance was exquisite, *mon cœur*. So much like your mother. You're becoming more like her every day. I'm glad to see your grandmother hasn't taken that much from you." The corners of her mouth pinched down. "I'll meet you at the carriage."

"But... can't we stay for an airship flight?"

"No. Promise me you'll hurry?" Without waiting for an answer, she brushed my cheek once with the back of her finger and turned away.

I felt like sails without wind. How much had Grandmother taken, and how much of my life had I missed while in her guardianship? I wasn't ready to leave the adventure, but even after I handed over the key, I still had the promise of more answers. And a home with Aunt Emma.

I maneuvered free of the crush and hurried across the lawn, up the steps, and around the veranda where well-groomed servants bustled in and out of a narrow side door. No one stopped me from entering the gallery. The shaded room was cool and smelled of wood oils and silver polish. The high windows let in little sunlight between clouds. Most of the cerussite rainbow refractions had disappeared, as had, it seemed, Mr. Keays and his companion.

I ventured farther inside toward the main staircase. My heeled boots tapped a light rhythm against the creaking wood floors. Darting quickly across the inlayed tram tracks, I peered into the library through the arched doorframe.

"Art said he'd enlisted the assistance of a third party," said a gravelly voice. "I should have known he meant you."

I spun on my toes. A man leaned against the nearest bookcase. Despite the change of setting, I recognized the cloth hat. Apparently, the gravel in his voice was natural. The shadowed and smudged features in my memory of his face were clean and chiseled in the light of day, and though he wore the livery of a house servant, his posture was about as lazy as a circus cat waiting to pounce. Clearly, his true position was nowhere near the lower rungs of working cogs. I didn't see the unusual, three-barreled gun, but it was possible the weapon was hidden beneath his shapeless tunic. Perhaps that was why he dressed as a servant? Gem fashions were much tighter and would conceal less.

I took another cautious step into the room. "I can't say my assistance has been particularly helpful. At least . . . Mr. Keays was rather upset with me."

"That's not what I heard. But then, he wasn't the only one fascinated by your performance."

I nodded. Lord Tackleton wouldn't remain ignorant forever. "Where is Mr. Keays?" I asked.

"Out to get more information, but he's looking in all the wrong places. He ought to check the upstairs study."

Without another word, he pushed himself off the bookcase and left the room.

What in all aether was that?

Feeling faintly unsettled, I exited the opposite direction, ascended the grand staircase, and slid quietly into the ladies' lounge. I was alone save several coatracks of draped shawls and reticules, with larger belongings scattered throughout the spacious apartment. The other guests seemed to be out savoring the last hour of sunshine.

Between my performance and my jaunt across the lawn into the manor, the stolen key had shimmied its way even *farther* down my embonpoint. Fortunately, my bodice was tight enough that the chain had stuck. I shouldn't need to unlace anything to reach it. I hooked a finger through a loop of chain and tugged, twisted, squirmed, and finally decided that the next time I followed adventure, I would spare myself the embarrassment and wear a dress with pockets. Of course, how could I have dressed for a highway robbery, an alliance with a Ruby Agent, and an impulsive act of theft? Spontaneity seemed impossible to outfit.

After dancing around like a bee in a tube flower, both chain and key popped free. I weighed the unusual key in my hand. The silvery, smooth bow-handle was commonplace, similar to the key for a lockbox in Grandmother's room; however, the entire bottom edge of the pin *and* shaft was lined with ornate combination of bits and teeth. The complex pattern of bumps and ridges would be nigh impossible to copy. Curious to learn what sort of lock would require such an extraordinary key, I wrapped the chain tightly in my fist and left the lounge in search of Mr. Keays.

I was somewhat familiar with the Hall. The wealthiest of gem families provided regular tours of their estate and land holdings. Aunt Emma and I had taken a full tour of Cerussite Hall three summers earlier. So I knew several of the upstairs rooms were luxuriously furnished apartments. Other rooms included an airy and colorful art gallery with an impressively displayed collection of outdated inventions, a billiard room that smelled like loamy cigar smoke, a disappointingly dusty music room, and Lord-Maker Tackleton's private study.

And I had what looked like the key to a private safe.

The highwayman's words suddenly sounded less cryptic and more like a dare. Or an opportunity. Perhaps I could remove the new make from the safe before Lord-Maker Tackleton noticed the key was missing? Had the highwayman given me the chance to make things right?

I bit the edge of my thumb. I'd made such a blunder obtaining the key. Would Mr. Keays be grateful for the help or upset by my interference? Still, how could I ignore the opportunity?

I hurried in the direction of the western corridor.

"You there!" a stern voice called from behind.

I froze halfway across the landing, one hand gripping the banister and the other fisted tightly against my skirts.

"Guests aren't permitted to explore the manor!"

A house servant had spotted my mad dash. Of course, I hadn't exactly been subtle.

There was only one thing I could think to do.

I burst into tears.

The great Dame Gemma cried on stage every night in her famous role of Lady Morganite. Surely my acting skills were enough to cry for the protection of queen and country? I yawned in the back of my throat, hyperventilated my breath a bit, then slowly turned toward the voice.

An abnormally stocky house servant was ascending the stairs to meet me. He reached the landing as the first, plump tear trickled down my cheek. He skidded to an abrupt stop. "Oh, uh, are you unwell?" he asked in a thick northern accent.

"It's nothing. I—no, thank you for your concern. It's just . . . I only meant to fetch my reticule from the lounge. After the performance—"

Another perfectly thick tear plopped down my wet cheek.

"I forgot my handkerchief, you see, and the embroidery is so very fine."

My breath hitched. "With little roses and daisies along the lace."

I sniffed. "But there is a letter inside. My reticule, that is. Not my handkerchief. But I could not eat the ice cream and—"

Sniff. Sniff.

"I didn't think to ask for an escort into the house! I am so very sorry."

The poor fellow fidgeted with his beefy hands, unsure how to help such an incoherent female. "No apology necessary, Miss. Allow me to show you to the lounge."

"Oh, thank you. I would be very grateful." But I couldn't have him waiting outside the room. I needed to buy myself more time. Blinking up at him through my watery vision, I bleated, "Don't tell anyone I made such a blunder."

In my mind, I pictured Grandmother's disapproving glare. *A gem does not make demands!*

The man straightened then nodded.

"I'll be fine in a moment," I said. "Unless . . . would you be kind enough to fetch my aunt, Miss Toussaint? She will know how to help."

"I don't really—"

"Please. I-I should like to stay in the lounge."

He sighed. "Of course. Where is your aunt?" he asked as he guided me back toward the lounge.

"I believe she is out walking by the lake."

"Won't take but a minute. Stay here," he ordered and closed the door behind me.

As Aunt Emma was *not* out by the lake, I was confident it would take more than 'a minute' for the servant to find her. Still, I could not afford to waste a single cent of my hastily borrowed time. I stretched a sudden cramp in my side, impatiently brushed the leftover tears from my lashes, and spent a few seconds with my ear pressed against the door until the sound of his steps fully retreated down the stairs. Quietly, I eased open the door. The hall was, once again, empty.

I didn't bother with stealth. My polonaise silk dress with copper-wire flowers would stand out anywhere, not just on the open landing above the grand staircase. I would be significantly less conspicuous walking the halls than if a servant caught me crouching along the wall. I could play the role of 'subtle' if I chose; however, the usual character of Audrey Clune was never subtle, and I'd chosen my costume to match.

I strode purposefully to the adjacent corridor, counted doors to the study, and paused to listen. Hearing no sound within, I turned the unlocked brass knob and hurried inside.

The room was vacant.

I quietly shut and leaned my back against the door and inspected Lord-Maker Tackleton's private study. The recognizably pungent smell of cigar smoke and brandy hung in the air and clung to every fabric, and the luxurious décor was decidedly masculine with dark leather furniture and blood-red accents in each of the gaudily framed paintings. A massive, intricately carved desk faced a partially curtained window which merged with an entire wall of shelves containing everything from books to leather cases to a collection of engraved figurines —nude men and women locked in lustful embrace. I averted my gaze to the floor.

Grandmother kept her lockbox on the floor beneath her desk. But there was more than one servant in the Hall, and one wrong step on a loose floorboard could give me away. Stepping lightly around the edge of the room, I bent and checked under the lip of Lord Tackleton's desk and discovered a conventional, black-iron lockbox. Unfortunately, the keyhole was conventional as well—circular on top with a flat base. The sharp-edged key digging into the palm of my hand had not been fashioned with an ordinary lock in mind. A different safe and lock had to be hidden elsewhere.

But where? The floor? I flipped up a corner of the scarlet rug with my toe but found only clean, secure slats of wood beneath.

I bent and replaced the rug. But when I straightened, I caught a swirl of movement from the corner of my eye.

Someone else was in the room with me.

I gasped and smacked a hand over my own mouth before I realized it was the other highwayman.

"Do you always charge into things head on?" he rasped.

I slowly lowered my hand from my jaw to my throat and exhaled. My pulse beat furiously. "You're so quiet. I didn't even hear the door."

"And you're quick. I went to fetch your bag. By the time I got back, the hall was empty." He closed the door and took two silent steps into the room, appraising me.

"I sent the house servant on a false search for my aunt, so that should give us some time. But there is no telling how much longer we have before Lord Tackleton notices the key is missing from his pocket."

"You sent away the . . . *servant*?"

"Yes." His tone nettled my suspicion. "So then, you knew?"

He raised a dark brow in question.

"You *knew* a man was watching the hall, yet you practically dared me to come up to the study on my own! Were you *trying* to get me in trouble?"

"Now why would I want to do that?" he asked with a faint smirk. He held up the blue and gold bag and swung it like a pendulum. "I'm simply returning your carpetbag."

"Fine." I dangled the chain by two fingers and swung the key back and forth in time with my bag. "I have the key but not the safe. Help me find it before we both get into trouble."

In answer, the highwayman propped my carpetbag against the closed door and skirted along the walls while I opened the short cabinets on either side of the desk. They were filled with stacks of notes and technical manuals. We searched the wall of shelves behind the desk, and heat crept up the back of my neck at our shared inspection beside the nude statues. Whether we were caught alone together or caught stealing from Lord Tackleton's private study, the damage to my reputation would be equally significant. But while I was keenly aware of the fact that I was behind closed doors with a man, he seemed thoroughly unimpressed with me in every respect. At least until he said, "Your performance of 'Le Voleur Voyage' was extraordinary."

Startled, I rattled a decorative Imperial egg but caught it before it rolled off the stand. "You recognized the piece?"

"Yes."

"Then . . . you speak Gallia?"

He nodded.

I groaned inwardly. Why hadn't I stopped to consider the meaning of the song? Impulse seemed to be taking over all my actions lately. Feigning a careless shrug, I asked, "Did you enjoy my little joke?"

His expression went unexpectedly dark. "You call *that* a joke?"

"But of course! A song about a highway thief. Ironic, wouldn't you say?"

He studied me a moment and resumed his search. "Try the far wall."

I tiptoed lightly over the wooden boards and said quietly, "You know, I just realized, I never learned your name."

He hesitated. "You may call me Harland."

"So, Mr. Harland—"

"*Just* Harland."

"Very well . . . Harland. Assuming we locate a safe, what is it you are expecting to find inside?"

He grunted, the translation of which implied a refusal until he countered my question with another. "What do you know of the Keyah mages?"

"I'm, uh, somewhat familiar with continental geography, but I don't believe I've heard of Keyah. Is that in the Accent Territories?"

"They are from the continent, yes." His dark eyes took on a distant look as he tilted and straightened a picture frame. "Keyah mages permanently ink the folklore of their people into their skin with colored dyes. The artistry is so lifelike that when they dance around the flickering fires at night, the ink on their bodies seems to move, too. They become a living story like watching a memory from someone else's mind."

My brain reeled to imagine it. "That sounds . . . magical."

"It is," he said quite seriously.

"But . . . how is that possible? I've only heard of magic conducted for healing." Granted, I knew very little about mages. I'd set foot inside a Magicstry only a handful of times. Despite her own condition, my mother insisted that I had no reason to visit when I was almost never sick. And when the Magicstry had failed to heal her . . . after that, I'd found even fewer reasons to convert.

Harland cocked his head to the side. Again, I was reminded of a caged animal waiting for the opportunity to pounce. I'd assumed Harland and Mr. Keays were partners, but a seed of apprehension planted in my gut.

"Conduction within the Parure is monitored closely by the Magicstry," he said. "Undisciplined magic is dangerous. Do you know what happens to those who conduct magic but refuse to convert?"

"Well, apart from what you just told me, I've never actually heard of anyone conducting magic outside the Magicstry."

"*Exactly.*"

A shiver trailed down my spine.

"You asked what I expect to find inside the safe," he said. "You should stop charging in headfirst, or one of these times you might stumble into something . . . truly dangerous." He went on before I could ask more. "You already checked under the rug. What about the desk?"

"Nothing," I answered. "Only a generic lockbox. And I am sure the secrets of Lord-Maker Tackleton are *much* too important to sit in a box on the floor. His Lordship would demand something more remarkable."

"Like this?"

I turned. Harland held the corner of another frame. The painting itself was a gruesome depiction of a battlefield washed in a blood-red sunset. The dismembered limbs and mangled bodies of dead soldiers were heaped before a giant, smoking flame. The part of me that longed to be Robin Renegade thrilled to imagine a war of good against evil— brave soldiers who chose death over surrender. The painting, however, was nothing like that. Rather, it was as if Lord-Maker Tackleton had chosen to frame humankind's capacity for violence—the cruelty of greed and bloodlust.

"Why would anyone hang that in their home?" I asked.

"This is an original Cabochon," he explained. "Worth thousands."

I pointedly eyed his loose-fitting costume. "And how exactly would a servant know the value of a Cabochon?"

He grunted and tipped the frame aside. Behind the painting was an inlaid metal panel with a small lock.

Quickly sweeping around a leather chaise, I held the key up to the lock. They were the same shape and size. "You found it!" I whispered, triumphant.

I fitted the thin key into the lock and turned. With a faint click, the panel popped open. I reached inside the dark cubby.

There was only one item.

My arm tingled like charged energy in a lightning storm as I pulled out a fist-sized drawstring bag made of deep, blue velvet. The lumpy object inside the bag was surprisingly heavy. I set it down, careful not to let it thump against the wood floor, quickly replaced the metal panel, and twisted the key in the safe with a soft click.

Harland straightened the picture frame and immediately bent to plunder the bag.

I lowered myself onto the floor beside him. "You still haven't told me . . . what is it?" I asked.

"I cannot tell you anything you do not already know," he said and unknotted the drawstrings.

"I know that you and Mr. Keays are attempting to intercept something dangerous. A new make that could change the Parure as we know it. What I *don't* know is why Mr. Keays is a Ruby Agent and you are not. You're not wearing the seal ring. Why are you here?"

He paused and gave me an appraising look. "I'm here to keep Art from getting us killed. He was wrong to trust you. You're . . ." He trailed off and frowned at the open bag. "Wait. Something isn't right."

And then I couldn't breathe.

Chapter Fifteen

AUDREY

I SWAYED ON MY KNEES, GASPING.

Like shouting against a strong wind, air forced its way into my lungs. I was suffocating in reverse—I couldn't exhale. I fell forward onto my hands. Fiery pain shot through my wrists, my arms, and flared at my shoulders. Unable to hold my own weight, I collapsed onto the floor in front of the blue velvet bag, which puffed out like a bellows whilst my lungs felt similarly swollen behind my ribs.

Somehow, impossible though it was, the bag—whatever was inside —was filling me with air.

I dragged myself away by my forearms, but the hard wood stung like whips of wind and lashes of icy rain against my exposed skin.

And still, I couldn't exhale.

Harland was standing over me. I reached for him, but the sharp features of his face blurred like chalk drawings in the rain. Colors ran through my fingers and pooled into muddy puddles around the edges of my vision. The pain was too much.

Then Mr. Keays was kneeling over me with warm hands cradling the sides of my head. "Miss Clune? What happened?"

The room was a hurricane of wind, but his hair wasn't even slightly ruffled. Couldn't he feel it?

"Miss Clune? *Audrey*, talk to me!"

Behind him, Harland was staring up at the velvet bag.

Had I seen that right?

Yes, the bag was bobbing along the ceiling like an impossible balloon.

Harland climbed onto the chaise and leapt. But as he caught the strings of the velvet bag, his body jerked to the side. By the way his hair stood on end, he looked to have caught the charged end of a lighting conductor. He landed hard and convulsed against the floor but did not let go. He somehow managed to knot the corded drawstrings. The bag whined, deflating, and went dead in his hand. He collapsed like the splayed soldiers in the bloody painting above him. Still, he reached a shaking hand toward me until his colorless features blurred, and the ends of his black hair curled into storm clouds that blotted out the sun.

But Mr. Keays stayed with me. He was saying something . . . only his voice was muted by the deafening wind in my ears. He pulled me upright with my face close to his. His eyes were bright, twin stars shining down at me through the gathering storm.

I stopped struggling.

Then everything went dark.

∽

"Help her, dammit!"

"I'm trying, but the make conducted too much."

"What was she doing here in the first place?"

Something heavy pressed against the sides of my legs. Hands clamped around my ribs. The wind crescendoed until, once again, I could barely hear above the storm.

"If she doesn't . . . punctured her lungs . . . I don't know what else—"

"Try!"

"It's not only damage to . . . but the magic . . . worse . . ."

There was nothing after that.

~

A GENTLE BREEZE BRUSHED MY FACE.

I gasped and jolted awake. I was sprawled on the floor with my back against a chair. Everything ached—my wrists, my shoulders, my ribs. Very little sunlight streamed in through the partially curtained window. How much time had passed? It couldn't have been long because Harland was slumped against the side of the chair beside me, shaking and pale, and Mr. Keays was still kneeling in front of me.

He again took my head between his warm palms. "Audrey—*Miss Clune*? Are you all right?"

I still felt a little breathless. After a few more gulps of air, I replied, "Someone will have heard that. We should leave. And then you *will* tell me what in all aether just happened."

"I take that as a yes," Harland rasped.

Mr. Keays let go and sank back onto his heels. He covered his face with a hand. His shoulders were shaking.

"Are you . . . are you *laughing* at me?" I asked.

"*No,*" he said in a pinched voice and clapped his hand more tightly over his mouth.

"You're laughing at me."

He took a deep breath, wheezing slightly. "Forgive me. Your tenacity is reassuring."

I couldn't help but return his wide smile, but I winced and gently felt my scalp. My hair was crusted with blood, probably from the hatpins that had been torn away with my sunbonnet. Half my hair tumbled down my back. But the worst abuse was a fiery pain that had settled deep into my joints—each seemed to grind directly against bone. My knees creaked loudly as I tried to stand. I swayed and dropped into the chair.

Harland seemed to be suffering as well. His complexion was pale and clammy as he clawed his way to standing and leaned heavily against the desk for several deep breaths.

131

I huddled in my seat as the threads of each clue pulled into a tightly stitched picture.

Harland had bandaged my coachman after his head was injured. From what I'd seen of the bandage, the head wound had bled quite a lot. But Harland had managed to stop the flow.

And then there was the dangerous make.

I brushed my fingers against my throat. I'd nearly suffocated. And my lungs had been punctured—I was sure I'd heard Harland say so— but apart from a deep ache in my joints, there was no residual pain of an injury. I couldn't even find scratches on my scalp beneath the dried blood.

Direct evidence of the Great Maker and the miracles of His magic.

My skin prickled with chills. The truth should have been obvious from the start. But once again, I'd been wrong in my assumptions.

"You're a very talented mage," I said softly.

Harland stiffened. "And *you* are a very talented musician." His dark eyes narrowed into a look that was both a threat and a dare—daring me to ask a question and threatening me if I did.

It didn't matter.

"Thank you, Mage Harland," I said, "for saving my life."

The tension went out of his shoulders like a snuffed match. "It's just Harland."

"Harland, then. Thank you."

"Don't thank me just yet." He crossed the room, limping slightly, paused to listen at the door, and unceremoniously stuffed both the wilted velvet bag—the dangerous make—and my sunbonnet into my gold and blue carpetbag.

"And the blueprints?" asked Mr. Keays.

"There were none," Harland answered.

Mr. Keays frowned. "That can't be right."

"There's nothing else in the safe."

The sudden anger in his voice was palpable. "There *has* to be. Or is this what you meant by a compromise? By Maker, I swear, if you're lying—"

"The blueprints aren't here," Harland said flatly.

"Give me the bag."

"Tell him, Audrey."

Startled by the use of my given name, I glanced between the men bracing for a fight. I'd originally assumed the highwaymen were partners in crime. I'd trusted Harland because I trusted Mr. Keays. But for the first time, I wondered if the two men were, in fact, competitors. As a Ruby Agent, Mr. Keays represented the gems while Harland was clearly a representative of the Magicstry. The Parure and Magicstry were two self-governing organizations with autonomous jurisdictions.

Ignoring the painful creak in my knees, I stood and positioned myself between them. "In point of fact," I said, "it's my bag. So I should be the one to take it."

As one, their ire turned on me.

"Absolutely not," Mr. Keays objected.

After brief consideration, Harland shrugged. "It's a compromise."

"It's too dangerous."

"But inconspicuous," Harland said. "If she leaves alone, she could easily carry it out of the Hall."

"As soon as you two are finished squabbling," I said, "I will take *my* bag with *my* belongings, and I'll return your precious make as soon as you answer *my* questions."

I grasped the handles but winced at the twinge of pain in my wrist when Harland didn't let go. He held fast, forcing me to meet his gaze. "Do *not* open this. Understand?"

I nodded.

He relinquished the bag.

"Harland is correct," I added. "Lord-Maker Tackleton's desk held nothing useful, and the make in a velvet bag was the only item in the safe. Why? What does it mean if blueprints are missing?"

In the sudden, bleak silence, Mr. Keays ran a hand over his face. When he looked up, his almond eyes were red-rimmed. "It means, Miss Clune, that things are much worse than I thought." He cleared his throat. "But we've lingered here long enough. We need to get you and your luggage somewhere safe. Where is your aunt?"

"She's waiting for me at the carriage."

"Good. We'll go straight there."

Harland twitched a black brow. "You can't mean to return her. Not looking like that."

"And not without answers," I added. I was irritated to be classed as a faulty appliance, but Harland was right. Strands of hair clung to the sweat on my face and collarbone, and my eyes felt dry enough to be swollen. Even as I adjusted my grip on the carpetbag, I swayed on my feet. The smell of spring air enveloped me as Mr. Keays wound a supportive arm around my waist. I tried not to lean too far into the comforting pressure as I hurriedly released the few remaining hairpins, rubbed away the crusted blood, and combed through my curls, wincing as the tangled strands caught against my aching finger joints. Unfortunately, nothing could be done for my crumpled dress. "Is anything else too amiss?"

"What do you think, Art?" Harland asked. "Do you find anything *amiss* with Miss Clune's appearance?"

Mr. Keays gave him an uncharacteristically dark look.

Harland huffed what could've been a laugh. "Don't be a fool. What do you think her aunt or anyone else will assume? At best, they'll question her reputation. At worst, she'll be caught up in the aftermath and blamed for the theft. The only way to ensure her safety is by bringing her back with us. Besides—" He smiled. A dangerous expression. "She has secrets to tell, too."

What did he mean by that? I opened my mouth to reply, but before I could speak, the door slammed open.

"No one move!" The stocky house servant from before lumbered across the threshold.

Unlike before, he was carrying a pistol.

Weapon in hand, the Northern servant looked far more like a street thug than a domestic. Clearly, there was more to his character than I'd originally assumed. Was there any way to talk ourselves out of such a compromising situation? I doubted a couple of deceptive tears would work a second time. Cautiously, I tucked the carpetbag beneath my skirts.

To make matters worse, Aunt Emma appeared in the doorway behind him. She raised a shaking hand to her colorless lips. "*Mon cœur!* What happened? Are you all right?"

"Stay back!" the servant ordered. "And you, I said don't move! What are you doing here? This room is restricted to guests." Entangled as I was with Mr. Keays, the servant grinned wide enough to reveal several missing molars. "Took me a wee bit of time to find your aunt, but I see you've kept good company while I was gone."

I shied back, face burning.

Mr. Keays moved to stand in front of me, but the servant aimed the pistol directly at his head. "*Nah*—I wouldn't do that. Kneel down."

"On the *floor*?" Mr. Keays replied. "Do you have any idea how much this suit is worth? The tariffs on fabric alone—"

"I said down! Keep those hands up. That's it. And you—get away from the desk!"

Harland didn't respond.

"*Oi*, cogs! What's your issue?" Aiming lower, the servant crossed the room. Without warning, he grabbed the back of Harland's head and smashed a knee directly into his face. I slapped a hand over my mouth to keep from shrieking as blood sprayed and Harland collapsed atop the desk.

Aunt Emma gripped the edge of the doorframe, eyes wide.

"Now what to do with you?" The servant licked his lips and eyed me. "Lord-Maker T. will want to hear about this. Of course, I might be persuaded to forget you were here. . ."

Behind him, Harland slowly pushed himself off the desk. Blood trickled from broken nose to his mouth, but he smiled—manic expression stained red—just before he lunged.

One moment, the stocky servant was leering down at me. The next, his face bleached of color as Harland gripped his wrist. The pistol fell from his stiff hand and clattered at my feet, and his knees hit the floor with a dull thud.

In the same smooth motion, Harland twisted and pinned the servant's arm behind his back. Only, when Harland let go, the servant's arm *continued* backward. His fingers curled, then his wrist, and then his arm at the elbow. Finally, with a loud *click* like a door snicking shut, his shoulder followed. The man let out a horrifying scream, which was instantly stifled by the crook of Harland's elbow.

The burley servant fell forward, kicked hard, and lunged for the fallen pistol.

I moved faster.

"Stop or I'll shoot!" I leveled the pistol at his chest. My hand was shaking, but my voice was firm. I took a deep breath—it was a wonder I had any room in my lungs. "Don't move a muscle!"

He froze in place—one arm outstretched, the other contorted behind—expression twisted in fury.

The sudden silence of the room was like the pressure of a storm against my eardrums.

Harland raised both hands in a calming gesture as he slowly straightened from a crouch. "It's all right . . . you're safe. You can let go now."

"Right . . . *sorry*." Trembling, I lowered the pistol.

The servant still didn't move.

"That's *enough*, Audrey," Harland growled. "Let him go."

"I . . ."

The servant's livid face had drained entirely of color and began to deepen into a bloodless blue.

"Why is he—"

"You're *killing* him." Harland charged forward but stalled as Mr. Keays blocked his path.

"She doesn't understand."

A gentle hand wrapped around my elbow, and Aunt Emma turned me toward her.

"Listen to me, *mon cœur*. You trust me, yes? You must tell this man to move. His heart won't beat. His lungs won't expand. Unless you order him to move again. Can you do that?"

Her words didn't make sense. Every time I grasped at logic, it sprang away. "Why won't he . . . I don't—"

"*Please*, just tell him."

How could I tell him anything? Apart from his expression, the servant looked dead. His eyes were glassy. His chest wasn't moving. In fact, nothing about him had moved. He was as grey and lifeless as carved stone.

I set aside the pistol and took a shaky breath. "You—you can move now. Or . . . breathe."

"Try harder, Audrey," Harland snapped. "Take a deeper breath."

"*Please* move."

"You have to mean it!"

I physically shoved the man with all my might. "Move!"

The servant collapsed to the floor in convulsions. His eyes rolled back into his head, and a foaming vomit spilled from his mouth down his chin.

Harland quickly knelt and pressed his hands against the man's chest with rhythmic compressions. Like a ghostly wail of fright, the man gasped. But gradually, moment by moment, the convulsions slowed then ceased, color returned to his face, his jaw unclenched, and his body slackened until there was only the steady rise and fall of his broad chest.

Wordlessly, all eyes turned to me.

Rage.

Grief.

Concern.

But no confusion.

What did they see that I couldn't? Even with so many pieces in place, the picture refused to make sense. I gripped the back of my neck and flexed my fingers. My limbs felt oddly numb, but the pain was gone.

"Will he be all right?" I asked quietly.

A tight nod from Harland.

"How is any of this even possible?"

Harland redirected his cold stare. "*That* seems like a question for your aunt."

"Aunt Emma?"

She looked so pale—like the colorless portrait of herself. Her chin trembled as she brushed a finger across my cheek. "You're so much like your mother."

The slow, creeping realization hit all at once, a leaden thud in my mind. "But why did she never tell me she was a mage?"

Chapter Sixteen

ART

Miss Clune was a mage.

And not just any mage if she could influence others with her voice. Most mages, including Harland, required physical touch to conduct magic through another person. And even then, they rarely possessed the creativity to influence the human body apart from healing the occasional broken bone. She was extraordinary in every way, and clearly, she hadn't even known.

I'd briefly wondered if Miss Clune was working with Harland to spy on me but immediately dismissed the idea. The mixture of shock and hurt in her expression thoroughly uprooted my heartstrings. Her lower lip trembled just before she turned away.

Harland forestalled compassion with all the empathy of a brick. "Escape first. You can explain yourselves later. At least until the Magicstry finds you."

"I remember you," the aunt, Miss Toussaint, said coldly. "You're the one who delivered the letter. How long have you been watching us—"

The distant sound of running feet thudded one floor below. As one, we held our breath until they passed.

"*Later*," Harland growled. He stood from a crouch, pinched the bridge of his nose, and dabbed at the blood on his face with a sleeve, but he was no longer bleeding. He'd already healed.

With silent steps, I disarmed and pocketed the pistol, closed and locked the study door, and wedged one of Tackleton's hideous chairs under the handle for good measure. When I turned back, Miss Clune still hadn't moved.

"Is that the only exit?" Harland asked, nodding toward the barricaded door.

"There's a balcony," I said. "It adjoins the next room, and I believe this wing faces the park. There's also a servant's stairwell at the end of the hall. If we're careful, we shouldn't be too visible."

"So, we sneak out through the servant's entrance, and then what?" Harland asked. "Make a run for the ship?"

"Possible," I said and nudged the unconscious man with the toe of my derby shoe. "However, there's more where this lump of muscle came from. Once he wakes, our secrets are out. We need a better plan. What do you think, Miss Clune?"

She was still facing whatever bloody ugly painting was hanging on the wall.

"Miss Clune?" I approached, grasped her arms, and turned her to face me. "*Audrey.*"

With a hitched breath, she finally looked up. Her sapphire eyes were even brighter beneath unshed tears.

"So, that's it, then?" I asked. "You're breaking our agreement?"

"Sorry?"

"Our agreement," I repeated. "You promised to keep my secrets, and I still need your help with my assignment. Can you do that? If not, well . . . you can forget about the pastries. That box belongs to me now, fair and square. Oh, and your bag. I'll take that now, too."

The hurt in her eyes remained. The tip of her pert nose was pink. But with a defiant tilt of her chin, Miss Clune set her expression like setting out the best china for company. She brushed away a stray tear and, assuming more of her usual confidence, gathered her carpetbag off the floor.

"Do you forget the terms of our agreement?" she asked. "If we make it out of here, you'll need a lot more than pastries to sate me."

"*When* we make it out of here, I'll even let you inflate the terms."

She held out a hand.

I shook it.

"Right," she said. "The plan. We take the balcony to the stairwell to the ship, but that still leaves several problems in our wake. The first of which is him."

"You could always just *tell* the man not to remember," said Harland darkly. "Why not let the magic take care of his memory for us?"

Miss Clune paled, but her voice was edged with venom. "No, I cannot *just* abuse his mind. I may not understand conduction, but I do understand free will . . . most especially the lack thereof. That is something I will never knowingly take, and certainly not for the sake of an easy solution."

The tight coil of Harland's anger seemed to unwind. He nodded in understanding and perhaps relief.

She took a steadying breath. "Besides, I won't need to."

I hadn't noticed the silver key until Miss Clune plucked it by the chain from beneath the chaise. She pressed it to her chin in thought. "We've been looking at this all wrong. Our aim is escape, when what we *actually* need is a way to salvage our reputations. To do that, we need to be *seen*."

Wordlessly, Miss Toussaint reached for Miss Clune to adjust her spilled hair and crumpled dress.

Miss Clune continued. "I'm sure you well know, Mr. Keays, reputation is merely the story others tell about you. We simply need to find a way to rewrite this story for our purposes."

I grinned. "So, what is the story this thug will tell? And how can we influence the retelling?"

"Exactly."

"What do you propose?"

"I have one idea . . ."

"But?" I asked.

"But I'm afraid it characterizes Harland as the villain."

I waved my hand, unconcerned. "If the gauche grey robe fits."

Harland shrugged. He knew as well as I did that the Magicstry could do almost anything and never face the consequences. Even with Judge Pinefoy's mysterious disappearance, Mage Citoyen would never be charged with murder.

"Very well," she said and handed Harland the silver key. "You will play our thief, and I believe it's your turn to be the distraction, Mr. Keays. Giving me time to steal away on the *Courtship* with *this*." She held up her carpetbag.

"*Et moi.* I'm coming with you." Her aunt's tone brooked no argument.

"All right. Aunt Emma and I will send away the carriage, then stow aboard."

"And trust you alone with the make?" Harland asked "Not a chance."

"But you and Mr. Keays have all the answers. We both have the advantage over the other."

"In that case . . ." I guided Miss Clune apart from the others where I hoped they couldn't easily overhear. I slid the gold and ruby ring from my finger to hers. She glanced down, holding the loose band in place with her thumb.

"Why are you giving me this?"

"An answer," I explained. "Mae will never let you on board without my permission."

"Mae?" she asked. "From The Jolly Cook?"

"The same. She should already be on board the *Courtship* waiting for my signal. Show her the ring and say the phrase—"

I hesitated only a moment before leaning in to whisper the honest truth—a truth that not only razed my defenses to the ground but handed Miss Clune a sharpened blade to hold over my throat.

"*As the Robin flies, the mage survives.*"

A line from the original poem, *The Renegade*.

She pulled back, eyes wide, and I held a finger to her lips—a plea for silence. The soft touch prickled against my skin even after I drew back. Was that magic? Or the current of something stronger? For the first time, I realized she wasn't already wearing a ring. Despite my despair at finding a make instead of blueprints, a new sprig of hope immediately sprouted inside me like a hearty weed that wouldn't crunch beneath my heel.

I kept my voice low. "You should be on your guard, Miss Clune. After everything is over and done, my next distraction may very well be in pursuit of that locket. I'd much rather steal something with lasting value over a single kiss."

She blinked and swiped a hand over her eyes. "Oh, for Maker's sake! Does *everyone* speak Gallia?"

I answered with a wide smile.

She peeked up at me between her fingers, a sly gleam in her eye. "If you remember the poem . . . the thief had no need to steal the locket. It was a gift willingly given."

That left me momentarily speechless.

"Of course," she continued. "I never saw myself as the lady in that story."

"No?"

"I always wanted to be the thief."

She left me there staring after her. I wasn't supposed to want to give away my locket.

After a last, grief-stricken look for the guard on the floor, Miss Clune straightened her shoulders and addressed the room. "Now that we each know our part, let's discuss the plot. It's time for another performance."

HARLAND SWIPED A HAND ACROSS MY CHEEK.

"*Argh!*" He hadn't hit me hard. But with the conduction of magic, I felt an immediate bloom of blood along the surface of my skin, and my eye instantly swelled shut. I gently prodded at my cheek. I already had a tender bruise. "Don't you think you're overdoing it?"

"I'll heal you after."

"But did you have to mark my face? I won't gain any sympathy for looking hideous."

He gave a noncommittal shrug.

"You're enjoying this, aren't you?"

Another shrug. Did he never change expressions? The man was harder to read than a Thornden novel.

"At some point," I said, "when we're not about to make a grand entrance, I'm going to ask for more of a reason to trust you."

Just around the corner, there was a commotion on the lawn.

"Ready?" I asked.

In answer, he held up the key and aimed a pistol at my chest.

"Wait, what are you doing?" I shouted. I stumbled back and turned to run.

Harland grabbed me by the jacket collar. He was shorter but clearly wiry with muscle because I struggled against his hold as we rounded the far corner of the manor.

"*Tackleton*," Harland shouted in a voice that clattered like an avalanche. "Where are they?"

Before us, the crowd gasped.

Nearly every garden party guest had congregated beneath the largest pavilion to avoid the looming threat of rain. At the front of the crowd stood my aunt and uncle Tackleton. Beside my uncle was the hired thug from the study. He clutched one arm to his chest. I'd worried he wouldn't recover. But apart from the arm and the unfocused gaze of a concussion, Harland seemed to have restored him to full health after Miss Clune managed to release him from the conduction of her magic. I also counted at least six more hired guards spaced throughout the crowd and across the lawn. Unfortunately, the greatest wildcard in our game was standing at the front of the crowd nearest my aunt.

"Arthur!" Mum shrieked when she saw me, nearly strangling Sweetpea in her panic.

"Hello, Mum. It appears as though I've caught a spot of bother, but not to worry—"

"Quiet!" Harland snapped and jabbed the pistol barrel against my ribs. I grunted in pain. Harland adjusted his grip on my jacket collar to display the safe key. "Where are the blueprints?" he demanded.

Tackleton's face was still red and ruddy, but he seemed to have sobered slightly. "Is this the mage?" he asked.

The thug slowly nodded. "I caught him in your study with the boyo and the woman I told you about."

"Well, clearly you *didn't* catch him if he's here."

Harland waved the pistol. "Shouldn't have dropped this. How's the arm? And the rest of you. Still feeling a bit cramped? I'm afraid I conducted too much."

The thug glared. Harland had redirected all suspicion of the magic conduction onto himself.

"Now, about those blueprints," Harland said.

Tackleton rolled his tongue around his mouth. "I'm afraid I don't know what you're talking about. But if you think to leverage my nephew, you're mistaken. You'd be doing me and the world a favor if you shot him—"

"I beg your pardon!"

"—You should've brought the girl instead. Where is she?"

The other guards were closing in. But it wouldn't help our plan to flee too soon. Miss Clune and her aunt needed enough time to send away the carriage before heading for the garden of moored airships.

"Can't help you there," Harland said. "I only needed one hostage. Clearly, I chose the wrong one."

"I'll have you know, I am *very* appealing!"

"It's true!" Mum cried. "He's not worthless at all! Lord-Maker, tell this ruffian to unhand my boy this instant!"

"Thank you, Mum. I'm sure that helps."

"Last chance," Harland warned as, once again, he painfully jabbed my ribs and started backing away. I was grateful the pistol was empty. Even knowing as little as I did about Harland, I wouldn't put it past him to shoot me thinking he could simply heal me later. "I've already confiscated your ill-gotten make. Now, where are the blueprints?"

"Clearly, you have no idea who you're dealing with," Tackleton said. "You're not from the Magicstry. Who are you working for?"

"The maker, of course." Grabbing my arm, Harland twirled us around and shoved me forward. The guards had slowly been closing in from the edges of the manor. We charged through an opening just before they boxed us in.

"Stop him!" Tackleton shouted as the first shot rang out.

The crowd screamed.

And we ran.

Dodging between a line of confused servants, we skirted closer to the Hall. "I'm going to fall now," I said.

"Do it."

I stumbled and tripped on the lawn into a graceless roll. Harland made a show of waving the pistol at me, then heaved me partway up by the shoulders of my poor, abused suit jacket. But a hired guard wearing the livery of a stablehand careened into Harland, and all three of us hit the ground. I scrambled far out of reach—I did *not* want to be anywhere near the conduction of magic—as Harland pinned the man's knee with both arms. My ears popped as the aether seemed to condense around us. The guard writhed and screamed as Harland instantaneously diverted all the blood out of his leg; his muscles cramped fast enough to shred ligaments and crack bone.

There was a loud pop and the guard slumped unconscious.

I'd seen the conduction technique before, but never wielded so militantly nor so skillfully. I tamped down my fear—a problem for later—as Harland tossed the guard aside by his mangled leg then sprang to his feet.

I waved my arms in mock protest. "Don't forget the pistol." It'd fallen to the ground during our scuffle.

Harland mutely scooped it up and once again shoved me into a run.

Ahead, the *Courtship* was ready to sail. I only hoped Miss Clune and Miss Toussaint had made it aboard safely. We rounded the first bend in the garden path as another shot rang over the lawn.

Harland grunted and stumbled into me. A streak of red painted my sleeve.

"Harland?" He listed to the side, and I caught him by the arm.

"Hit a lung," he wheezed. "I . . . had worse."

"No need to brag." However, I immediately traded our places. I hadn't considered that in running behind me, Harland had also been shielding me with his body. The mage had very likely saved my life.

We ducked inside the gazebo, and Harland ascended the ladder ahead of me—one arm limp at his side—as angry shouts chased us upward to the skies.

"Mae?" I called and loosed the docking line.

"Aye."

"Cast off!"

We dove onto the deck as the *Courtship* sailed upward.

My stomach dropped, and my feet dangled in empty air for several terrifying seconds before Harland and I finally managed to drag ourselves fully on deck.

Mae was the only pilot I trusted with the *Courtship* other than myself, even if she did fly like a madwoman. Would anyone be suspicious that my ship had been prepped for flight before I'd been taken hostage? Even if Tackleton somehow managed to follow, the *Courtship* could outfly every other make. At least, every other make I'd already raced against.

A sudden ping of bullets ricocheted against her hull. I covered my head, wincing, but at least the guards weren't smart enough to puncture *her* lungs. That was the only possible way to slow her ascent.

Somehow ignoring the incoming fire (and bleeding hole in his side), Harland heaved himself up to stand at the taffrail, straightened his shoulders, and surveyed the crowd like a king at court. "Looks like I *did* choose the right hostage," he shouted. "Your man was generous enough to lend me his ship. Deliver the blueprints at the Maker's Gala tomorrow night, or he dies!"

Harland crouched out of sight and sat. We slumped back-to-back on the deck.

"Good show," I said.

He coughed.

"Except for the part where I die tomorrow. That felt a tad heavy-handed."

"That was the best part."

"Was *that* a joke?"

Mae's grim face suddenly filled my vision, and her eyes bugged behind a pair of flight goggles as she loomed over us. Her wild curls frizzed out from beneath a tied scarf, and the safety harness over her *blouson* was only halfway buckled. "Are you dying? Can I have the *Courtship*, then?"

"No one is going to die."

"He might." She pointed to Harland. "Is that blood dripping on the deck? Yeh better not expect me to clean that up."

Harland nearly made a human expression of exasperation. I got to my feet and helped him to stand. "Did they make it?" I asked.

"Yeh collect the oddest people," she replied. "All these mages on one ship. I mean, really, Art. At this point, yeh might as well start yer own religion."

"Mae . . . who's flying the ship?"

"She can fly herself for a bit." The *Courtship* bobbed alarmingly low.

"Just get us safely home, please," I said.

"Aye."

We cleared Trolleywood Park as the humid sky thickened into a gloomy drizzle of rain. The party guests would be drenched; however, thanks to our show, the party itself would be the talk of the ton. Maybe it would even detract from the rumors circulating about Cecily. Though I couldn't distract my mind from the thought of leaving her and the palace behind. Anxiety twisted my stomach into knots.

With one last look over the city, I slung Harland's arm over mine to shoulder the bulk of his weight and together, we staggered belowdecks.

Chapter Seventeen

Audrey

THOUGHTS CROWDED MY MIND LIKE DOZENS OF UNINVITED guests—every one a stranger.

Mr. Keays was the Renegade. The *real* Renegade. He had to be—with the Gallia fashion, the fast ship, the secret assignments. Above all, the permanent character he wore like a mask to cover a limitless depth of sincerity. Then again, I put on the confidence of Robin Renegade to cover the fact that Audrey Clune was falling apart inside. Both of us Renegades, and only one of us an impostor.

Because I was a mage.

Had I used magic in the past without knowing? In Gallia, heretic mages who conducted magic outside the Magicstry were executed. In the Parure, mages were forced to convert. Neither prospect was appealing. Would Harland send me to the Magicstry for training? There was too much I didn't know and a crowd of strangers surrounding me.

Aunt Emma took my arm as soon as we were out the front door and out of earshot of the servants. We'd put on a show of tears and trauma in front of the staff before making our escape.

"We can't go home," she said in low tones. "They'll be expecting us there. We should go directly to the station then to the docks. There's always a steamer to the Accent Territories this time of year. I have some money saved—"

"What are you saying?" I asked.

"We need to run."

"Yes," I said. "To the *Courtship*. We don't have much time."

"But I thought . . . you're not actually thinking of going with them?"

"It was *my* plan."

"*Mon cœur*," she said, tugging me to face her. "You don't understand."

I roughly shrugged free of her grip. "Of course I don't understand because no one ever explained things to me!"

"He's a mage. You cannot trust him."

"I can't trust *him*?" I choked on a laugh. Every emotion inside me finally reached a boiling point. "I may not understand everything, but I understand very well that magic would've killed me if Harland hadn't saved my life. Even worse, magic—*I*—my ignorance—could've killed someone else. The only person I don't trust is *you*."

She fell back a step.

"Where else do I direct my anger?" I asked. "If Mother was a mage, why didn't she tell me? I'll never understand because now I'll never be able to ask her. Grandmother *certainly* knows the truth about me. After every slight, every indignity, every abuse I've suffered whilst trapped in that Maker-forsaken house . . . I *finally* understand—she was using me! The entirety of my life finally makes sense! But Grandmother isn't here. And even if she were, I'm not sure I'd be brave enough to confront her." I angrily wiped away the tears fogging my vision. "So that leaves only you. You who I love more than any other person in the world. You who I write twice each week and visit at every opportunity. And yet *you* never told me the truth."

I tightened my grip on the handles of my bag. The loose ring dug against the sides of my fingers. "Harland saved my life. And Mr. Keays has never given me anything apart from the honest truth. What's more, both of them trust *me*. And unless I ensure the safety of this bag, magic may very well become even more dangerous. So now I am going to the carriage and then to the ship with the people who can give me the most answers." With effort, I softened. "I understand if you don't want to come. I'd much rather you were safe."

I turned and crossed the rest of the drive to the carriage. It appeared that Ivo had returned to Maker Malowney's townhouse because John was waiting alone. He held open the door, but I waved him away. "I can manage, thank you."

The distraction wouldn't last long. I had only a brief window of opportunity to enact my plan. I fumbled with the interior seat and retreated from the carriage.

Aunt Emma reached around me and closed the carriage door. "John, would you please return the carriage?" she asked. "We'd like to spend a little more time in the city."

"It looks like rain, Miss."

"Don't worry. We'll take the streetcar home. But if anyone should ask, you drove us home. A carriage loitering among all these fine steam autos is scandalous enough."

We'd made quite a show of tears with plenty of servants watching. If we stayed to explain, we'd only draw more attention, and we needed to leave fast to board the airship before Harland and Art made their own hasty exit. Aunt Emma would send a letter to Lady Tackleton by way of further explanation and to corroborate our stories. It was a calculated risk, but one that I hoped would keep the rumors at bay while also leaving less opportunity for disputation of the day's events.

John tipped his hat, and I nodded, grateful for his discretion.

"Very good, Miss. Your secret is safe with me! You ladies enjoy your outing."

I gave a friendly wave to John as he returned to the box but spoke under my breath to Aunt Emma. "You don't have to come," I repeated.

Aunt Emma hugged—mostly dragged—me closer until we were crushed together. "Of course I'm coming with you. See? You can't get rid of me!"

"But I'm still angry," I said with my face squashed against her shoulder.

"I'm glad. You should take your time forgiving me, too. *Je le mérite.* None of this is your fault."

"No, that's not—"

"See? Even now you're trying not to be angry. Stop that."

John urged the horses forward, and Aunt Emma released her stranglehold. Keeping the carriage between us and the servant positioned at the front door, we followed the curve of the drive and ducked behind the veranda. We carefully made our way around the side of the house toward the gardens.

"Your choices have always been for the happiness of others," Aunt Emma said quietly. "You took care of your mother when the Magicstry would not. You make choices to appease your grandmother. Where did you get this idea that you need to take care of me, too? *Hm?* I much prefer to support the choices you make for *yourself.*"

I didn't have an answer to that.

I led us to the same path Mr. Keays and I had followed only an hour earlier. The painted figure of Miss Conduct still pursed her lips down at us in a wicked smile. Would she tell our secrets? A woman like her would most certainly be more loyal to herself than a lover.

No one else was watching as we quietly entered the gazebo.

The guardrails had been removed with only a rope ladder leading up to the ship's deck. Managing my dress while ascending the ladder was a struggle, but I eventually reached the top only to be blocked from the deck. The same girl I'd seen at The Jolly Cook stood at the entrance. She was a younger, female copy of Mr. Jolly with wide, rosy cheeks and a sturdy build, albeit slightly less *jolly* than her father. Her overall appearance was haphazard—loose harness over a jacket buttoned halfway— apart from her keen eyes. She was looking down at me with the same detached assessment as before. I couldn't read her opinion, if she had one at all.

"Mae?" I asked.

"Aye."

"Good to see you again." I had no doubt she remembered me. She didn't seem like the type to forget anything. Pinning the bag between my stomach and the ladder, I raised one hand and showed the ring. "Mr. Keays asked me to show you this."

"And?"

"And to tell you, *As the Robin flies, the mage survives.*"

She folded her arms. "So?"

"So . . . we can come aboard?"

"No."

"Pardon?" I asked. "Mr. Keays sent us ahead, but he'll arrive momentarily."

"Oh, I believe he sent yeh." Mr. Jolly had a thick, rural accent. But when Mae spoke, she sounded like she was attempting to fit every vowel into each word. "I just don't agree with him. Art likes to collect strays, but yeh look like yer more trouble than yer worth."

"There'll be even more trouble if you don't let us aboard," Aunt Emma called testily from behind me.

Mae rolled her eyes but let us board without further convincing. Apparently, she'd simply wanted to make her displeasure clear. After standing back to observe our graceless climb in party gowns, she showed us to a set of stairs leading belowdecks. "Stay down here. It's not my job to keep yeh from falling overboard."

My heart sank. The only good thing about this situation was that I was on an airship. I didn't want to miss my first flight. "If I could just—"

"No."

That time, her tone brooked no room for argument. Aunt Emma patted my arm as, glumly, I descended below.

Safely stowed away, all we could do was wait.

The surprisingly spacious interior cabin was furnished like a comfortable parlor with a tasteful pair of sofas built directly into the floor. The room was well-lit with gas lamps spaced evenly along the walls, and a galley bordered the far third of the cabin. I inhaled the strong smell of coffee and cedar and took the opportunity to snoop before the men arrived (or before Mae decided to blind me for looking).

A deep metal tray was affixed to the galley counter. Inside was an empty paper box that looked suspiciously like my box of pastries from The Jolly Cook. The rest of the cabinets were filled to the brim with emergency foodstuffs.

I wandered next to the far doors which led to a complex-looking boiler room. Too afraid to touch anything, I closed the door without exploring further. An arched hallway led to cozy berthing compartments. Several rope hammocks hung from the roof, each cradling a comfortable mattress and woven blanket. Bolted cabinets were evenly spaced around the walls. Peeking inside, I discovered that most of them were filled with simple clothes of various sizes and toiletry essentials. Refugee supplies, I realized, for the mages the Renegade brought across the border.

The cabinet farthest from the door was more like a costume closet of contents—vests, cape cloaks, glasses, and a diverse collection of hats. Even a small box of makeup and false facial hair. I smiled to myself imagining Mr. Keays wearing a thick mustache and false, bushy eyebrows. He was a decent actor. With a thorough disguise, I believed he could blend in almost anywhere.

Pushing aside the cloaks that smelled like lavender sachets, I deposited my carpetbag at the back of the wardrobe and closed and latched the door.

Overall, the ship was used but clean. I assumed most of the furnishings were a personal touch from Mr. Keays. *Courtship* was as close to the real Mr. Keays as anything I'd seen from him so far. I felt a thrill of warmth that he'd trusted me enough to allow me aboard . . . to share his secret.

I returned to the parlor-like area where Aunt Emma had chosen a seat on the far sofa. I huddled beside her.

We didn't have long to wait.

The shouts outside were loud enough to be heard even above the hissing boiler room bellows. I perched nervously at the edge of my seat as the whine of the boiler suddenly intensified.

The *Courtship* swayed like balancing supports had been removed. And without any further warning, we soared upward.

I careened into Aunt Emma, and we tumbled into the arm of the sofa.

In the absence of fresh wind on my face, I felt like the spoke of a spinning wheel. My stomach seemed to summersault inside me.

The ping of gunfire racketed against the hull like a violent hailstorm.

I dove for the floor as Aunt Emma flattened herself on the couch.

Thankfully, the bullets didn't seem to puncture the thick hull, but I immediately worried for Mr. Keays. Were he and Harland in harm's way? And where had all the shots come from? Lord Tackleton had more hired guards, but apparently, I hadn't realized just how many. Had I known, I never would've sent them into danger against such odds—just one more gap in my understanding that sent me into a spiral of shame and worry. I wrapped my arms over my head and lay on the floor.

The moment the *Courtship* leveled into a less frantic ascent, I pushed myself up and bunched my full skirts until I could finally stand.

"Aunt Emma?"

"I'm all right."

I dashed to the stairs but pulled up short as I nearly collided with Mr. Keays. He and Harland staggered down the final step and into the cabin.

"Are you hurt?" Impulsively, I reached for Mr. Keays and ran my hands up the lapels of his crumpled suit jacket and clasped the sides of his neck to examine his face. One eye was crinkled into a smile. The other was nearly swollen shut, and a dark bruise had already started to form.

"I'm fine," he said.

"But your eye—"

"All part of the performance."

"What happened?" I asked. "We heard the gunshots, and I worried . . ."

"Go on."

"Well, there's no need to look so smug. You're fine." I lightly slapped his healthy cheek and took a large step back. My hands and side felt hot where I'd pressed against him. But under the bright humor in his gaze, my face felt scorching.

Harland grunted. "I'm bleeding out, thank you for asking."

"You are?" I exclaimed.

"Tell me you at least have the make," he said.

"Yes, it's safe."

He pushed past us and limped to the sofa.

Mr. Keays reached to stop him. "No, not the—"

Harland plopped onto the cushion. Water, blood, and whatever else soaked into the expensive fabric. "Send me a bill," Harland said flatly.

Aunt Emma glared at Harland but pinched her lips together without comment.

"He'll be fine," Mr. Keays said.

Would he? *Fascinating*. Was that what magic could do? Tentatively, I followed him to the sofa and hovered at Harland's side. "Can I . . . can I help? With magic, I mean."

"I doubt it. Not unless you've studied human anatomy."

"Can't I help by . . . conducting or . . . something?" I asked. Aunt Emma shifted in her seat, but I kept my attention firmly fixed on Harland. I wanted *him* to answer my questions.

He rolled his gaze heavenward and leaned forward with his elbows on his knees. "All right. Let's say you breathe in the aether and, with it, a massive charge of magic. Then what?"

"Well . . . of course I don't have an answer. I only just found out I've been conducting magic at all."

He sighed like a disappointed tutor. "Conducting is the process by which we guide magic to a specific connection point. Am I correct in assuming that in spite of your youth and general good health, you are in frequent pain? Your joints ache. You have difficulty breathing. Your ribs often feel like they've fused together."

My lips parted in shock. I instinctively massaged my hands—they ached at the reminder. "How did you know?"

"Your pain is a result of improper conduction. Without a fixed outlet or connection point, excess magic will often pool in the joints and around the lungs. Conduct too much magic this way, and your body enters a healing crisis, and symptoms become . . . a great deal worse."

"Is that what happened in the study? I conducted too much magic?"

"*Mm.*" Harland sank back into his seat. "Right now, I need to concentrate on healing a hole through my side. But if you were to, say, accidentally conduct magic to my heart . . . my heart would beat stronger, I'd bleed out faster, and I'd lose consciousness before I ever got the chance to heal."

"Right . . . I won't help, then."

"I appreciate the neglect." Harland leaned his head back and closed his eyes.

Mr. Keays rounded the sofa and took the seat beside my aunt. In a comfortingly familiar gesture, he patted her hand. My heart warmed at the small kindness.

The ship bobbed in waves beneath my feet as I alternated between pacing and hovering anxiously at Harland's side. But in a surprisingly short amount of time, color started to return to his face. His chest rose and fell in deep breaths.

"Even with training," he murmured, "I doubt you'd be able to help. Your method of conduction appears to primarily affect cortex polarity and other areas of the brain that control inhibitions and free will."

"That sounds . . . *very* specific," I said. "How can I conduct magic to something I don't even understand?"

He shrugged and winced. "Raw talent. Instinct. Blood mages like me are as common as the branches in my family tree. But you are something else entirely."

I rested a hip against the edge of a sofa. "You're making it sound as though I'm inhuman."

"You are what has been termed a Charismage," he said. "Influential. Powerful. And exceptionally dangerous. Especially without Magicstry training."

"*Entraînement?*" Aunt Emma firmly broke in. "You mean subjugation. The Magicstry is equally dangerous to the mages they collect like cheap *trophées*. The masters push their novitiates beyond what they can bear. They preach protection, but Audrey . . . they put your mind and body at constant risk. You would never be free or safe."

I looked to Harland. His eyes remained closed, but his expression showed a new tension. "She's not wrong."

Aunt Emma narrowed her eyes. She'd stepped into the ring for a fight, but her opponent was already defeated. In fact, he looked as though one punch had laid him out on the floor.

"Are you going to turn me in?" I asked quietly.

After an extended silence, Harland swiped a hand over his brow and opened his eyes.

"It was easier when I thought you were simply cunning or cruel. But now . . . ignorance won't save you. Even if I choose not to report you, it's a miracle you've escaped for this long. *When* they catch you, they'll force you to convert, and I'll be punished for my failure to inform on you. For years, they've been searching for a new Charismage to plant inside the government. Someone to influence the queen. You are a powerful commodity."

I laughed cynically. "I wish that were so. But apart from conducting magic in the study, I've never done anything influential *or* powerful."

"No?" he asked. "Let's review your actions *before* stealing the make. How do you explain your ability to influence so many people? How easily you bend them to your will. Your performance of 'Le Voyeur Voyage,' for example. The entire audience was enthralled."

"There's nothing magical about an ear for music and years of hard work," I said.

Aunt Emma gave me a sad smile.

Harland continued, "Then explain why Lord-Maker Tackleton, perhaps the most greedy and paranoid man in the entire Parure, would freely share information with you. Not only did you steal his attention, but you also managed to acquire the key to his private safe."

A sliver of doubt creeped into my voice. "I tricked him into telling me. I asked if he was working on any new projects, and then I . . . it was just a distraction."

"Outside the study?" he asked. "You sent away the guard."

"I thought he was a servant! I-I pretended to cry and asked him to find my aunt so he would leave."

"You're telling me that a couple of tears convinced a well-paid criminal to run an errand?"

"Maybe?" I wrapped my arms around my middle.

Harland didn't let up. "Do you think that sort of behavior is normal?"

"Well, no . . . but—"

"Do you honestly expect people to indulge your whims just because of a pretty face?"

"*Harland*," Mr. Keays warned.

"See? You've wrapped Art into a neat bow around your finger and bewitched him into doing whatever you please, including decisions that compromise his own sister!"

"Enough!" Aunt Emma stood. Her frail frame shook with fury. "Clearly, the great Magicstry doesn't know everything. *Mon cœur*, I cannot make up for lost time. But please, let me tell you some of what your mother could not. Most mages need physical touch to conduct the magic to someone else. Amalie discovered that her singing could also conduct magic, but only when she fully believed the words she sang. I think, without fully meaning to, she taught you this skill as well. You *are* powerful. Even your words conduct magic. But unless you conduct an immense amount of power like with music, intention doesn't work. You can't impose your thoughts on someone else. You can only influence others with *direct* statements or commands." She pinched Mr. Keays's jacket sleeve. "Did you tell him to fall in love with you?"

"What?" I protested. "Who said anything about love?"

"*Exactly*." She rounded on the men. "Don't blame Audrey for *your* problems! Her talent for magic is not a scapegoat!"

While they bickered in the background, no one noticed as I sank to the floor with my back to the sofa cushions. My limbs shook. I felt ill as I reexamined each encounter. My ribs ached after my run-in with Lord-Maker Tackleton, my hands ached after my performance, and I'd fought a twinge in my neck after sending away the servant or . . . the hired guard. In each instance, I'd felt an expanding confidence like deep lung-fuls of air followed by an inexplicable pain.

The clear reflection I saw of myself in life's mirror cracked and fell away. How long had I been conducting magic without knowing? Yet if I had the power to influence others, why did I lack the freedom to make my own choices? I couldn't understand how it was possible for the misery in my life to be lies and truth all at once.

"Audrey?" The cabin had gone silent.

"Is that why Grandmother does not allow me to make direct statements?" I asked quietly. "Because I take other people's choices?" I looked up through the blur of tears. "Was she right to silence me?"

No one gave me an answer.

"Enough of this." Mr. Keays stood and abruptly left for the berth.

Chapter Eighteen

AUDREY

I STARED BLANKLY AFTER MR. KEAYS, BUT HE SHORTLY returned holding out an armful of dark clothing. He'd also removed his hat and other party trappings. Without the kohl lining his almond eyes, he better suited our surroundings. He looked like my highwayman again with ruffled hair and travel-worn clothing. The bruising only made him look more like a rogue. He leaned his swollen face within reach of Harland. "Do you mind? I'm not in the habit of being homely."

Harland rolled his eyes and not-so-gently slapped a hand over Mr. Keays's eye.

Mr. Keays rubbed his face, but the swollen bruise miraculously disappeared, leaving only healthy, golden-brown skin. He took my hand and pulled me to my feet. "No more lies and no more feeling sorry for yourself," he ordered. "The only tragedy here is that you're missing your first flight. Now put this on." He held up a flight *blouson* of midnight blue and cream-colored leathers.

Was he taking me outside? I knew what I *should* feel, but I couldn't seem to work up an enthusiasm. My bleak mood stuck.

Mr. Keays sighed, turned me around by the shoulders, and slid my arms inside the stiff sleeves. "A near-perfect fit," he said. "Thread the buckles there. Yes, that's it."

As I slowly fit the buckles to my frame, the ruby ring spun loosely around my finger. Mr. Keays donned a similar-looking jacket dyed a deep green. He offered me a hand.

I placed the ring inside his open palm. "I should give this back."

"Ah, yes." His brow furrowed slightly as he replaced the ring on his finger. "I almost forgot. You'll want to leave room for another ring, I expect."

I tilted my head, uncomprehending.

"Your engagement to Malowney," Harland clarified. "Felicitations."

"Why would you assume *that*? We're not engaged."

Harland and Mr. Keays shared a glance. "You're not?" Harland asked.

"I ought to know." But the matter raised even more questions. Where had they gotten their information? Did Maker Malowney know about my ability to conduct as well? What had Grandmother told him?

Mr. Keays straightened. "Well, that changes things considerably. Again."

"We need better information," Harland said.

"And a new plan," Mr. Keays agreed. "In the meantime, we're going out." Once again, he offered me a hand. Hesitantly, I placed mine within. He laced our fingers together and set off to the exit.

"Try not to kill each other while we're gone," he called over his shoulder.

Aunt Emma and Harland didn't reply.

The stairs were slick with rain as we ascended to the deck, and a thin drizzle fell at a slant. I was grateful for the *blouson*. My hair and dress were immediately misted with rain, although my hair was already tangled and the dress fabric might've been beyond saving anyway. A trickle of water dripped down my spine, and I shivered.

Peering glumly through the gloom, I could barely make out the landscape view. Apart from the slight sway of the ship and staccato tap of the rigging, I might as well stand on a windy hilltop and pour a bucket of water over my head. "How is this any better?" I asked loudly. "I can't see anything."

Mr. Keays kept us close to the center of the deck as we made for the bow. "Mae!" he called.

"Aye?" she answered from the helm. I hadn't seen her through the rain.

"We're here to relieve you."

"I already set a course. We shan't even change altitude till Collet."

"Go below and make sure our passengers stay civil."

"Not my job." But after a look at me through a pair of fogged goggles, she wound a sopping rope around the helm and did as he'd asked.

Mr. Keays led me to the same gearbox as before and directed me to sit on the drenched deck. Resigned, I knelt in a pile of my wet skirts. After dumping a few items in front of me, he clipped a snap hook with a line onto the railing running from the mast to helm. He looped the first tether at the shoulder of my flight *blouson*.

I should've used a wrap to secure my hair like Mae. Even though the flight jacket provided insulation against the chill of a higher altitude, I shivered as the wind whipped tangled wet strands across my face.

"Allow me." Mr. Keays met my gaze in question. I nodded permission, and he gently placed both hands on either side of my head. He smoothed my hair back into a twist and tucked the tail of hair into the high collar of my jacket. His warm fingers lingered around the inside of my collar.

"Are you cold?" he asked.

Another kind of shiver rippled down my spine. "Yes."

He continued to hold my stare as his hands slid over my shoulders and down my arms, grazing along my sides. "In that case . . . it may help to tighten these."

My breath hitched as he tugged me closer by the buckles along my stomach. I slid forward until our knees touched. His gaze roamed over me. Exploring. Suggesting. Lingering.

"I don't feel cold anymore."

Slowly, he bent his face to mine. His quickened breaths brushed my lips.

"May I?" he asked.

I wanted him to kiss me. Was that what *he* wanted?

If I'd somehow conducted magic, would Mr. Keays even know? Our past conversations raced through my mind. Had I made any direct statements regarding my desires? Was there even the slightest possibility I'd compelled his affections?

A thin rivulet of rainwater dripped from a curl of his hair and down my cheek like an icy tear. The chilling sensation was enough to bring me back to reality. I shoved away from him, scrambling back. "No, this isn't right!"

"Forgive me! I shouldn't have—"

"No—it's just—I don't want to take advantage of you!"

"You don't . . ." He pinched his lips together, trying and utterly failing to hold in a laugh.

"I mean it!" I insisted. "What if Harland is right? Have I been conducting magic to you? Have I manipulated your choices? I forced you to include me on this adventure. What other explanation is there for me to be here? But that person . . . the woman you met on the road. She doesn't exist. I was playacting. I put on confidence like a character. You've never met the real me because I never introduced myself." I wrung my hands with worry, but that didn't stop all the words from pouring out. "Audrey Clune is quite different from the Renegade I've pretended to be. I'm really very . . . *small*. And sheltered. And I never had much choice in the direction of my life. What if . . . what if I forced you to see me as I wished, not as I am? I never meant to steal free will. I won't manipulate your interest any more than I already have!"

I drew in my legs and put my chin on my knees. Water dripped down my nose. I'd never felt more miserable. The magic. The shame. It all soaked into me like the cold rain.

"Are you quite finished?" he asked.

I grumbled into my skirt.

He scooted and sat beside me, pulled over a harness, and adjusted the tether lengths. "I was out of line when I said you were shameless in your methods to steal the key from my uncle. But it was because I knew that silly flirt wasn't the real you. I thought, why would such a mighty woman play dumb when she's smart enough to do anything she wants . . . to *be* anyone she wants? I wondered why you didn't think to use your strength instead of fear. I've never met your grandmother, but my opinion of her is quite low if she repressed your spirit—made you believe that you are weak when I know you to be quite the opposite. *This* is who you truly are, Audrey. Clever . . . daring . . . *beautiful.*"

He set aside the last tether. "Even if you *have* conducted magic to me," he continued. "You are not responsible for my desires in this moment."

I glanced sideways, dimly noticing he'd purposefully sat against my side to better block me from the slant of rain. "I don't want to steal from you," I said quietly.

"You can't steal something that's willingly given." He brushed a hand over my hair and got to his feet and grinned down at me. "As regards a kiss, at least. Now that you're aware of your magic, I trust you not to deliberately bewitch my more tender affections. *Hm?* At least, not any more than you already have. There's plenty of that already without magic involved." His tone turned unexpectedly serious. "This . . . *attraction* between us. It can't be more than it already is. I owe too much, and I—I can't afford to—"

"I understand." He already carried so much weight on his shoulders. How could I ask to add more, and would I even want to? I'd already postponed an unwanted marriage. Admitting that I liked Mr. Keays would only bring more complications. I'd only be tied to him, too.

In a sudden shift, the teasing rogue was back. "My locket stays with me. Or before I know it, I'll be giving you my ship, too."

I massaged my hands with worry. "How can I make a promise when I don't fully understand how my magic works?"

"Let's try this." He took a hand and lifted me to my feet. Winding an arm around my waist, he drew me in close. When I opened my mouth to protest, he lightly pressed his warm fingers to my chilled lips. "You conduct magic with your voice. Therefore, I'm not under the influence of magic now, am I?"

Hesitantly, I shook my head.

"So, kiss me. I give you my permission."

"Wha—" My voice muffled as he emphasized the gentle press of his fingers against my lips.

"You don't have to now. Kiss me anytime. Wherever and however you please. You don't need to worry about taking advantage of me because I've already given you my unreserved, unconditional permission in advance. I want you, Audrey. And that is the honest truth. Have I made my opinion clear?"

I nodded numbly.

"Good." He dropped his hand. "I look forward to your response."

Before I could react, he handed me the flight harness. "Now, let's tend the helm. Mae set us on a good course, and I think the rain is about to clear."

Feeling dazed, I strung my arms through the harness. I *tried* to observe as Mr. Keays fitted the tethers and buckles to the correct measure and *not* observe the firm pressure of his steady hands on my shoulders and waist. I hoped to commit the flight gear to memory so I'd be able to replicate the process myself. Thankfully, the design did not require a knowledge of aero-knots because metal rings were already sewn throughout the jacket. It would be easy to tie-off, or rather clip, a line from myself to the metal railings that reached from mast to mast across the ship.

But when Mr. Keays leaned over me to clip the line, my breath hitched, my pulse quickened, and my gaze immediately centered on the proximity of his lips from mine. Every thought was absorbed in him. I wanted to know the feeling of those lips against mine. Across my skin. He'd given me permission, hadn't he? If he would only tilt his head . . .

He grinned.

"Oh dear," I muttered. "Now I see your game."

"Game?" he asked brightly.

He'd given me permission . . . *and* he'd found another way to tease me.

The rake.

"Let me see if I understand the rules," I said. "You want to see how long you can bait me before I finally give in and kiss you? Is that right?"

He clasped his hands behind his back with a casual shrug.

"What if I don't want to play your game?" I asked seriously.

His hands fell to his sides. His expression fell, too. "I apologize. I gave you a choice but not the freedom to make it."

"I don't want you to tease me."

"I understand."

Wrapping my arms around his shoulders, I dragged his ear to my lips. "I want only the honest truth between us."

Then, I gently pressed my lips to his.

OUR FIRST TOUCH WAS CHILLED FROM THE RAIN, BUT OUR shared breaths warmed the kiss into more. I moved against him, savoring the softness of his mouth, the light pull of skin as I angled my head, the strong flex of his shoulders beneath my arms. Everything inside me tightened with desire. Humming a sigh, I slid higher against his chest.

And he stilled.

My lips trailed over his chin as I pulled back and studied his reaction.

For a long time he simply looked at me—almond eyes full of indecipherable thoughts.

My stomach twisted, and I wanted to apologize. Had I made a mistake? Did I play the wrong game?

But before I could speak, he enfolded me in his arms and kissed me back. That time, there was no gentle caress and nothing teasing about the way his hands flattened against me to crush our full bodies together. He tugged at the edge of my *blouson*, anchoring my hips against his, and fell back into the mast. Tightening my arms around his neck, I dragged his bottom lip between my teeth until finally, he opened his mouth to mine.

There we tangled together, wound fingers through each other's clothes and hair, and whispered more truths between each fierce kiss until both of us were gasping for breath.

He gripped my upper arms, pushing us apart.

"Don't stop!" I panted.

"I don't want you to miss—"

"What?"

In one smooth motion, he spun me toward the railing, and I gasped as the unconstrained landscape suddenly stretched before me. The rolling hills far below were like a woven carpet of moss. A flock of birds as small as a swarm of insects launched upward from one of the trees. Streams of sunlight burst between shadows of clouds and trickled over the landscape like gold veins.

I hadn't even noticed the rain had stopped.

Mr. Keays wrapped his arms around my waist and settled his chin against my shoulder. I leaned into his touch and played with his fingers, pausing on the band of his ring. "How did you become the Renegade?" I asked.

"I'm not *the* Renegade." He teased my ear between his teeth. "There's more than one. Or do you think I'm nearly one hundred years old?"

"Did you inherit the job? I always thought the rumors were just cogs telling stories. It's surreal to meet the actual person."

"Disappointed?"

"Very. I admired the Renegade more when she was a woman."

"Robin Renegade was real. The Magicstry tried to suppress her part in the Gallia revolution, but the best they could do was turn facts into stories. What the stories leave out is that Robin had a first mate, her husband. After her death—old age, by the way, not trapped in a barn fire set by mages—he trained an apprentice to continue her work. And so the smuggling business continued until the previous Renegade, a man named Earnest Fletch, found me and offered me the job."

"That, I'm certain, is a fantastic story." I twisted around and faced him. His hair was silk between my fingers.

He shrugged and pressed a kiss to my temple. "A drunken night in Caleti with my university mates . . ."

A kiss to my jaw.

"A *fête* gone wrong . . ."

My neck.

"Shipwreck into a Magicstry cathedral . . . nothing much to tell."

I laughed. "Is any of that true?"

"I have to keep some of my mystery," he said.

"I want to know why you chose this."

He quietly considered. "The opportunity to help innocent people wasn't one I could ever turn down. When it comes to mages, the

Magicstry enforces their own form of government. Even to this day in Gallia, any mage conducting magic outside the Magicstry is executed. Here, in the Parure, they're at least given a chance to convert or immigrate to the Accent Territories."

I wilted, but he tipped my chin up to his mouth. "Or they live in secret."

"Like you?" I asked. "Nearly your entire life is an act."

"Not with you."

I trailed my fingers along the planes of his face. "Thank you for the truth," I whispered and skimmed my lips lightly against his before the tight desire again drove me to greater passion—a delirious dance of strokes and commands as I pulled his lips between mine and traced his smiling mouth with my tongue.

Eventually, I wound my wandering hands inside his jacket. Drawing him in closer, I rested my head against his heaving chest.

"They say the aether is richer the closer you are to heaven," he murmured against my hair. "The sky was Made as a reservoir of magic. Whether you knew it or not . . . clearly, you were always meant to fly."

And perhaps, for the first time in my life, I believed it.

Chapter Nineteen

ART

WE STAYED ON DECK UNTIL THE SUN KISSED THE HORIZON, and then Miss Clune kissed me again, and then I really *did* need to steer the ship before we sailed straight across the channel or so far north that we crashed into an ice-capped mountainside.

Our desires were clear, but the weight of everything else still pressed heavily on me. Every landmark we passed marked the growing distance between me and Cecily.

The flight with Miss Clune felt like a balm, but also a reminder of the distance between us, too. There were truths we still hadn't spoken. The more difficult feelings—the complications. I wasn't used to giving my trust. But any sting of betrayal I might've felt had immediately dissolved the moment I saw the utter shock and terror on her face. She was more afraid of her magic than I was. It wasn't magic itself that frightened me but the mages who conducted without conscience.

And somehow, I trusted her more than anyone I'd ever known.

How could I admit a truth I barely understood myself? But perhaps she already knew? I'd never been able to hide from her. From the first moment I'd stepped inside her carriage, she'd seen straight through to the core of me.

I'd told Miss Clune I wanted her. Should I have used more words?

Before I got the chance (or the nerve), the temperature had already dropped with the sun. Miss Clune wrapped her arms around me from behind, but even then she was shivering. I slowed our descent long enough for us to return belowdecks and trade places with Mae.

Miss Toussaint was already waiting. I immediately tensed for her reaction. Anyone with eyes could see that Miss Clune and I had been up to no good . . . or a *whole lot* of good, depending on perspective.

We'd done the sort of thing that would've sent any dutiful aunt into a faint—unchaperoned company and an intimacy far beyond what was considered proper.

"*Mon cœur*! You're soaked through and so flushed! Do you have a fever?" She said all of this with a wicked smile.

Miss Clune did indeed look flushed despite the rain-chilled wind. Her eyes sparkled with humor as we shared a glance. She didn't look away or duck her head. She simply looked happy. "I feel just fine."

How she didn't trust her own confidence was beyond me.

Harland poked his head out from one of the galley cabinets. For a man who'd recently been shot, he was certainly spry. "Art, didn't I already heal you? Why does your lip look swollen?"

I narrowed my eyes at him. "*That* was a joke."

"Cut the cackle." Mae stomped past me to the stairs. "While yeh were out snogging in the rain, yeh left me stuck down here with these two."

"I see no one died," I said.

"I showed great restraint," Mae shouted as she stomped up the stairs. "Though I'm surprised yeh didn't crash the ship and kill us all regardless."

Miss Clune took her aunt by the arm. "All right if we pilfer some fresh clothing from the wardrobes?" she asked.

"Be my guest," I said.

She led her aunt away. "I should probably tell you how Mr. Keays and I really met . . . and a few more important details." Miss Clune smiled at me over her shoulder as they left.

"Notice she hasn't told us where she put the make," Harland said. "I haven't seen her bag."

"I trust her."

"An extremely powerful, untrained mage is now in possession of a functional magic make. What could go wrong?" Harland leaned against the counter with folded arms. "Did you also forget I'm planning to kill you in less than twenty-four hours, or was that *rendezvous* with Miss Clune your last meal?"

"Is death still the plan?"

"Did you think of a better one? Why do I feel like the only one here who cares about your sister?"

We'd only flown a short distance from the capital, yet the distance between Cecily and me felt like an entire ocean. I'd allowed myself to fly free with Miss Clune. Now that the truth of our feelings was clear, the weight of everything else landed heavily on my shoulders once again. I sighed and ran a hand down my face. "Too many questions."

"Then I'll use statements." He ticked each one off on a finger. "Your sister is captive to the queen. Our lead to find the blueprints in exchange for her release turned out to be false. And Malowney somehow had access to the blueprints long enough to build *and* smuggle a working model."

"But now we're back to questions," I said. "Where are the original blueprints? Did Malowney make copies, and is there more than one working model? If we can't find a way to contain the information, Cecily will pay the price. Oh, and did I forget to mention? Belwater, the queen's spymaster, is working against me. If he finds the blueprints first, I've lost my leverage to free Cecily. If I somehow find the blueprints, the queen will steal her make regardless. No matter what I do, Cecily is the victim."

"Her make works." The unexpected note of fear in his voice made me turn. His expression hadn't changed, but his hands were fisted tightly against his arms, shoulders tense. "I couldn't contain the amount of magic the make conducted, and I barely opened the bag. But proof of a working make won't save your sister. Public knowledge won't save her. She's forever changed the authority of magic. She's innocent, but Mage

Citoyen will still find a way to kill her for heresy. I don't know how to stop him."

"I think that leaves only one more question."

"Which is?"

"Why are you here?"

His brow furrowed.

"We agreed to find the blueprints," I said. "When that failed, I assumed you'd leave or steal the make for yourself. Instead, you helped us escape. You agreed to save Miss Clune's reputation. And mine. You saved both of our lives. And now you want to save my sister. Why?"

For the first time, a flicker of discomfort crossed Harland's expression.

"Is it Miss Clune?" I pressed. "Are you planning to turn her in?"

"No."

"I've seen enough of your actions . . . I want to believe you. But without our compromise, what reason do I have to trust you?"

"Catching a bullet for you wasn't enough?" He considered me for a long moment. "I always admired the Renegade. If mages are part of some holy crusade, why are they exterminating their own soldiers?"

They not *we*?

"What cause demands the blood of their own?" he asked. "Mages are rare enough. And women like Cecily are rarer still. She doesn't deserve to die." He pushed off the counter and headed for the deck. "I have my own reasons for wanting that make, but they're not in competition with yours. I have no reason to harm you or yours. If you can trust that, then I believe we have a new compromise."

A SHORT TIME LATER, MISS CLUNE EMERGED FROM THE berth wearing a plum-colored travel vest and skirt. She'd dried and plaited her hair into a single braid over her shoulder. My favorite part, however, was that she'd chosen a spare flight jacket to complete the look. Clearly, she meant to stay airborne.

"You look troubled," she said. "Did something else happen during the five minutes I was gone?"

"Same problems . . . no new solutions."

"I'm here to help."

I pulled her into my arms before remembering that, although Miss Toussaint had accepted our time in the rain with surprising equanimity, I probably shouldn't ravish Miss Clune directly in front of her aunt.

Miss Toussaint emerged from the berth, and she raised an amused brow as I hastily let go of Miss Clune. "Mr. Keays?"

"I—er . . . I should change, too."

"By all means."

Our small party regrouped on deck as we reached our destination. With Mae at the helm, docking was more of a sudden drop than a gradual descent, but she positioned *Courtship* perfectly within a long line of ships anchored to the harbor roof.

"The Jolly Cook!" Miss Clune exclaimed. "I should've known that's where we were headed."

Both the inn's rooftop harbor and steam auto garage were full to the brim with every last-minute straggler motoring into Diadem for the gala. Even outside the social season, and even though Jolly had only recently acquired the inn, suppertime was a crowded affair. The Jolly Cook was the perfect waypoint between the Gallia border and Diadem City, so I never felt conspicuous during my frequent stays.

However, the closer we descended to earth again, the heavier gravity pulled against me. We'd flown only a short distance from the capital, yet the distance between Cecily and me seemed infinite. How could I possibly protect her now? With the weight fully settled onto my shoulders once more, my heart felt compressed as well. I turned to address our small party.

"This is your last opportunity to leave. I believe Harland and I gave a convincing enough performance. You no longer need to be involved. I can book transportation for your safe return to Diadem tonight."

"Are you trying to break our agreement?" Miss Clune asked testily.

"From here, there are only more problems. And more dangers."

"Well, I *was* warned." She gave me a wide smile. "I knew that any involvement on my part would be dangerous. That won't keep me away. More importantly, I want a voice in what happens to the magic."

"Is *he* coming in again?" Mae interrupted, eyeing Harland warily. "Da won't like that."

"Harland saved Miss Clune, and he saved my life. I trust that we want the same things. But Miss Clune, I haven't told you everything yet, so you can't know the full extent. You still don't know who—"

"Are you quite finished?" she asked. "I can smell Mr. Jolly's cooking from here, and you still owe me. Does the rooftop connect with the upper balcony?" She immediately rushed down the slanted platform to find out.

Miss Toussaint unexpectedly pinched my cheek affectionately as she rushed after her niece. "I go where Audrey goes," she called.

Harland and I exchanged a glance. He shrugged, and the three of us followed at a more moderate pace.

The inn was filled with loud chatter and the bustle of guests. Descending the stairs, I caught at least three different languages plus many more accents among dozens of conversations. As usual, I kept an ear open for gossip, but nothing immediately stood out. Mostly because the smell of fresh bread and hearty scouse claimed the bulk of my attention. I pilfered a roll off a table as I wove my way to the bar counter.

By the time I caught up with Miss Clune, Jolly already had her wrapped into a tight hug. "I warned yeh not to get caught up with this riffraff," he was saying.

I smiled. "Hello, Jolly. Are you talking about me?"

"What are yeh doing back here so soon?"

"I'm your best customer."

"But clearly not his favorite," Miss Clune said with a teasing scrunch of her nose.

"There's a truth. Oi, Mae!" Jolly called over the din.

"Whatcha want now, Da?" Mae yelled over the first-floor railing.

"I need yeh in the kitchen!"

"I only just got back!"

"Then get back to the kitchen!"

The four of us watched the exchange with varying smirks until Miss Toussaint graciously stepped into the fray. "I'm capable enough in the kitchen. I'd love to help."

Catching his first sight of the handsome woman, the poor man flushed a ripe, strawberry red.

Miss Clune grinned with barely repressed mischief. "May I introduce my aunt, Miss Emmaline Toussaint."

"Mr. Jolly, I presume?" she asked. "Pleased to meet you."

"Merciful Maker," Jolly breathed. "Another diamond." He rubbed a hand over his bald head. "I could never let yeh into my kitchen—"

"Of course, you could," I interrupted. "In fact, we'll all help. Harland can cook the vegetables just by glaring at them. The rest of us have something rather urgent to discuss, and seeing as you have a full house tonight—"

"Miiister Jooolleee?" A grey-haired woman seated several tables over waved her serviette.

"The kitchen might be best," I finished.

Jolly eyed Harland warily. "I've already got help in the kitchen."

"I know," I answered. "But I need everyone, Harland included."

Jolly's fingers fisted and flexed, and I imagined he was wishing for a butcher knife to threaten the mage. "I'll be in to check on yeh soon. Li and Dem are helping tonight, so there's no need to watch what yeh say. And, uh . . . *au plaisir de vous rencontrer, Mademoiselle Toussaint. Mon nom est Varney Jovial.*"

"*Tu parles gemme!*" she said. "*Quelle surprise!*"

He blushed again.

"*Jovial?*" Miss Clune asked quietly. "Everyone here speaks Gallia. I'm surprised I didn't see it sooner."

"See what?"

She flicked her braid at me as she passed.

Jolly's kitchen had easily become more of a home to me than my own flat in Diadem or Mum's floral parlor. The smell of fresh pastry dough was like a welcome mat, and the tension in my shoulders eased a fraction as I ducked inside the doorway.

Miss Clune seemed to love the Jolly sanctuary as much as I. The way she was looking at the hearth of my heart with unmitigated delight moved me almost as much as watching her elation to sail the skies.

The woodblock countertops were clean but cluttered with trays of food, rising bread, and stacks of half-cut vegetables. The great, black stove was lined with pots and pans of various sizes, and a cauldron-like vat of souse stayed steaming and warmed inside a separate brick oven. Every available wall space was lined with shelves packed with anything from potted herbs to cookware and dishes to Jolly's charming collection of carved bird figurines (mostly robins). Wooden crates packed with burlap sacks of every kind of produce from summer greens and roots to currants to an early crop of sweet corn. Beside those, a thin, slatted door led down to a cooler cellar for the wines and endless collection of jarred fruits and vegetables for the winter months.

The twins, Liana and Demi, were already working—together and inseparable, as always. Demi was in the process of dishing out soup to a tray full of ceramic bowls while Liana prepared a fresh pot of tea and two mugs of ale. Spotting me, they beamed but instantly subdued in the presence of our newcomers.

Demi took Liana by the hand. After a silent moment, Liana nodded as if in agreement.

Both girls had dark shoulder-length hair and a sprinkle of freckles across their nose.

Both were secretly mages.

I could only tell the twins apart because Demi had raised scars over her palms and the backs of her hands. I still didn't know her method of conduction. I'd never heard her speak. She simply held her sister's hand and Liana would speak for her.

Liana had an extraordinary talent for conducting bone. Unfortunately, a neighbor reported her conduction to the Magicstry after they saw her heal the broken foreleg of her beloved horse. So I'd smuggled the twin sisters across the Gallia border. (It'd been quite the feat to smuggle the horse as well, but he lived happily in the back pasture behind the inn.) At the time, they were barely old enough to work, let alone make their own way through the world, but Jolly agreed to take them in. They were only a few years younger than Mae, and the three girls became fast friends. After Jolly acquired the inn, the girls stayed on as maids. Liana served food while Demi mostly kept to the kitchens, but they'd also become two of my best informants. They simply listened to the inn's patrons and remembered details.

Miss Clune gave the girls a small wave, but the room seemed to freeze when Harland, slowly but purposefully, crossed the kitchen. The girls watched wide-eyed like wild rabbits about to bolt as he approached. Harland unbuttoned and rolled up a sleeve.

Straight white scars streaked his forearm like tick marks. Dozens upon dozens of cuts.

"They cut me faster than I could heal," he said in a surprisingly gentle voice. He held out a palm to Demi and waited like offering breadcrumbs to a fearful wild animal. She hesitated and placed her hand atop his. He tilted his head as if listening. After a moment he nodded. "I understand."

I hadn't noticed Jolly standing behind us. Evidently, he'd watched the entire exchange before he nodded, wiped his hands on his apron, and returned to the dining hall.

Mae took his place at the head of the kitchen and immediately began giving orders. "Might as well roll up yer other sleeve, mage. Yer on dish duty." She pointed to a towering stack of dishes and tubs of water in the lower scullery down a short landing of stairs. Harland did as she commanded. His opposite arm was covered in scars as well.

Without instruction, Miss Toussaint found a spare white apron, tied it around her waist, and checked the souse. After adding a pinch more salt and a handful of carrots to the large pot, she cut and plated the cheeses at the sideboard. Mae wordlessly handed her a larger knife.

I wandered to the sideboard and popped a small tomato into my mouth.

"Eat after yeh cook," Mae ordered. "Dice those potatoes. Da didn't prep nearly enough." She flung her arm as a barrier and stopped Miss Clune in her tracks. "That's close enough. I don't want yeh two near each other. Yeh can slice the new loaves at the opposite table."

Miss Clune widened her eyes at me in mock fear.

I winked.

WE HUNG OUR JACKETS, TOOK TURNS DRAWING WATER AND washing up in the scullery, and set about our tasks. Mae and Jolly frequently put me to work, so cutting potatoes wasn't new. At least I'd moderately improved at the task. Liana rushed in and out of the kitchen as each new tray and plates were prepared while Demi pointed to each of the items Miss Toussaint would need next. Our party quickly found an efficient rhythm in the comfort of food.

"Is it truly safe to talk?" Miss Clune finally asked.

"We're safe here." The kitchen was one of the only places I felt free to lower my masks.

"I've already told Aunt Emma everything I know," she said. "But I still don't understand why you robbed my carriage in the first place." Mae turned her back, and Miss Clune surreptitiously slid a slice of bread to me across the counter.

"I'll have to go back further than that."

"To the Exhibitions?"

"And the magic make." I snuck a bite of the bread. "My sister is the maker."

Miss Clune fumbled. Bread went flying over the tabletop, and she scrambled to gather up the slices. "That's an important detail for you to leave out!"

"Or well . . . Cecily is technically my cousin, but she and I were raised together."

"Your *sister* is the maker!"

"I was worried for her safety if I shared any details of my assignment." I gave a brief summary of all that had transpired at the Maker Exhibitions.

Our mad dash to the Jeweled Palace.

Irritating mages and our audience with the queen.

The missing blueprints.

Cecily as a hostage. "The Magicstry can't get to her . . . for now. But that doesn't mean she's safe."

"We'll get her back, don't yeh worry!" Jolly said as he breezed into the kitchen, maneuvered the crowded space, and left with an armload of cheeses.

"Mage Citoyen wanted to kill you both in the street," Harland added from the scullery landing. "I convinced him that your sister's immediate death would only make her a martyr. But Cecily has forever changed the authority of magic. The moment the gems let down their guard, Mage Citoyen will find a way to kill her."

Miss Clune reached across the space and clutched my arm. A fraction of the weight lifted simply feeling her there with me. "If the make is already beyond his control, why direct his anger at the maker?" she asked. "It's not like he can force her to recant a working model once it becomes public knowledge."

"Mage Citoyen considers the title of maker to be the greatest blasphemy," Harland explained. "There is only one Great Maker. To take the Great Maker's name in vain—to claim godlike dominance over earth —is a terrible sin."

"Do you agree?" Miss Toussaint asked. Her tone toward him had improved considerably, but her mistrust of the Magicstry was clear.

Harland moved a stack of bowls to a tub of clean water, but his gaze was unfocused—his thoughts far outside of the inn. "There was a time, before the Magicstry, when I was taught differently. Wanting to become like the Great Maker, following the work of creation, was seen as a holy act of devotion. But Citoyen will never see this. Ironic that he will stop at nothing to destroy . . . all in the name of the Maker."

"And you?" Miss Toussaint asked. Her tone made me wish Mae hadn't given her the large knife. "What would you do in the name of the Maker? You were sent to kill Miss Keays."

If Harland noticed the tension, he didn't react. "Everything I've done since has been to protect her . . . to prevent the exploitation and misuse of her make. And," he muttered, "keep everyone else from getting themselves killed."

Miss Toussaint's gaze was sharp, but Harland didn't elaborate, leaving the weight of unspoken reasons hanging over the room. Regardless, I was certain his motives were rooted in the execution of mages, his respect for the Renegade (perhaps not me personally), and something deeply personal like the jagged line of scars along his arms.

"What exactly is the make?" Miss Clune intervened. "How does it work?"

"Cecily could explain it better," I said. She *should* be there to explain. "From what I understand, the make acts as an artificial conductor of magic. Combined with another make, the Conductor becomes an unlimited power source—watches won't need to be wound, boilers won't need to be fueled, that sort of thing. We were searching for the stolen blueprints, but we never expected to find a working model."

Miss Clune rubbed at her collarbone. "I didn't even touch the make, but it felt like . . . almost as if a great wind was rushing through me."

"That's an apt description," Harland said. "Conducting is like taking a full breath without releasing the air. After a while, your lungs burn. The make conducted an entire windstorm while forcing us to hold our breath. I diverted the magic away. The pain you felt afterward was a bare remnant of the magic you'd conducted. When you ordered the guard to stop breathing, the magic was amplified by what was left in your body from the make. Cecily was smart to realize the human body is a fragile conduit compared with sturdier material."

"She is brilliant," I agreed. "And inexperienced enough to be completely reckless."

The dishes clattered loudly as Harland tossed another bowl onto the pile. "She may be your younger sister. But one of these days, you'll figure out Miss Keays is also a woman. I don't believe she's as reckless as you think."

I stilled. I hadn't missed the way he'd said her name—like someone who'd formed his own opinion. Harland didn't meet my gaze. He scrubbed a plate a little too roughly, jaw tight. He knew he'd said too much, but he didn't seem at all repentant.

"Her make launched an entire war of mages and makers," I said. "The gems want to be sole investors to the makers so that the crown retains power. The Magicstry wants sole control of magic. Cecily should have realized her make challenges both of those authorities."

"How else could she have exhibited her make?" Miss Clune asked. She took a bite of bread, chewing slowly. "That kind of magic is too dangerous for one faction to claim, but she can't simply ignore the discovery of magic machines. Perhaps she was right to reveal her make in such a public setting."

"The Magicstry repressed the spread of information," added Miss Toussaint. She waved away steam and looked inside the largest of the pots. "Are those potatoes ready?"

I pushed them to her side of the table.

"I heard about the Exhibitions directly from Hattie," she continued. "But most gems think the make was some sort of elaborate hoax. Does that mean the Magicstry currently has the advantage?"

"Not the Magicstry," I said. "Not even one faction. There is currently only one person in control of the make. That person *should* be Cecily. But until the queen grants her a makership, the proprietary rights of her make are directly linked to the paper records, namely the blueprints. My patronage supports her credibility. However, someone else has the blueprints as well as the means to send Tackleton a working model."

"Do we know who?" Miss Clune asked.

I hesitated. Was there a delicate way to approach the topic?

"Your man, Malowney," Harland said.

Miss Clune choked.

So much for tact.

Mae thumped her hard on the back, confiscated her piece of bread, and directed her to the tea station.

"Maker *Andrew* Malowney?" she croaked. "*He* stole the blueprints?"

"The one with straight teeth?" asked Miss Toussaint.

"The very same," I said.

Miss Clune dazedly poured herself a cup of tea.

"Malowney is the reason we found you. His great-uncle Pinefoy was the officiate judge for Cecily's blueprints before they went missing. And before he went . . . missing," I said at the same time Harland said, "He's dead."

Miss Clune blanched.

"Yes, *thank you*, Harland. Malowney also happens to be the sole heir to Pinefoy's estate. He paid his uncle a visit and departed rather suddenly to the country just prior to the Maker Exhibitions. After we learned where he was staying, Harland and I staged a robbery to search an antique carriage conveying a rather cheeky woman—"

Miss Clune raised her teacup in mock toast.

"Your bodyguard had a letter on him."

"Who?" she asked.

"Your jarvey," Harland clarified. "The ugly one."

"Ivo?" Her face hardened into a frown. "Maker Malowney insisted I needed another escort to Diadem. He was using me."

I grimaced. How many people had misused Miss Clune, and how many blows could she take in one day?

"Based on the letter," I said, "we assumed Malowney sold and delivered the blueprints to Tackleton, but we found a working model instead. Which means . . . Malowney still has the blueprints." I sat on the edge of the center table. "That's one problem. Let me see if I can summarize the rest."

"Shell these while yeh do," Mae ordered, handing me a bowl of peas. "Emma's doing all the work."

Indeed, Miss Toussaint hadn't exaggerated. She knew her way around a busy kitchen. With Liana and Demi's help, the rushing dinner service flowed flawlessly. What would Jolly make of that? He might even let Miss Toussaint lend a hand with the pastries. Jolly wouldn't let me so much as look at the sweets before they were ready to serve. But for Miss Toussaint, I had a feeling he'd make an exception.

"Mae, do you have paper and pencil?" Miss Clune asked.

"Aye."

"May I please use them?"

Mae rolled her eyes but complied.

"All right," Miss Clune said with pencil poised. "I'm ready for more problems."

I smiled despite the subject. The woman must be plated with iron.

"Malowney had the blueprints long enough to create a working model," I said. "If there's already a working model, how many people have access to information about the make? If that information is too widespread to contain, we lose our leverage to free Cecily.

"She's in grave danger from both factions," I continued. "Mages and makers. Not only do we need to steal back the blueprints *and* all information regarding the make, we also need a safer way to exchange the blueprints for Cecily and her deserved title as maker while somehow keeping her safe from Mage Citoyen."

"Can't you simply tell the queen?" Miss Toussaint asked. "If her own makers have the blueprints, the gem at least has the advantage over the Magicstry."

"The queen won't be happy to learn her own makers were the ones to steal the make," I explained. "The Maker Exhibitions are structured as public funding, patrons with systematized government oversight. Essentially, Maker Malowney and Tackleton undermined the queen's authority in pursuit of private funding."

"Again, we need leverage to free Cecily," Harland said. "And better information."

"Before tomorrow?" I asked. "The queen expects me to return the blueprints by the night of the gala."

"Tackleton still owes Malowney money," Harland said. "And we also know he'll be at the Maker's Club at seven o'clock."

"What else do we know?"

The conversation suspended as we realized Miss Clune had stopped writing. Throughout our exchange, she had tapped the pencil against her lip—lost in thought.

"Audrey?" Miss Toussaint prompted.

"*Hm*? Oh . . . I think we're looking at the wrong problems again," she mused. "At Cerussite Hall, we didn't need to escape. We needed a distraction to tell a better story."

She turned the paper for me to see and scrawled a few additional lines in a tidy hand. "You're still trying to appease the queen. But in doing so, there doesn't seem to be a favorable outcome. Unless the queen decides to relinquish her advantage over the Magicstry, Miss Keays is almost assuredly trapped and without control over her make. As for the mages . . . well, it doesn't seem to matter whether we contain the make or not. That problem won't be solved with secrecy. However . . ."

She circled one word.

I left the table, Harland left the scullery, and Miss Toussaint left the stove to encircle Miss Clune and read her notes.

"Neither mages nor makers are counting on a third faction to intervene," she said. "While they're distracted fighting each other, the Renegade has a chance to win the game."

I startled as Mr. Jolly slapped a hand on my shoulder from behind. I hadn't noticed his return to the conversation. "It's about time cogs had an advantage!" he boomed. "What's the plan?"

Miss Clune grinned. "The blueprints, the model, all of it is a distraction. The *real* problem is how to ensure Cecily's safety. Then we help take back her make."

"We keep everyone else fighting over blueprints while we steal her back," I said.

"Don't forget, you're still a hostage," she said. "I'll keep everyone distracted at the Maker's Club while *you* steal Cecily."

I looked at each of the faces around me—our small league of renegades—and the weight on my shoulders lessened.

Miss Clune offered me the paper. I snatched her fingers instead. "I ought to tell you, Miss Clune, your relentless attempts to make me fall in love with you are wearing away my resistance. I ask you—have some self-control!"

"You're one to talk," Harland mumbled.

True. My heart was a worn and polished gem inside a gifted locket. We'd kissed, but I wanted more. If only I could admit my fear that starting something real might shatter everything I was supposed to hold together. The weight of everything I carried pressed down on me.

Miss Clune smacked my hand away. "We three have our parts. Now, let's discuss the plot."

Chapter Twenty

Audrey

Mae finally let us eat. Mr. Jolly made extra pastries specifically for me and chided Mr. Keays for stealing. We talked late into the night until the rowdy inn was silent and all the guests were asleep in their rented rooms before we quietly crept back to the ship.

The general plan was simple.

Harland would continue to play the villain and distract the mages long enough for Cecily to escape. Once free, we could make more permanent plans to keep her safe from the Magicstry, even by fleeing to the Accent Territories if necessary.

I would act as a second distraction by keeping close to the makers with Maker Malowney. He had the most information, and I was in the best position to steal it. If I could persuade him to admit me to the Maker's Club, I could also steal evidence for the queen.

Mr. Keays would operate independently, raising questions for mages and makers alike. Most notably: why had he been released as a hostage? He would distract the queen and her agents long enough to steal Cecily. He also hoped to deliver both the blueprints and the make to the queen in exchange for public recognition and a title for Maker Cecily Keays.

Further than that, we were still missing too much information. The bulk of our conversation was a discussion of contingencies and what ifs and "what happens when" until the best thing for us to do was rest and await the morrow.

With the rain cleared, Mr. Keays and Harland offered to sleep on the deck while Aunt Emma and I took hammocks. They could take turns flying us home to Diadem—in time for the gala. Truthfully, I would've liked to sleep under the stars . . . curled in the arms of Mr. Keays. I didn't want to say goodnight. I didn't want to leave him alone with his worries. But what more could I say? The truth of our attraction was unmistakable, but the future held so much uncertainty. The adventure that brought us together also seemed to hold us at a distance. How could I entwine my life with his without first untangling the darker story threads?

Aunt Emma retired belowdecks ahead of me while Mr. Keays and I said goodnight. A slight thrill of nervous energy rushed down my spine as he pressed my hand to his heart and tugged the edges of my flight jacket closed.

"It suits you," he said.

I preened. "I like the look."

"Not that. The confidence. Never take it off."

"But . . . I'm also keeping the jacket."

"Thief."

I grinned up at him.

"You're getting better at your distractions," he said. "I almost didn't notice when you stole the make."

I tensed and carefully weighed my words. "I hid my carpetbag inside your wardrobe."

"Your bag . . . but not the make?"

I tensed, waiting.

He tipped his head back and laughed, unconcerned. "You don't need magic to fit words to your purpose. You're already a renegade. Where did you really hide it?"

"In my carriage," I admitted with a cringe. The make was gone even before Aunt Emma and I boarded the ship. Uncertainty and guilt gnawed at my insides. "I didn't know who to trust."

His eyes still held laughter and kindness, but something more serious stirred beneath the surface of his words. "All the same . . . the make belongs to Cecily."

I nodded, solemn. "What is Cecily like? When she's not changing the world, that is."

His expression instantly softened. "Oh, Gears is always causing a stir. That part isn't new. She's a whirlwind of chaos. She can't walk through a room without leaving something out of place, yet she never forgets a single fact. I may be older by seven years, but I struggle to keep up. She read through all my university textbooks at eleven. I only passed my sciences because of the notes she left in the margins."

"Will she attend Diadem University?"

He shrugged. "If that's what she chooses. Social situations can be . . . difficult for her. As are new experiences. I can only imagine what she must be feeling these past few days."

The fear in his expression squeezed at my heart. "We'll get her out."

"We have a plan." He smiled wearily. "If I weren't otherwise occupied, I'd steal you for the first dance."

"You have enough to steal already. Don't worry about me."

He ran a hand over the back of his neck. "I'm not supposed to . . . I shouldn't want . . ."

His halting thoughts were interrupted as Harland crossed the deck.

"A word?" Harland asked me.

"Now?"

"Mm."

I fought back a sigh but nodded.

Mr. Keays ran a hand over his neck once more. He turned and left for the upper deck.

Harland took my arm and led me back out onto the platformed roof of The Jolly Cook. The summer breeze from the rooftop felt like a cool embrace. I inhaled deeply—scents of recent rain and earth. My ribs and fingers tingled with liberating anticipation.

Almost like magic.

"Wait . . . stop that!"

Harland's hand flung away from my arm as if I'd physically shoved him. I clapped a hand over my mouth trying to sever the conduction. The magic immediately settled into the joints like thorns between my fingers.

"Why did you do that?" I asked from behind my pinpricked hands. Tears of anger and pain hazed my vision. "Why did you make me do that?"

"I wanted to see how long it would take you to identify the magic."

"You're testing me?" I asked bitterly. Out of habit, I massaged my aching hands.

Harland took my wrists in a light grip. "The amount of magic you've conducted in a short amount of time is uncommon. Picture each pain like a cluster of branches caught while flowing downstream. Let the current of water gently break them free. Release that buildup of magic back through your body and out into the surrounding current."

"I'm too angry."

"Concentrate."

I gritted my teeth. "Fine."

Closing my eyes, I focused on each pinprick of pain as he'd instructed. But no matter how I tried, I couldn't imagine the water. My mind wandered away from the metaphor. Harland conducted blood, so a water-flowing analogy made sense. But my conduction felt different. I needed something more specific to my reasoning.

I took a deep breath and instead envisioned magic like a song. Each pain became the relative minor of my song—the notes were the same, but the key signature was different. I hadn't played the song of magic incorrectly. I simply needed to let the music continue. I hummed quietly, letting the music move through me—through the air around me.

When I opened my eyes, the pain was gone.

"Impressive."

I threw off his grip on my wrists and flexed my fingers. "Did I pass the test to your satisfaction?"

"You should know how to find an outlet. Keep practicing."

"Why? I'm not planning to conduct again."

"And one minute ago?" he asked. "You weren't planning to conduct magic then."

"That was you! I already told you, *I* won't steal free will. My conduction is too dangerous."

"Ignorance is dangerous. Corruption and evil intent are dangerous. Magic itself is impartial." He leaned on the railing of the platform and folded his arms over his chest. I finally understood the frequent gesture. He self-consciously hid the horrific scars along his arms. "We've made a good plan, but the people we're up against don't follow your same morals. I know you won't conduct magic with intent to harm, but what if others hurt you? If I fail, the Magicstry may come after you. You need the means to defend yourself. And you'll need to make some difficult choices."

I folded my arms against the railing and stared into the darkness. I could just make out the faint outline of rolling hills. The real beauty was in the sky. Holding to the railing, I tipped my face up to the stars. "I know my conduction would be an easier solution to all of this," I said quietly. "But absolutes of power, at least where Miss Keays is concerned, are exactly what we're fighting against."

"You understand what this make really means. Mortal conduction of magic will almost always be accompanied by corruption of morality. You're led by practical considerations, so you may not yet realize that Art is an idealist. He tries to hide his hope, but he still thinks everything will be solved if only Cecily reclaims control of her make."

I considered him. "The make I understand. Why do you care about what happens to Cecily?"

He didn't answer for a long time. "She's an idealist like Art. They don't understand."

The exhaustion of the day seemed to leach into my muscles all at once. I sagged against the railing. "We'll all need to make difficult choices."

"Your conduction of magic is a choice, too."

"Goodnight, Harland."

Returning to the ship, I descended to the berth and settled into the hammock nearest Aunt Emma.

Harland's words made me consider my role. I was a distraction for the makers because of my connection to Maker Malowney, but I could also play the perfect distraction for the mages even as the thought of conducting magic to bend the will of others left me feeling sick.

Melancholy and memories and plans and worries all vied for a place in my thoughts.

Aunt Emma's breathing was steady. I thought she'd already fallen asleep until she whispered quietly into the dark. "*Mon cœur?*"

"Hm?"

"You can still be angry with me, but I want you to know . . . I meant to tell you everything. I didn't realize how much your grandmother kept hidden from you. About Amalie, your magic, your inheritance . . . all of it. *Je vous promets*, I always meant to tell you."

"Will you tell me now?" I asked. "I'm too worried to sleep." My hammock swayed as I rolled to face her.

"I will do my best."

The patient silence between us was filled with distant waves of wind and flap of the sails.

"Amalie was always my protector," she began slowly. "Our *père*, your grandfather, was not a good man. But at a very young age, Amalie learned that she could sing to calm his fits of anger. When we were hungry, she sang to the people in our village and they would give us food. At first, we didn't know it was the magic. Amalie conducted as easily as breathing. But as her talent grew, the village began to notice . . . *père* noticed. She ran away before he could sell her to the Magicstry. And because she protected me, I followed her everywhere . . . always moving to stay safe, on the road, to join a traveling actors troupe, and eventually across the border to Diadem.

"In Gallia, talent like hers was not a good thing. But in Parure, the people adored her for it. We were lucky. She kept her magic hidden under the guise of talent. And for the first time in our lives, we had a home and patrons to protect us. After the queen herself became a patron, Amalie married into a prominent gem family, and your father protected her with his name. By the time the Magicstry finally realized her secret, they could do nothing. Many times they tried to force Amalie to convert, but I believe they were more concerned that the public would learn of her magic. The Magicstry feared losing control more than keeping one mage."

Her hammock creaked, and her low voice was clearer as she turned toward me. "Even after everything we'd endured, Amalie believed magic was her gift, not a curse. She shared that with you, *sa joie*. And she protected you, too."

She hesitated. "One day, Amalie conducted too much. She knew the very hour that the magic broke her body. I have a letter from her telling me so."

"Her sickness was the magic?" I asked. "Why did she let me believe she was ill?"

"*Tu sais*, it was easier for Amalie to say she was sick rather than tell you she was in pain. She didn't want you to be scared to hug her."

I thought back to each time I'd climbed into her bed to hug her and read. How much pain had she been made to endure? She'd hidden it all from me.

Aunt Emma's voice choked with emotion. "The Magicstry finally won in the end. Because she refused to train as a mage, they refused to heal her. They let her die as punishment."

The darkness hid our shared tears, but she reached a hand across the space between us and clasped mine.

"I thought . . . I *hoped* you were happy with your grandmother. She could provide much more, you would be safer there than in the city, and . . . I was scared. Amalie was always the protector. Without her here to counsel me, I feared I would fail you." She laughed bitterly. "And what a miserable failure it was. I ought to have taken better care of you. I should have told you the whole truth from the beginning."

"It's not your fault." I sniffed a wry laugh. "If I'd moved to Diadem, Grandmother wouldn't have sent a monthly living from my inheritance. I wouldn't have been able to support us."

She went silent.

I squeezed her hand. "What did I say?"

"Audrey, I've never received so much as a single note from your grandmother. And even if I had, I would not have accepted it. I saved my own modest living. Enough to keep me comfortable and close to my friends. Where did you get the idea that you need to care for me?"

I sat up, feeling dizzy. The sway of the hammock was no longer comforting. I steadied myself as I haltingly relayed the details I'd tried so hard to keep private. "She—she told me you couldn't afford to support yourself, let alone support me. Mother left my inheritance in trust, but I can't access it until I marry. So I asked Grandmother to send a living on my behalf. Last month, she refused to pay any more unless I agreed to marry Maker Malowney."

"I see." Aunt Emma squeezed my hand tight enough that I thought she might snap bone. "Listen to me, *mon cœur*. There is no trust. Your mother bequeathed everything to you at the time of her death. That *woman* has been stealing your money."

Everything inside me went numb.

Grandmother had lied.

Stealing was about distraction. How could I have allowed myself to be distracted long enough for Grandmother to steal my choices—my very life—away from me? How was I so blind? But reason whispered truth. I'd been a grieving child when she took me in . . . and when she took everything else. She'd used my youth and my grief for the loss of my mother as her distraction.

A gem of the right set does not make demands.

But how many times had she instructed me to make demands on her behalf? Grandmother disciplined my conduction but used me for her own purposes. My only guardian had crushed my spirit, stolen every decision, and exploited her advantage over me in every way possible.

I could never be at fault for that level of cruelty.

Still, I sobbed a gasp as I felt the full impact of my fall. "I never had a choice."

Aunt Emma left her hammock and sat with me. She gently unbraided my hair. "You've always had a choice," she said quietly. "Many choices, in fact. But I never allowed you to make them. I see that now."

"I have choices." If I repeated her words, maybe I'd believe them.

On paper, Maker Malowney was a good prospect. He would allow me to live in comfort as a gem—better than the life to which I'd grown accustomed. Needless to say, a supposedly better life did not guarantee a happier one.

I could choose magic. Harland had already given me that choice. If it were possible to ensure a place with Harland, I could join the Magicstry as his novitiate. My words weren't just figurative weapons—they were truly lethal. I'd feel safer mastering control over such a weapon. But then, the Magicstry would claim the right to wield me however they pleased. The choice to conduct would never be my own.

Beyond a doubt, the most apparent choice was Mr. Keays. Somehow, if only for a brief time, Mr. Keays made me believe that my actions mattered—that I mattered. I longed to play a more meaningful part. Mr. Keays wanted me, but did he want me in that way?

But no . . . that choice wasn't right either. Why was every decision dependent on other people? Specifically, the men in my life.

I didn't know how much money I was worth or how much Grandmother might've stolen. Any amount was enough for me to find independence. Where would I go?

I'd always wanted to live with Aunt Emma. Did I want that now?

Diadem University accepted women. Should I go there?

Aunt Emma kneaded her fingers against my head. "I can feel the gears in your mind turning," she said. "No one is forcing you to make a choice tonight."

"Everything was a lie. It helps to want something real."

"A real choice. *Hm*, that can only come from your heart." She hummed. "Does it help to know you always have a home with me? I love you and, of course, I want you with me always. But only if that is what you choose. You already cared for your mother when the Magicstry would not. You inherited her talent, but you don't need to take on her role as my protector, too. You need to be free to be your own person. Forget your grandmother, forget what you think your mother might have wanted, and please forget me. None of us deserves your attention. Leave aside expectations and consider . . . what do *you* want?"

Was there a choice that was mine alone?

My immediate answer was ridiculous. I shook my head.

"Please tell me," she said. "What was your first thought?"

"I hardly know."

She waited patiently.

"Robin Renegade," I admitted quietly.

"Mr. Keays?" she asked. "Have you fallen in love with the Renegade?"

"No, not him. I mean—" I smiled at the tentative flutter of hope in my chest. "I *do* like him. But my first thought was of Robin Renegade. She traveled the world and fought injustice and . . . I've always loved to imagine that I could play the part of a heroine like her. I want to live independently and travel the country, or even outside the Parure. I want to sail overseas to explore the Accent Territories. I want to help mages like me or help Cecily with her make. Together we might do some good with magic. I've been playacting for so long and following the script that others wrote for me that now . . . I'd love to enact my own adventure."

Aunt Emma wound her arms around my shoulders. "Then I will do everything in my power to support your choice."

It was all so very idealistic—exactly what Harland warned against—but that small light of hope was enough to brighten my whole world of darkness. I wiped my face free of tears and wound my loose hair at the nape of my neck as Aunt Emma settled back into her hammock and I burrowed deeper into mine. I couldn't remember when I'd been so comfortable. Grandmother's house was a relic. That included the flat mattresses.

Softly, Aunt Emma hummed a tune my mother used to sing. Something from their childhood in Gallia. I wrapped my arms around myself, holding tight to my new resolve. I'd always dreamed of becoming Robin Renegade, but I'd never considered that a dream might become a choice.

Eventually, Aunt Emma and the gentle creak and sway of the ship sang me into a peaceful sleep.

Chapter Twenty-One

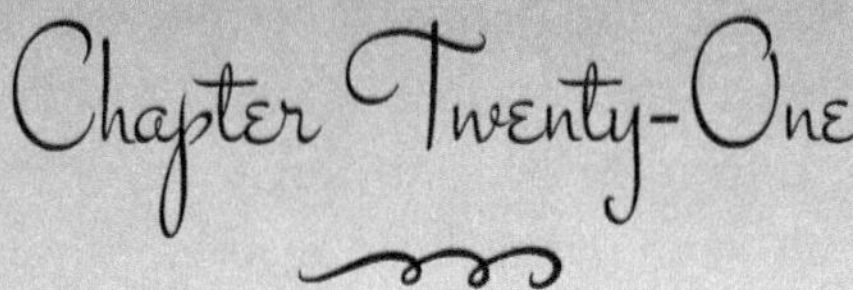

Audrey

We flew the *Courtship* to the edge of Diadem and took a hired steam car back to the townhome. There we collapsed for a few more hours of sleep before the gala, but our rest was interrupted when Ivo arrived with a delivery.

What else did he do for Maker Malowney if he'd acted as jarvey and now courier? In light of all I'd learned, he was clearly a bodyguard as well with those scarred knuckles.

"For you, Miss Clune." He handed me a multilayered, cut-paper box with silhouettes of doves tied with pink and white ribbons.

"How beautiful!" I exclaimed.

"His Makership and Lady Clune will be here to collect you this evening at five o'clock."

"Thank you, Ivo. Would you also be kind enough to fetch John while you're out? I'm afraid my aunt isn't feeling well enough to join us. We had quite the ordeal at the Tackleton garden party yesterday, and I don't want to leave her unattended."

I felt the moment when a slight current of magic trickled through my words. The magic was impossible to ignore now that I'd learned to identify the sensation. I immediately tamped down the feeling like clenching my jaw against a wide yawn. It would take time to sing freely. Aunt Emma needed to take the carriage, but surely I could convince Ivo without conduction of magic? A servant, even a fake one, couldn't very well turn down my request.

Sure enough, Ivo shuffled his feet reluctantly but agreed. "Yes, Miss."

"Do you know . . . does Maker Malowney intend to dance or will he hide himself away at the Maker's Club all evening?" I pouted. "I know what these great social events are like. All business and no pleasure."

"I doubt he'll want to leave your side, Miss."

"Good! I plan to keep him there. Thank you again, Ivo."

With a friendly wave, I closed the front door.

Rejoining Aunt Emma in our cozy pile of knitted blankets and pillows, I wordlessly handed her the box and peered over her shoulder as she peeled back the delicate clasps of the lid. Inside was a small corsage of matching pink and white roses clipped together by a silver bracelet with fluttering bird wings.

"What a poor choice of flowers," I said. "Pink roses won't match my dress at all."

"I suppose you'd better wear them anyway."

"True." I sighed, pulled a pillow to my chest, and traced a finger over the embroidered threads. The scene was of tiny sparrows flitting between tree branches and a colorful balloon floating between sunset-tinted clouds. It was a good reminder of what I really wanted.

"It's a shame about the color." Aunt Emma sat up suddenly. "But come to think of it, I have just the dress to match!" She tossed the box aside, pulled me by the hand to the spare room, and rummaged through the wardrobe. At length, she produced an unwieldy bulk of fabric the shade of sick peas. "*Parfait!*"

I fingered one of the trailing long sleeves.

"It belonged to your mother. Lovely, isn't it? I thought you might want to wear it one day."

"It's green. And is that . . . a pouch?"

"Pockets. Look at the puffs." She prodded the lumpy skirt with one finger. "Amalie would have loved for you to wear it, and I'm sure the style will come back *encore* in another twenty years. You can preempt the fashion!"

"You probably should've trimmed it back every once in a while to keep it from taking over the wardrobe. Please return it to the dark before it decides to grow any bigger."

She laughed merrily. "Not until you try it on! Mr. Keays will fall all over you."

"He will fall ill."

But Aunt Emma coaxed and teased me into my mother's hideous dress. The waist was tight but the puffed skirt poofed as wide as the circumference of a carriage wheel around my hips. The frilled ends of sheer green sleeves straggled nearly past my fingertips, and a high, scalloped collar pushed stiffly against the back of my neck. I looked like a walking juniper bush and smelled like camphor mothballs.

Mother had been several inches taller, so I minced around the dressing partition on my toes. The skirt bounced with each exaggerated step. Draping my body across the bed pillar, I fanned myself with the bed curtain tassel, but the dress tipped my balance. I fell into Aunt Emma, and we both collapsed into a heap on the floor in a fit of giggles.

Eventually, I wrestled the dress until I could sit up high enough to see over the puff of my skirts. "You know . . . you've given me an idea. I know just what to wear tonight."

"I wasn't serious about the dress."

I laughed. "Maker no! Will you help me sew a pocket? I got into trouble in my last dress."

"That may be wise." Aunt Emma considered me. "Will you be all right tonight? The Malowney man is one thing, but I hate for you to face your grandmother alone."

A swell of anger rose within me. "The hardest part will be staying in character, but I have a plan."

"*We* have a plan. I am here with you now. Neither of them will be able to steal any more than they already have."

❧

THE REVUE-RED STEAM AUTO ARRIVED AT PRECISELY FIVE o'clock, and Ivo came to the door to collect me. Aunt Emma silently hugged me farewell. I took a deep breath, straightened my shoulders, and resolutely stepped out of our home and into battle.

"There you are, my dove!" Maker Malowney waved from the auto window, glanced distastefully over the surrounding neighborhood, and withdrew his hand as if the *bourgeoisie* were catching.

I blinked at the sight of him. Maker Malowney had dressed to match my corsage of roses with a white suit coat and pink vest. His hair was slicked to the side with militant precision except for one stiff curl against his forehead. A flock of silver doves perched on his arms fastened with silver buckles. A silver-rimmed monocle framed his left eye, and to top off the entire picture, he wore a matching pink rose in his lapel.

I couldn't help but compare. Mr. Keays acted the part of a dandy but never a fool. Maker Malowney might have been the genuine gem, but he looked like a cheap counterfeit compared to the polished brass of Mr. Keays.

My spine went rigid as Grandmother leaned forward from the opposite seat. She wore a displeased expression that overpowered whatever gown she'd chosen.

I pasted on my best smile, descended the steps, and allowed Ivo to hand me into the auto.

Once seated, Maker Malowney kissed my hand with a loud smack. "Together again at last!"

"What are you wearing?" Grandmother immediately asked.

The modern style primarily consisted of lighter pastel fabrics, but I'd specifically ordered a more daring cut and color (with some last-minute adjustments made by Aunt Emma). My gown began with a rounded neckline of sapphire blue and sleeves of draped gold resembling shoulder pauldrons—armor for a knight striding into battle. The fabric gradually darkened into a deep, apatite teal at the waist and continued down until the sweeping ends of my skirt became a midnight blue. I wore no gloves, but thin threads of interlaced gold dripped over my arms like falling stars against the night sky of my gown. Aunt Emma had helped me pile half of my hair into a loose bun beneath a similar net of gold threads. The woven gold of my hair and threads cascaded gracefully over one shoulder.

Grandmother ought to be grateful I hadn't chosen to wear my mother's old green gown instead.

The only thing out of place was the band of pink and white roses around my wrist and silver, fluttering bird wings. The band felt like a manacle around my wrist as I held it aloft. "I'm wearing the most beautiful flowers, of course! Maker Malowney, I should've known you'd be thoughtful enough to match my gift."

Maker Malowney smiled tentatively. "The corsage looks well, but I had hoped you would dress to match. I'm positive I mentioned the color. And I ordered them from Citrine, you know. Cost me a fortune, but Diadem hot houses simply won't do. Not in matters of true *quality*." He eyed the surrounding neighborhood again. "What a terrible time you must've had here." He tapped the roof to signal Ivo and added, "We heard the most fantastical rumors."

The steam auto chugged to life and glided smoothly through the paved streets. I put my back to the window to avoid temptation. I needed to focus on Maker Malowney, not daydream about the city scenery. "What about?" I asked.

"Everyone is talking about the Tackleton garden party."

"Only half a week gone," said Grandmother, "and you've ensphered yourself in scandal. What were you thinking?"

I laughed. "Well, it's not as if I *chose* to be held at gunpoint."

I realized my mistake when Grandmother stiffened in appall. The previous few days, I'd chosen my own character. I'd forgotten how difficult it was to return to the role of *dutiful granddaughter*. I swallowed and dropped my gaze to the floor. "My apologies, Grandmother. You must've had quite the shock. Will you tell me what you've heard? Perhaps I might alleviate some of your fears."

She sniffed, unforgiving. "Where do I begin?"

"You were keeping company with Arthur Keays, the rakehell," said Maker Malowney.

I faltered. "He . . . intervened on my behalf, yes. A mage attacked one of Lord-Maker Tackleton's servants. He threatened me and Aunt Emma, too. Mr. Keays enabled our escape."

"A mage." Grandmother's eyes narrowed into wrinkles. "What did he want?"

"The mage said he was looking for blueprints," I said. "Something about a new make. For some reason he thought *I* might know where they were."

Maker Malowney looked thoughtful. "How very odd."

"Is that all?" Grandmother flicked a hand dismissively. "More to the point, you were seen in company with a *cog*. This little rebellion about your aunt was bad enough, but deliberately mingling with the wrong set? Lord-Maker Tackleton said you were behaving . . . *informally*. Poor Andrew was quite despairing."

Maker Malowney nodded dejectedly.

"I-I am sorry to have caused so much trouble. I'm glad we're together now. I promise I shan't leave your side tonight."

"That promise might look better if you'd worn the right dress," said Grandmother.

Chapter Twenty-Two

ART

I trekked to the Jeweled Palace on foot. It was slowgoing with a limp and a heap of laundered clothing tied to my back, but the disguise was necessary. Ruby Agents could be anywhere. I was positive Belwater had ordered them to keep an eye out for me, and I couldn't afford to be recognized . . . yet. I needed to delay word of my appearance until after I snuck in to see Cecily.

My nerves tightened with each step. Palace security had been heightened to prepare for the chaos of the gala. Every visible entrance was guarded. I joined the line to approach the guard stationed at the staff entrance for palace custodians—opposite the kitchen entrance. It was time to see just how many doors the seal ring of a Ruby Agent would open to me.

"Next, please."

"Laundry service," I explained. My cheeks and jaw were stuffed full of cotton so my pronunciation sounded innately dull. I'd tied a large bundle of clothing to my back with the company name *Lavendure* printed in bold red letters, and my head hung forward from my laden shoulders. I was draped in the loose overcoat and scarf of a working cog. To top it off, long strands of the black hair of my wig escaped the tail at the nape of my neck and hung around my swollen face.

The young guard ran a finger down his list. "No laundry delivery today," he said.

"They's expecting me inside," I insisted.

The guard kindly checked the list again. "I'm sorry, no. There's no laundry delivery scheduled. It looks as though you've come a long way, but I'm afraid you'll have to return again tomorrow."

"Even with this?" I asked and held out my hand. The ridges of my knuckles were caked with dirt, but I subtly twisted the ring so the gold-encircled ruby glinted in the sunlight.

The guard's eyes widened with recognition. Such was precisely the reason why I didn't carry a ring or other identifying signet as the Renegade. Even a low-level guardsman stationed by the servant's entrance knew what the ring meant. Ruby Agents relied on the queen to open doors for them. In some cases, that level of recognition was useful—my uncontested reputation in society as a useless dandy, for example. But for the most part, I worked best in anonymity with a close league of trusted compatriots.

Of course, Miss Clune had changed all that with her wildly overt performances. Despite circumstances what they were, I was curious to see what she had planned for that evening.

The guard glanced around and pointed to his papers with a stilted performance of casualty. "Oh! I *see* . . . let me check again." Devious the boy was not. "Yes . . . *here* it is! Of course you may enter. Right through here."

"Very kind of you," I said, tipping my forelock in thanks, and hefted the clothing higher on my back and entered the palace.

There was some sort of poetic justice to using the gem's own tool against them.

Moving through the bustling traffic of palace caretakers and custodians, I flashed the ruby ring at as many people as possible to ask directions. Only one guard thought to search the bundle on my back but, finding nothing other than clothing, let me pass. Eventually, I reached a suspicious number of guards compassing a secluded wing of the palace.

"Stop there! That's far enough."

The guards had taken every precaution against the mages. A barrier stretched across the hall—I couldn't get within arm's length—and every guard was armed with at least one ranged weapon. No mage would come close enough to conduct. Maker help us if the Magicstry ever got ahold of someone like Audrey who could conduct without touch.

Ox was there, too. The captain had planted himself in front of a door like a tree. His rifle looked almost the size of a regular firearm when slung across his broad chest. My initial reaction was to tease him with my new character; however, one wrong move and Ox wouldn't hesitate to shoot me. Especially when the stress of guarding Cecily had clearly taken its toll. Rings of worry circled his eyes, and his customarily smooth head and jaw were peppered with stubble.

He'd protected her when I could not.

"Laundry service," I called and again, boldly flashed the ring. "I have this."

Ox frowned as he scrutinized my face. He didn't recognize me until I smirked. Then, Ox rolled his eyes.

"Let him through and no one else until I return." He beckoned me forward, and I limped through the tunnel of stoic guards. Pulling out a ring of iron keys, Ox unlocked the door, half shoved me through, and locked the door again behind us.

Straightway, I dumped the laundry load onto the floriana rug—muffling the space beneath the door against any prying ears—and arched my sore back in a stretch. The apartment was comfortably furnished in pale yellows and lavenders with only one obvious scorched burn mark on the far sofa cushion. Apart from a few cushions, most excess fabrics had been removed.

"That ring may have gotten you in," Ox said, "but you'll never get out again. Not with Cecily in tow."

"I don't need out," I explained. "Not yet. I've caused enough of a stir, and you can handle the rest. If the queen and Belwater think I'm a threat inside the palace, they'll transfer Cecily to a more secure location. I need you to make sure you're the officer on duty tonight."

Ox took the information in his usual calm stride. He bit his cheek and nodded thoughtfully. "I can do that . . . but if your plan is to steal her during a transfer, there are too many agents watching."

"Leave that to me. Where is she?" I moved farther into the room to where the curtains nearest a side room had been tied back.

Ox followed my anxious gaze and jutted his chin. "Her workshop is through there." He didn't move to follow.

"Cecily?" I called and stepped inside the adjoining room.

Something glass shattered on the wall above me. I instinctively ducked as shards rained down over my head. "Wait, Gears! It's me!"

"*I know.*" Another glass shattered to my left. I covered my head and face with my scarf. "I heard you talking," she said.

"Then . . . will you please stop throwing things at me?"

"I'm angry."

But when no more breakables came flying, I peeked out between the folds of my scarf. Cecily's lips were pressed in a tight slash of annoyance. One hand was on her hip while the other held a glass beaker shaped like a large carafe. With a sigh, she dumped the glass back onto the large, cluttered work table beside her. "Why in all aether are you dressed like that?" she asked. "I've never seen you look so . . . plain."

Without an answer, I stood from my crouch, shook out my scarf, and crossed the room and yanked her into a tight hug. I breathed the first true sigh of relief in days.

"I can still hurt you," she muttered into my shoulder.

"That's fine. As long as you're safe."

She slouched against me. "I thought I had everything under control, but . . ."

I held her tighter.

"Art, I think . . . I think that judge changed my application."

"Come away from the breakables and tell me."

We retreated to the sitting room. Ever the soldier, Ox stood at attention near the door, while I made for the sideboard for a biscuit. It snapped in half between my teeth like a stale strip of tree bark. I spat it back out. "Maker! If I'd known how they were feeding you, I would've rescued you sooner."

Cecily ducked her reddening face and burrowed the toe of her boot into the rug.

"You asked her to save you a biscuit days ago," said Ox. "She wouldn't let me touch those."

"Not true!"

My heart unexpectedly warmed. I dug inside my coat and retrieved a small velvet bag. "I saved something for you, too. Or, well . . . a friend saved this."

"What is it?" she asked.

I held my breath as Cecily unknotted the strings and peered inside, but the magic make didn't come to life like when Harland and Miss Clune opened the bag. I'd already tested it inside the carriage house after I'd found it tucked beneath Miss Clune's carriage seat cushion.

"Uncle Tackleton was hiding that in his safe," I explained. "We found—"

"What has he done to my make?" she cried. I recoiled in alarm as Cecily roughly shook the bag upside down, and the conductor make clattered loudly onto the table. It was a small, palm-sized device of polished brass, with adjustable clamps and copper filaments curled around a bellows-like core—like veins around a pair of artificial lungs.

Cecily's lip curled with intense disgust as she inspected the make from several angles. "Horrible man . . . clearly, he has no idea what he's doing. This is *extremely* volatile."

"Is that right?"

She reached down and, with a deft twist, popped the make into two pieces.

"Wait a moment." I closed my hand around hers to stop her. An awful resolve began to settle into my gut.

"It's wrong," she said flatly. "I need to fix it."

"Actually . . . could you leave it the wrong way? Just for now," I hurriedly added. "I promise you can fix it later, but this adds another precaution if the make somehow falls into the wrong hands."

She adopted an air of forced calm. "Whoever stole my blueprints didn't read them correctly. See this part, here? Do you see what's missing?" When I smiled helplessly, she rolled her eyes. "What's *missing* is a regulator. That means there's no sure way to stop the magic once the make begins conducting. An entire steam plant wouldn't need that much conduction. This make is extremely dangerous, almost like he made it a weapon."

"May I?" I held out my hand.

Glumly, she twisted the make back together. I returned it to the velvet bag inside my hidden coat pocket.

"We don't have much time together," I said. "Why do you think Judge Pinefoy changed your application?"

"Ox told me that you only stepped in as a patron because I hadn't listed one on my application. But that's not true . . . I *did* list a patron."

"Who?" I asked.

She bit her lip. "Well . . . you and father complain all the time about the inequality between factions. While the giant gems and mages are fighting, the little cogs get trampled beneath their feet. So I thought, why not use a powerful invention to change that? If the cogs could publicly invest in the conductor, they would legitimately have access to both the Maker Exhibitions and magic. And if my conductor can be mass produced, everyone has an equal opportunity."

My mouth hung open. Belatedly, I pried the cotton stuffing from my cheeks and turned a querying look to Ox.

He shrugged. "I told you to talk to her."

Cecily fidgeted with the rumpled lapels of her work dress. "I approached a specific . . . my application listed a cog union as my first patron. Once I presented my make at the Exhibitions, I hoped similar organizations would join. Of course, that didn't exactly go to plan."

I pressed a hand to my jaw and wordlessly poured myself a drink of wine from the sideboard. I gulped the full glass, but my mouth was still dry from the cotton and the shock. I may have kept my identity a secret, but that hadn't stopped my sister from taking notice of my revolutionary ways.

With that knowledge—cog involvement in her make—everything else made sense.

"Pinefoy . . . no, not him," I muttered to myself. "He ran from the Exhibitions. He was framed. *Someone* else . . . Malowney . . . saw your application and didn't want the cogs to invest. Instead, he doctored your application and gathered his own private funding. But then . . .

why would Pinefoy approve your application if your make was already stolen?"

"He didn't," Cecily answered. "Not at first. Initially, I was rejected from the Maker Exhibitions. But later, I received a letter saying my application was approved."

I clenched my fist around the wine glass. "Malowney wanted you to be the public face of the make so the mages would come after you. Meanwhile, he could find investors, produce working makes at a faster rate, and ultimately control the profit." My mind raced through the possibilities. "I'll need to find more evidence than just the blueprints."

"What's the likelihood he left any evidence to find?" asked Ox.

"If he did, I know where to find it." Miss Clune wouldn't be alone in the Maker's Club. I needed to find my way inside, too. Fortunately, I'd brought several changes of clothing with me. I replaced the glass at the sideboard with a resolute clink. "Do you have somewhere I can wash up? Oh, and a writing desk?"

"In the bedroom," she said. "Why?"

"I need you to deliver a letter for me." I went to the door, sorted through the bag of laundry, and held up a clean, white uniform. "Here's for you, Gears. Like I said, be ready to move soon."

"Where will you be?" Cecily asked.

"Me?" I grinned. "I'm going to the gala."

Chapter Twenty-Three

AUDREY

OUR STEAM AUTO ARRIVED AT THE MAKER'S GALA AS THE low sun tinted the clouds pink and orange.

Less than one hour before the meeting at the Maker's Club. I needed to keep Maker Malowney distracted and somehow gain entrance to the club.

As we entered the Jeweled Palace, a smartly dressed butler relieved us of our wraps and accessories and stiffly directed us to a line of guests. I resisted the urge to bounce on my toes as we waited for our introduction by the Master of Ceremonies. Too many emotions jumbled around my insides—my extremities had difficulty staying still.

Eventually, we reached the arching doorway to the ballroom, and Maker Malowney presented our cards to the Master of Ceremonies. "Maker Malowney, Lady Clune, and Miss Audrey Clune." His booming voice echoed throughout the ballroom as we emerged arm-in-arm at the top of the grand staircase.

With a flutter of whispers, nearly every head turned to observe our arrival. Wide eyes filled with curiosity and barely concealed amusement followed me. Apparently, the story of our misadventures at the Tackleton garden party had spread like seeds on the wind. I caught fragments of whispers like "how frightful" and "that poor girl." Thankfully, not the part where Mr. Keays and I had been keeping company. Despite Grandmother's perspective, the crowd seemed titillated by the excitement, not the scandal.

That was promising. I took a deep breath and held my chin high. Descending the stairs was simply another performance, although the real challenge was to avoid gaping at the view. The ballroom was stunningly modern. Rotating ocular amplifiers lit the room from every angle in a wash of soft, gold light. Automated tea trollies trundled around the edge of the room bearing trays piled high with decadent, sweet hors d'oeuvres from rare, imported fruits to perfect pastries. A magnificent gold and jeweled throne sat on a dais before a towering three-story stained glass window depicting the outset of the industrial revolution. Below that, rows of lower chairs indicated where the newest makers—the guests of honor—would sit after they received a title. Pedestals were spaced every few meters with make-prototypes encased in glass.

I'd been isolated in the country too long—I felt like such a hayseed when faced with the full wealth of modern innovation.

A waft of perfumes permeated the air like a blooming tropical greenhouse where every Diadem City gem packed around the vacant dance floor. The orchestra was beginning to rosin their bowstrings and test pitch. My mind had every reason to focus elsewhere, yet I still hoped for an opportunity to dance. Social dance put me at ease. It was a way to use my talents from the theatre without the pressure of putting on a performance. What a pity the man at my side was not my dance partner of choice.

Countless servants in ruby red uniforms bustled to and from the kitchens, through the crowd, and along tiered balconies. I searched, but Mr. Keays did not appear to be among the crowd. Neither did Harland. I reminded myself that was a good thing. We were each busy with important tasks, although doubtless mine was the most unpleasant.

"Smile, Audrey," Grandmother ordered at the same time Maker Malowney gave an insincere smile to a passing trio of gems.

We were met at the bottom of the staircase by Lady Tackleton and her friends. "Don't you look stunning, Miss Clune!"

"*Ah*, the venerable Lady Tackleton!" Maker Malowney interposed. The ridiculous row of silver doves perched along his shoulders bobbed with each of his movements. "But where is your husband this evening? The Lord-Maker and I have some business to discuss."

I tightened my grip through his arm. "Business already? La! And we haven't even left the staircase. I thought I had you all to myself this evening."

"Elias left to fetch a drink." Lady Tackleton eyed the corsage on my wrist but made no comment. She was backed by a familiar coterie of gem ladies. Sequestered in the center, Mrs. Hattie Keays stood with her pug dog cradled in the sling of her arm. She put on a brave face. But apart from an exquisite saree in satin shades of cream and pink, the poor woman looked a mess. Her previously elaborate hairstyle was gone. She wore only a simple braid, and her beautifully golden-brown complexion was splotched with red. Her tearful gaze never landed on any one spot for long as she searched the room. I was anxious to see Mr. Keays. I couldn't imagine how anxious she would be to see both her children.

Without thinking, I went straight to her and took her free hand in mine. She blinked up at me. Mr. Keays must've gotten his height from his father. "Oh, my dear Miss Clune." Her voice was slightly hoarse. "How beautiful you look."

"You as well." I scratched the dog behind one stubby ear, and he immediately snorted and blissfully slumped to the side.

"Nonsense." She waved a hand. "It's a relief to see you. Are you well? We were all quite worried about you."

"I am well . . . thanks to your son," I said.

"He didn't try to do anything too heroic, did he?" she asked.

"He didn't want to wrinkle his suit."

She laughed, and some of her tears spilled over.

"But he also protected me."

Her lower lip trembled.

"Please don't be troubled," I reassured her. Maybe if I said it, I would believe it, too. "Everything is going to be all right."

She squeezed my hand. "When all this unpleasantness is over, I hope we'll have the pleasure of your company at our Beryl home. I'm sure my son will want to see for himself that you are hale and safe. I don't believe I've ever seen him so solicitous before. He seems quite taken with you, my dear."

"With me?"

I tried to imagine the Keays family life. The senior Mr. Keays was obviously successful in his profession—the family had both wealth and connections—while Hattie Keays practically overflowed with affection. I longed to see Mr. Keays and his sister reunited. He spoke of Cecily with such protectiveness. I could easily picture the disagreements and the laughter between them.

Of course, Mr. Keays wouldn't want to share that part of his heart. I was part of the adventure, but I doubted Mr. Keays would allow me to intrude on his ordinary life, too. I shouldn't want more. Something of my sadness must've shown on my face.

"Oh, forgive me!" Hattie Keays said. "I shouldn't have presumed. Clearly, you're already taken."

How could they know? Were my feelings that transparent?

"What lovely flowers," Lady Tackleton kindly prompted and tapped my wrist.

"Oh!" She meant Maker Malowney. I was already taken by Maker Malowney. I fought the self-conscious urge to pick at the pallid roses. "Yes, thank you!"

"Audrey, you're being rude," Grandmother snapped.

Maker Malowney smoothly reclaimed my arm. "Won't you introduce me, my dove?"

"Of course." I cleared the rasp from my throat. "May I present Maker Andrew Malowney and Lady Clune. This is Mrs. Keays. And, of course, you already know Lady Tackleton."

With the exception of Hattie Keays and Lady Tackleton, the surrounding ladies tittered with delight. Maker Malowney was an impressive title and personage for any social circle.

"The roses are from Citrine," Maker Malowney explained for the second time that evening. "Cost me a fortune, but Diadem hot houses simply won't do."

Lady Tackleton smoothly stepped in and introduced the rest of us.

"Mrs. Featherton, Mrs. Boxfourde, and Mrs. Garnet. You remember Miss Clune." She glanced up the staircase. "But where is Emmaline?"

"I'm afraid Aunt Emma is at home this evening."

"Convalescing?" Lady Tackleton asked. "That doesn't sound like her. She must be in great distress after yesterday. I'll be sure to call on her tomorrow."

"You mean to visit Tourmaline?" Maker Malowney asked, disbelieving.

"What a frightful encounter!" I recognized Mrs. Featherton as the elderly woman from the front row of the audience at Cerussite Hall even before she said, "And after such a triumph! Your performance yesterday afternoon was simply splendid, Miss Clune!"

"Performance?" Grandmother asked sharply.

I cringed but quickly masked the expression with a smile.

"Why yes," Mrs. Featherton chirped. "A charming Gallia piece. Something about dark roads leading to love . . . I'm unfamiliar with the lyrics, but the emotion . . . I felt as if I understood every word. Such talent! Why have you never played for us before, Miss Clune?"

"My granddaughter is only permitted to play for private parties," Grandmother said in a carefully controlled tone. She would reserve her anger to use on me later.

"We were fortunate, then, that Miss Clune agreed to play for our little party," Lady Tackleton said kindly. The ladies chuckled at the joke. The annual Tackleton garden party was technically a private one, but the number of gems in attendance was second only to the Maker's Gala.

"I'm glad you enjoyed the piece," I said quietly.

"Are the rumors true, then?" Mrs. Garnet clasped her slender hands. "Will you perform here this evening?"

Grandmother glanced over sharply.

"Nothing has been made official," I offered vaguely.

"You will excuse us," Grandmother said abruptly. "We won't monopolize your time any further." She rapped Maker Malowney on the arm. "Drinks," she ordered, and without another word, Maker Malowney obediently escorted us away. I gave one last wave to Hattie Keays and her pug over my shoulder.

A champagne fountain of at least twenty tiered silver bowls flowed freely beside stacked towers of multicolored glasses. The alcohols in glasses were organized by jewel color. Ruby was the mildest followed by fire agate, amber, emerald, sapphire, and amethyst. The strongest drink was represented by a clear, pure diamond-faceted glass. Grandmother demanded a flute of the flowing champagne from one of the attending servants, and Maker Malowney automatically selected the diamond for himself and a ruby glass for me. I took a wistful sip, wishing for something stronger than watery punch.

Glancing around, I noticed a concentrated cluster of Makers in our particular corner of the ballroom—primarily older gem men who, like Lord-Maker Tackleton, wore makes on their suits like epaulets. Maker Malowney didn't feel so out of place with the bobbing silver doves perched along his shoulders. Perhaps they'd claimed exclusivity over the liquor? More likely, the fountain was nearest the arched hallway which led to the Maker's Club—a private wing of the Jeweled Palace that supposedly housed a smoking room, gaming tables, library, and a meeting hall.

"Perhaps we should move farther into the ballroom?" I suggested. "We won't want to miss the queen."

"Traditionally, Her Jeweled Majesty won't arrive until just before her bestowal of makerships," explained Maker Malowney.

"Will the dance begin soon?"

A maker with a waxy complexion and unlit cigar between his yellowed teeth nodded to Maker Malowney and retreated down the hall to the Club.

"I believe, Andrew, you have other business to attend to?" Grandmother asked.

"Ah, yes." He knocked back the diamond drink in one gulp and deposited the glass onto a passing tray. "I'll return momentarily, my dove."

"You're leaving?" I stopped myself from adding "so soon?" There was still time before the Maker's Club was scheduled to convene.

"The Maker's work is never done. You know what these parties are like."

"But we've only just reunited."

He made a pouting face. "I have no desire to leave your side—"

"Then I'll stay with you," I said brightly.

"Don't be absurd," said Grandmother. "Leave the man to his business."

A slight current of magic trickled into my lungs. I immediately resisted the feeling. "I don't want to break my promise. Let me come with you," I pleaded.

"Audrey," Grandmother hissed. "A gem of the right set does not make demands."

As anticipated, a fanfare of music proclaimed the first dance of the gala, and the most prominent gem couples filtered onto the floor. I tugged at his suit coat. "Won't you at least stay for the first dance?"

He hesitated. But the moment he made up his mind, he slid out of reach. "Needs must, my dove. Our minutes apart will feel like hours."

He made for the exit, and my heart sank. Short of ordering Maker Malowney with magic, how else could I convince him to stay? Should I force my way into the Maker's Club?

"I say! No pure gem could possibly turn down such a lady."

Startled, I looked up.

Directly into the almond-colored eyes of Mr. Keays.

Chapter Twenty-Four

AUDREY

THE WHISPERS OF THE CROWD SWIRLED AROUND US LIKE
buzzing insects.

Mr. Keays smiled down at me as I took in his whole frame. He was
wearing a formal sherwani in a hazy, twilight-blue brocade. The seams of
his jacket cut diagonally across his broad chest and hung open around
the thighs of his dark, fitted trousers in an inverted V-shape. The collar
fit snugly around his neck, and the sleeves were expertly tailored to his
wrists with leather bands around his palms. In fact, the cut and color of
his suit was so understated as to be effortless. The only true sign of his
rake character were the rings (including the ruby ring), a drape of gold
chains around his neck, and kohl around his eyes.

Somehow, he'd dressed to match me perfectly—a nighttide sky of
golden stars.

"You're not supposed to be here!" I hissed.

He grinned. "May I have the first dance?" he asked loudly.

Without waiting for my answer, he deftly spun me out from

between Grandmother and Maker Malowney and led me onto the dance floor.

"What are you doing? Maker Malowney is about to leave for the Club."

"Is he? Because it looks to me as though we've made the perfect distraction."

I glanced around his shoulder. Maker Malowney had followed us to the edge of the dance floor, face mottled red and seething with jealousy.

"I doubt he'll let you out of his sight after this."

"Thank you for the help," I said grudgingly. "What are you doing?"

"Stealing a dance."

"You know what I mean," I muttered through my teeth. "What are you doing *here*. You're supposed to be a hostage."

"And now, Malowney is wondering the same thing. If I'm here, does that mean the Magicstry somehow got hold of the blueprints? Why did Harland let me go? It's the perfect excuse to keep the villains preoccupied with each other." He casually glanced around and admitted, "I need something else from the Maker's Club."

Mr. Keays tightened his arm around me and led me to a free spot of floor just as the orchestra played the first few notes of a waltz. My heart fluttered in time with the music. Unlike the more traditional assembly dances, a waltz would place me directly in the arms of my partner.

He was looking down at me with a flash of mischief in his almond eyes.

"Oh dear, I know that look."

"What look?"

"The one you're giving me right now. You're about to do something rakish like leap into a carriage or drive me to *distraction*."

"Good to know a simple dance could drive you to distraction."

He stepped in close, and my body was suddenly awash with sensation—the light trail of his fingers on my waist, the curve of his warm hand around the small of my back before pressing up between my shoulders, the pull of his gravity until I was only one deep breath away from standing flush against his broad chest. I automatically draped my left arm and held up my right hand like a frame. The muscles of his shoulder flexed beneath the grip of my fingers, but he didn't immediately take my hand.

"I like these," he said. The drape of gold threads ran through his fingers as he caressed the underside of my arm, dragging my hand into place. His fingers cupped mine. His thumb pressed gently against the tops of my knuckles.

Then, the music began, and the world spun around us.

Mr. Keays was a strong lead. He kept the steps simple but precise; however, his movement also held a deep passion like the hidden ring of gold around his almond eyes—only I was close enough to see. I was grateful for years of dance training. The muscle memory still held, even if my mind was as foggy as the night we'd met. I couldn't think or speak or feel beyond the sway and pull of the music and the movement of our bodies between spaces.

He led me into a turn, but with a deft flick against my wrist, the corsage of roses went flying and skidded across the floor. I bit down on a giddy laugh. "You shouldn't have done that. Those cost a fortune from Citrine."

"So I heard. Diadem hothouses simply wouldn't do." He grinned at my expression. "Mum told me."

"I'm so relieved you spoke with her! She was worried for you."

"Was she? I got an earful about how I'd spoiled her skin regimen but nothing about my disappearance." He spun me inward and cradled me against his side. With a serious look, he said, "She also told me to confess my feelings for you before it was too late."

With an awkward laugh, I tucked beneath his arms and led myself into the basic waltz position with more distance between us. But again, he pressed us closer, hand splayed between my shoulder blades. His thumb subtly hooked into the low backline of my gown. My entire body prickled at the small but intimate touch.

"I am sorry for the way I left our conversation last night," he murmured. "There was more I meant to say." But he said no more as he twirled us around the edge of the floor.

Our bodies were perfectly balanced within the gravity of each other. The tight pull in my chest went taut like a string as we spun apart, then coiled again as we reconnected. Every touch was like the sensation of magic—the air of an open sky, the wind on my face, the freedom of flying.

The music swelled. He held my waist in both hands, and I arched back until he caught me in a full embrace. My leg pressed against his as, slowly, he dipped me back.

We held there, neither of us willing to let each other go—a truth neither of us had spoken aloud.

Dimly, I became aware of the sounds of the crowd.

The song had ended—I couldn't remember when.

Mr. Keays and I were alone on the dance floor draped together in a graceful pose, and the crowd was applauding.

With some dismay, I stood and curtsied. True to character, Mr. Keays flourished a rather excessive bow and blew a kiss. Several of the ladies fanned themselves.

Maker Malowney hadn't moved from his spot at the edge of the dance floor. His face was no longer red, but his eyes had hardened into a concrete glare. He moved to intercept our path as Mr. Keays led me off the floor.

"We're leaving." Maker Malowney took my arm in his and all but dragged me to the arched hallway. I stumbled over the tapestry-woven runner rug and skidded on the marble threshold as Maker Malowney flung open the double doors to the Maker's Club hard enough that the affixed brass plaque rattled. He stormed inside with me in tow.

The first room of the club was similar to a conference room with arching doorways that branched into more rooms including a billiards hall and a library. A large table surrounded by padded chairs took up the center of the room. Only five of the chairs were full. The closest was already taken by Grandmother, and Lord-Maker Tackleton sat beside her. The far side of the table was rounded out by two more gents and one lady with vaguely familiar faces. I must've seen them from behind the piano at one of Grandmother's parties.

Maker Malowney shoved me forward toward an empty chair.

"Sit," Grandmother commanded.

"Is there a problem?" Mr. Keays asked behind us. He'd followed us directly into the club.

Maker Malowney rolled his shoulders into a steadier composure and made a show of inspecting Mr. Keays through the tinted lens of his monocle. "Are you lost?"

"No?" He glanced at his feet. "No, I'm standing exactly where I intend to."

Maker Malowney pursed his lips and tossed his slicked hair. It didn't move. "This club is members only, and I don't believe we've been introduced."

"Mr. Keays, this is Maker Malowney," I said and rubbed my sore arm.

"*Ah*, yes. I have heard of you."

Lord-Maker Tackleton stood smoothly. "I'm surprised to see you. How did you manage to escape the mage?"

Mr. Keays shrugged and casually strolled to the far side of the table. "He let me go. I didn't ask why."

Lord-Maker Tackleton looked troubled by the news while Maker Malowney sneered. "I ought to thank you for intervening on my fiancée's behalf . . . but she's no longer your concern. Now, if you will excuse us, we have some business to take care of before the makerships are bestowed." He forcefully gripped me by the upper arm. I winced as he pinched skin and stuffed me down onto the chair.

"Maker Malowney," I said with forced calm. "You know very well an engagement has not been finalized. There are no promises between us."

"Bite your tongue, girl!" Grandmother spat.

"Why?" Mr. Keays challenged. "Is there a reason you prefer her to keep silent?"

Grandmother stiffened.

Maker Malowney ran his tongue over straight teeth and laughed bitterly. "I see the rumors are true. You do keep other men hidden under your skirts." I gasped, and he gripped my arm even tighter. "Particularly if this cog knows your more, shall we say, *intimate* details. I am nothing if not a gracious man, but even I have my limits. I did not resent you these diversions, so long as you allowed me the same *discretion* after we married. But I will not be made a cuckold. I've invested too much in our marriage for you to throw me over."

Mr. Keays's jaw tightened at the same time mine dropped. I yanked my arm free of his grasp and backed away until all eyes were facing me. "Grandmother? Did you know about this?"

Maker Malowney's mustache stretched thinly across his upper lip. "Know what? That your skirts are as loose as your ill-bred mother's or that I don't care?"

Everything inside me went still.

"You always were a willful child," Grandmother sneered. "This time, you *will* do as you're told."

"She said you might require certain . . . *persuasions* to stay in line. But it won't come to that, will it, my dove? Just keep your mouth closed unless I tell you otherwise. And keep my business and your whoring affairs discrete."

My insides were numb, but every inch of my skin prickled with feeling. The hairs on my scalp tingled. I breathed, and my lungs filled with magic.

"I've seen all I need to." Mr. Keays stood beside me. "If you don't tell him to stop breathing, I will."

I could.

The whole of the aether was mine to conduct.

The magic only needed an outlet.

Great Maker only knew what showed in my expression because Grandmother immediately paled. She pointed a shaking hand. "*Audrey.* Don't—don't say anything you might regret."

Lord Tackleton and the others looked around, confused.

Maker Malowney was a bit slower to catch on. But once he realized the threat, there was no doubt he'd already known about my ability to conduct. He tripped over his own heels to back away from me. His veins beat a visible pulse beneath his pallid skin. "No, wait . . . you aren't supposed to know."

"Know what?" I asked. "My own mind? I'm not supposed to know *exactly* what I want? I'm not supposed to make my own choices? Or were you referring to my inheritance? I'm not supposed to know that you and Grandmother tried to force an engagement to steal my money? Or . . . could it be that you've been using me in another way? The business negotiations. The piano recitals. The constant control."

It was the first time I'd seen Grandmother and Maker Malowney speechless. A fissure of pride broke through the numbness inside me as I stared down Grandmother directly. Her stony expression was nothing more than a crumbling monument.

"Allow me to enlighten you because *you* are the one who doesn't seem to know . . . I have all the power here. I won't be manipulated. I won't speak at your command, and I won't be silenced. I'll never again be forced to play a weak character."

I held my breath a moment longer, savoring the thrum of magic in my veins. Even more, the confidence.

"Well?" asked Mr. Keays.

I *tsked* with false regret. "They already told me everything I need."

Slowly, I exhaled the magic back into the air like a song.

Grandmother sagged with relief, but too soon. I addressed the room at large. "Lord-Maker Tackleton, you've been led here today under false pretenses. Despite the fact that you're obviously the source of rumor and the disparagement of my character, I refuse to let Maker Malowney and Lady Clune swindle you. All of you."

"Swindle—what are you saying, gel?"

"You privately invested an advance payment for a stolen make, did you not?" I asked. "While I don't know the particulars of your agreement, I do know that Maker Malowney and Lady Clune are unable to obtain the money for their investment. They've only taken yours."

"What's this?" he asked.

Malowney held up a finger, defensively backing away. "No, no . . . now technically, that money is mine."

"Only if we marry," I said. "And that's never going to happen."

After my conversation with Aunt Emma, it had been easy to see their plan and why Maker Malowney had so suddenly proposed. They'd hoped to conclude multiple deals.

Tackleton rounded on Grandmother. "Is this true? What about our contract? I should have majority ownership."

"No, I-I have an *alternative* inheritance coming," Maker Malowney argued.

"From your great-uncle, Pinefoy?" Mr. Keays asked with a smirk. "I wasn't aware he'd been declared dead. Then again, you must've known the Magicstry would kill him when you framed him for the theft of the blueprints. Or was that simply an added bonus to your bank account?"

An argument erupted, each patron shouting over the other.

Grandmother stood and rounded the table. She bared her greyed teeth. "Ungrateful girl. After all I've done for you, this is how you repay me?"

"You're right," I said. "It's less than you deserve. I should tell the queen that her precious gems were the ones to steal the magic make."

I turned on my heel, and Mr. Keays followed me to the exit.

"Don't walk away from me!" she screeched. "Andrew, stop her!"

The patrons were in an uproar.

"The queen will be grateful!" Her shouts followed me through the double doors and down the hall. "I've kept a valuable weapon out of the filthy hands of cogs *and* mages like you and your lusterless mother. I should've turned you in to the Magicstry as well. Your blood was always too polluted to preserve!"

We reemerged into the ballroom.

"Audrey?" Mr. Keays asked quietly.

"I'm fine." The bitter taste in my mouth wasn't one of surprise; however, as I glanced around the ballroom, the feeling only worsened. Something about the scene was wrong. The guests were clustered around the edges of the room.

My skin prickled, and I rubbed my arms. There was a pressure against my ears like a sudden lift aboard the *Courtship*.

Was I conducting magic?

The feeling was similar to magic, but the notes clanged through the air around me like cacophonous funeral chanting. I wrapped my arms around myself, trying to shield from the harsh turmoil of such discordant music.

Mr. Keays and I pressed forward to the edge of the crowd—oriented in one direction.

Slowly, I turned toward the grand staircase.

Two mages descended the steps, the hems of their grey robes floating on an unseen breeze.

Harland wore his customarily hardened expression, but his gaze held an unfamiliar remoteness. The only color in his face were the dark bruises shadowing his eyes. And although he hid it well, his posture warped as if favoring an injury. Or several.

My chest tightened. What had the Magicstry done to him?

The second mage was undoubtably the master, Mage Citoyen.

I drew in a sharp breath.

With a sudden snap of his head, his eyes locked with mine. Numbly, I wondered if the cruel twist of his lips was hiding rows of sharpened teeth. The Gallia mage would tear into my throat without hesitation.

"You were right." His words carried over the crowd with a tone as bitter as poison. "The Renegade and a mage. Perhaps my novice is not so unworthy as I believed."

The prickling feeling penetrated my skin and stung my heart with cold dread.

"She's also hiding a working make," Harland said. "Now you have everything you need."

Chapter Twenty-Five

ART

THE WORLD WAS TINTED RED. MY THOUGHTS SCRAMBLED TO keep up with the dull pounding in my ears as Harland and Mage Citoyen smoothly descended the rest of the staircase and stood directly before us. Even then, Harland wouldn't meet my stare.

A cascade of astonished whispers echoed around the room, but the signification was the same throughout.

I was the Renegade.

Miss Clune was a mage.

We would never again be completely safe or overlooked.

Because Harland had told him everything.

Anger burned like bile in the back of my throat.

Mage Citoyen tilted his head and regarded Miss Clune. Ever the confident woman, she raised her chin to meet his gaze.

"Spirited and beautiful," the mage murmured. "How long did you think you could conduct without the authority of the Magicstry? *Can ye verily say that your conscience is clean before the Great Maker? Will* you confess your sins?"

Fast as a cobra, he clamped a hand over her chin.

"No!" I lunged for the mage, but Harland intercepted. I spun out of his grip. But in that one touch, Harland had already conducted magic. My limbs went numb, and I careened into an astonished cluster of gems. Harland caught my arms and pinned them behind my back—shoving me to my deadened knees. My muscles and veins strained against my skin as I struggled to break free, but I was forced to watch as Miss Clune went completely rigid. Her eyes rolled up into her head until only the whites were showing. She covered her ears for a noise only she could hear. Her mouth stretched into a silent scream, and she crumpled to the hard floor.

"Help her!" I shouted above the screams that echoed throughout the hall as gems scrambled back and widened the circle around us.

"She can help herself," Harland muttered. "Watch."

I clenched and unclenched my numb fists beneath Harland's grip until, sure enough, Miss Clune gradually uncurled from the fetal position. Sweat beaded her brow, but she met my gaze with a subtle nod of reassurance. I exhaled a breath of relief as she pushed herself up with trembling arms. Her fingers left bloody streaks along the wood of the dance floor. She'd torn open the skin of her palms. But gathering her skirts, she once again stood and defiantly raised her chin and faced the mage.

"Intriguing." Mage Citoyen looked grossly pleased by her defiance. He turned to Harland. "Where's the other one, the maker-girl? Did you find where the queen was keeping her?"

Harland pointed to a side hall. "That way is the fastest."

"No!" I thrashed against his grip.

"Take us there."

Palace guards finally arrived at the scene, but their progress was stalled by the panicked crowd, boxed tightly along the edges of the room. The guards seemed reluctant to push through. Would they directly intervene in Magicstry matters, or would they hold their ground as tension simmered?

Mage Citoyen seized Miss Clune around the waist, but she fought him as well as whatever magic he was conducting. Her brows creased and her lips mouthed a song—too low for me to hear above the din. Mage Citoyen snarled and again gripped her jaw. The air pressure dropped as he breathed in—conducting even more magic.

Miss Clune again went rigid.

"Wait!" I shouted. "I'll give you everything, the make and the blueprints. Only let her go."

"You're lying."

"We have the blueprints," Harland said.

My mind raced. "From Pinefoy? I bet my hat that what you found was a decoy. I stole the real ones directly from the Maker's Club." A stack of blueprints and contract papers lay on the table, ready to be signed. While Miss Clune distracted the patrons by confronting her grandmother and Malowney, I'd quietly slid the correct documents from the table and into my suit jacket.

Mage Citoyen paused, and Miss Clune sagged. After brief consideration, Mage Citoyen jerked his head, and Harland obediently released my arms. Some of the feeling returned to my limbs. I staggered to my feet—out of reach from Harland—and withdrew the velvet bag and a thin roll of papers from the folds of my jacket. I held both up for Mage Citoyen to see and tossed the papers to the floor between us. I held up the make.

"Let her go," I repeated. "And I'll give you the make."

"Do so and die!"

All eyes turned to the dais. The queen pointed down at us from her golden throne, quivering with rage. Belwater stood like a shadow at her side, and a square of guards dressed in red encircled them. "That make is mine!" she screamed.

The crowd gasped and belatedly dropped to their knees. The guards were well and truly boxed out from our position at the center of the room. They wouldn't open fire either—not into a room full of civilian gems.

Mage Citoyen bared his teeth in a smile. "We have a deal."

But he hadn't released his grip on Miss Clune. He still planned to kill her—or both of us—as soon as I gave up the make.

Betrayal burned inside me. Harland's treachery stung like a fresh wound, and a hollow ache settled in my chest. How could I have been so wrong? The queen's fury was a blaze threatening to consume my sister whole. And Miss Clune . . . I'd failed to keep her safe. Did she know my locket was hers? Cecily and Miss Clune were the last people who would intentionally misuse power, yet they were both captive to those who wanted to take away the power they'd earned.

Would they ever forgive me for misusing that same power to save them?

I met Miss Clune's eyes, and she gave me a small, sad nod.

So, I put on a rogue's smile.

"Here's the problem," I said to Mage Citoyen. "A simple cog like me can't conduct, but you shouldn't have any trouble getting this to work."

In one smooth motion, I opened the bag and tossed the make.

Time seemed to hang heavy in the air.

Mage Citoyen reached for the make.

Miss Clune dove for the floor.

My ears popped from the sudden change in pressure in the room as Mage Citoyen caught the make midair. His eyes widened in shock, then fierce triumph, then fear.

The mage let out a horrifying scream. It rattled the chandeliers and abruptly choked off even as his mouth stretched open in silent agony. There was no outward change—no rushing wind or visible tempest of magic—as his lungs swelled with aether. He fell to his knees and crawled toward Harland. "Help me!" he choked out.

Harland seemed to be holding his breath. He watched stoney-faced as his master mage writhed on the floor toward him.

I raced to Miss Clune and dragged her huddled form to the edge of the packed crowd—as far away from the make as possible—slid to the floor beside her and propped her head against my shoulder. Her eyes were glassy and unfocused. Even if she could fend off the effects of the make, Mage Citoyen had already conducted a painful amount of magic through her. I could do nothing for her as she coughed then spasmed. Weakly, she pointed to Harland.

He'd refused to help her before.

Again, she pointed.

I fisted my hands. "Harland, help her!"

For a moment, Harland didn't move. He stared at Mage Citoyen with a hollow expression, as if trying to make sense of what he was seeing. Then, with one last, empty look down at the mage, he turned his back. Mage Citoyen clenched his teeth in a soundless snarl and frantically reached for him. But Harland ignored him as he crossed the room, knelt on one knee before Miss Clune, and gripped her wrist.

The make suddenly half-lifted Mage Citoyen off the ground as if his arm were on a string. Only his toes dragged along the smooth wood of the dance floor. He convulsed, and his chest bloated unnaturally large as the aether filled his body beyond capacity.

With one final spasm, Mage Citoyen went limp. The magic deflated from the make, and his lifeless body smacked against the floor.

The room held in stunned silence except for the sound of labored breathing beside me. "Audrey?" I propped her higher against my chest.

She sat upright, testing her balance. "I-I'm fine. Harland?"

He coughed.

"Close enough." With one last brush of my fingers against Miss Clune's hand, I stood, returned to the center of the room, kicked the make out of the stiff fingers of the mage, and replaced it within the velvet bag inside my jacket. I retrieved the papers and knelt before the queen on her dais.

But before I could speak, the spymaster Belwater signaled, and the ring of Ruby Agents aimed their rifles down at me. "Her Majesty ordered you not to give up the make."

"Forgive me, Your Majesty," I said loudly. "I've brought you the magic make and the blueprints. Please allow me to explain." Every occupant in the room was listening, and there wasn't any use in pretending to be useless. Not after Harland had revealed my identity as the Renegade. I shoved down a sudden swell of sorrow. "I found the blueprints as well as a working make, but the model is faulty. The design was stolen and corrupted by another maker."

The crowd murmured, and the queen's beady eyes took in the full room lingering on the dead mage. She waved off the agents. Belwater almost looked disappointed when they returned to attention.

"Take away the mage," she ordered. "But don't touch him. I don't want any more surprises."

It took a minute, but three guards rolled the mage onto a stretcher and carried him from the ballroom. Once out of sight, the crowd relaxed slightly from their tight huddle along the walls, although the center of the dance floor remained markedly empty.

The queen's next words were to me. "If what you say is true, you've done the Parure a great service."

"A service, Your Majesty, but not a favor. The make and blueprints come with a price. I'll return them and tell you everything you need to know in exchange for recognition . . . for the *rightful* Maker Cecily Keays."

"You're in no position to make demands," said Belwater.

"Judge Pinefoy was filling both pockets," I explained. "He was an informant for the Magicstry and also worked with his nephew, Maker Malowney, to commit fraud. The judge rejected cog maker-candidates and stole their makes for Malowney. I found several unpublished research papers and blueprints that Malowney later claimed as his own makes including auto design and weapons manufacture."

I turned and spoke to the room at large. "Judge Pinefoy and Maker Malowney stole the blueprints for the magic make!"

More murmurs rippled around the room. Apparently, Malowney had been standing within the crowd because sounds of a scuffle reached me as he tried to make a break for freedom.

"He's right here!" Mum emerged from crowd. She held Sweetpea under one arm and swatted Maker Malowney upside the head with the other. "Take that, vile man!" She harangued and chased him until two guards caught him by the arms.

"Unhand me!" he whined.

I grinned and continued. "Malowney knew that once news spread of a magic make, the Magicstry would intervene. He wanted to profit, but he didn't want to be a target for the mages. If Cecily presented her make at the Exhibitions, that would buy him more time to develop a working model and manufacture the make at a faster rate. He also knew that as an informant, Judge Pinefoy would be framed. And if the Magicstry killed him for it, Malowney would inherit his estate."

The guards brought him forward, and Malowney dropped to his knees. "But, Your Majesty—"

"Silence," the queen ordered. "Get this traitor out of my sight." She put a veined hand to her temple. "Thank you, Mr. Keays. This is distressing news, indeed—"

"I wasn't finished." I raised my voice and pointed an accusing finger up to the dais. "I also have evidence that Judge Pinefoy and *Maker Belwater* were working together to reject cog maker-candidates. Your Majesty, your own advisor has been working against you."

The queen looked aghast while the crowd gasped in shock. Belwater, however, remained eerily calm. "Your Majesty, you can't believe—"

"Judge Pinefoy wasn't the only one with access to the vault," I said and held aloft the roll of papers. "Belwater lied when he said he checked the vault for the blueprints. I have here the original blueprints, a contract for a private investment between gem patrons independent from the Maker Exhibitions, and *two* copies of Cecily's application. In her original application, Cecily listed a cog organization as her patron. Pinefoy and Belwater denied her application and brought her blueprints to gem patrons instead. Of course, Pinefoy couldn't know he was marked as the martyr, so the forged application was later signed and approved by Maker Belwater."

"Is this true?" Her shrill voice rang through the silent room. "Can you deny your own signature?"

Still, Belwater didn't abandon his calm. The wraithlike man regarded me with a faint smile. "Your Majesty, I'm surprised," he said. "Do you truly intend to trust the word of a delusive thief? The word of a *renegade*?"

The circle of Ruby Agents glanced among themselves but didn't intervene as Belwater glided down the steps and joined me. He spoke quietly so only I could hear. "I said I'd keep an eye on you. You're surrounded by every Ruby Agent in the palace. I *alone* command them. Did you really think I wouldn't notice when you used the ruby ring to sneak into the palace? I relocated your sister as soon as you arrived at the gala."

"Did you?" I asked.

"I warned you. What I do is for the good of the Parure. My loyalty is pure. Whatever evidence you think you have won't be enough to besmirch my character. And unless you recant your lies, I can ensure you never see your sister again. So, Mr. Keays . . . do you still think it wise to threaten the man holding the winning cards?"

I nodded thoughtfully and tucked the papers inside my jacket with the make. "That's a very good threat. A delusive thief like me doesn't stand a chance."

I scanned the crowd for Miss Clune, torn between wanting to say goodbye and relieved she was already gone.

"But if all the agents are here," I asked, "then who's watching Cecily?"

That finally broke through his exterior calm.

When the queen believed there was a threat inside the palace, she ordered Cecily moved to a more secure location. I hadn't needed to know where they'd take her. I'd just needed to flash the Ruby Agent ring around the palace halls and force their hand. That gave our hidden players a chance to enact their roles.

I hadn't expected Harland to reveal my identity. That was a painful blow. Belwater's involvement, however, came as no surprise.

I'd feared I might have to sacrifice the life I'd built as the Renegade. But if that sacrifice was the only way out for Cecily, it was a price I was willing to pay. With my vigilantism exposed, there would be no escape for me.

Belwater fell back a step and glared from sunken eyes. "Filthy cog!" he shouted. "Guards, arrest him! I'll see to it the Renegade never flies again!"

Gasps rippled through the crowd as Ruby Agents and guards surged forward—closing in around me.

"Is that so?" A new voice rang out, sharp and clear above the noise of the ballroom.

All eyes turned upward to the orchestra balcony. Miss Clune stood at the railing overlooking the entire room. She'd somehow donned a flight jacket over a slimmer version of her bold gown and convinced the orchestra to lend her aid. The ends of her hair fluttered on an imperceptible breeze as the orchestra played the opening notes of a familiar tune. "You want to stop the Renegade? You'll have to catch me first."

She smiled as I gaped in amazement.
Then, all was lost to her song.

They seek her near, they seek her far;
Over sea and under star,
They seal the gates with barricades
To try to catch the Renegade.

They say she sails from Parure skies;
As the Robin flies, the mage survives.
And with this hope, the sinner prayed
For Maker to send the Renegade.

THE MUSIC SWELLED, WEAVING IMAGES OF NIGHT SKIES AND daring escapes between each stanza. Her voice rang out clear and infinite. Her song was like a rising tide of emotion, but the sadness didn't resurface as I'd expected. I only felt relief. Cecily was safe, Mage Citoyen couldn't harm her, and every prominent gem—everyone attending the Maker's Gala—knew that she was the rightful maker.

They seek her far, they seek her wide;
Through vale and over mountainside.
E'en so the mages have mislaid
Each trap made for the Renegade.

The people hail and praise her name
While the evil search for who to blame.
Yet with each sly disguise arrayed,
They cannot find the Renegade.

HER SONG WAS AN INFLUENCE BUT NOT A VIOLATION. SHE'D chosen to protect herself. I believed with all my heart that no one there could catch her. Belwater could seal the palace gates, but nothing could hold her. The mages could search every hillside, but not one would find her.

The magic mirrored the rhythm of my heart and entwined with every part of me. The music crescendoed until the final stanza resonated pure and true.

They seek her thither, they seek her yon;
    She flies at dusk and sails at dawn,
    Every snare she will evade
    Our fearless Robin Renegade.

I HELD MY BREATH, MESMERIZED, LONG AFTER THE LAST notes of the orchestra had faded.

The magic of her song gave me a choice, but how could I believe otherwise? I was the Renegade. But somehow, Miss Clune was and always would be Robin Renegade—the confident leading lady of her own story.

It was impossible to say how long the crowd stood frozen in a trance of music. But slowly we revived with hushed and reverential whispers. "The Renegade *and* a mage." Among the whispers, I recognized the exact phrase spoken by Mage Citoyen—Miss Clune had used his words to her advantage.

I shook my senses free, but too late.

Miss Clune was gone.

"Where is she?"

"Was that Dame Gemma?"

"Could she be . . ."

". . . the Renegade all along!"

Without another thought, I pivoted on my heel and sprinted from the room. Shouts of the magic-muddled guards followed me, but I soon outpaced them as I careened into a side hallway into the service wing. I followed a similar path—the same route I'd taken that afternoon—through the scullery and the frenzied kitchens and out the service entrance.

The *Courtship* hovered above the courtyard, and Miss Clune held one end of a dangling rope ladder.

A smiling Cecily waved down at me from the ship railing. She was standing arm-in-arm with Harland.

I skidded to a clumsy stop. "Is this a joke?" I shouted.

Harland's typically impassive face cracked into a wide smile. "I said I worked for the maker."

"How—"

Shouts echoed behind me from the kitchen. Miss Clune glanced over her shoulder and stepped onto the lowest rung. I raced across the courtyard, even though after her song, I knew I'd never be able to catch her.

Fortunately, Miss Clune caught my hand in hers and pulled me close. The ladder swayed as she hooked an elbow over a rung and arched down and kissed me with full passion—her lips parted into a shameless smile. Her hand gripped my neck then my jacket as her mouth claimed mine.

We were yanked apart as the *Courtship* ascended higher. Miss Clune clung to the rope ladder as Jolly and Miss Toussaint appeared at the taffrail and reeled her aboard.

Guards dashed into the courtyard behind me. But even if their ships launched fast enough to pursue the *Courtship*, they would be too late to catch the Renegade after her musical conduction of magic.

"Thief!" I exclaimed with a laugh. "I give you my locket, and you steal everything else! You won't get away with this!"

"Is that a threat?" she called. Her wide smile flashed like a shooting star against the night sky.

"It's the honest truth!"

Several guards encircled me, but Ox entered the ring. He gripped my shoulder with a reassuring hand. "Stand down! We were ordered to arrest the Renegade. He's no threat."

The guards fumbled with their weapons and glanced around as if looking for answers as the white sails of the *Courtship* faded into the hanging mist. Soon, she was lost to the dark.

Only then did I notice that the make and blueprints were missing from my inner pocket.

Robin Renegade had distracted me with a kiss.

Chapter Twenty-Six

AUDREY

I GAZED OUT OVER THE TAFFRAIL, EYES FIXED ON THE glimmering lights of the Jeweled Palace until Diadem City was no more than a flickering candlelight in the distance. Gaslamps creaked on their iron hinges as Mae sailed the *Courtship* higher—rocking against the airwaves.

My heart ached to leave Mr. Keays, but I hoped I'd stolen any remaining leverage the queen and her advisor could wield against him. To be fair, everything ached after the torture I'd endured from Mage Citoyen. I breathed deeply. The aether was thick with magic.

"Miss Clune?"

I turned to a new yet familiar face. Miss Cecily Keays looked so much like her cousin my heart ached anew. Harland stood at her shoulder.

I exhaled the magic back to the aether and replied, "Please, call me Audrey. I'm so happy to meet you, Miss Keays. Or should I say, *Maker* Keays."

Her eyes widened in shock. "Thank you for saving me."

I wanted to pull her into a giant hug—like a little sister I never had —but Art had mentioned she was uncomfortable in social situations.

Her gaze was focused somewhere around my left shoulder, and she dipped her head as she spoke. "Who would've thought my brother could be in league with the Renegade?" she asked.

Harland and I exchanged a glance.

"It seems we have a lot to talk about," I said. "But let's get you a flight jacket and harness first. You must be cold in that day dress. Oh, and I believe these belong to you." I pulled the make model and blue-prints from the pocket of my skirts and placed them in her delicate hands. "Just don't—"

She tore open the bag and swiftly twisted the make into two sepa-rate pieces. "I need to fix this."

When nothing happened, I pressed a hand to my rapidly beating heart.

Harland huffed a dry laugh. "Warn us before you test that."

Maker Keays abruptly looked into my face. "Audrey . . . or should I say, Robin? You have the most perfect face. Mathematically speaking, of course. Oh! I've just had an idea based on the Golden Ratio. I need paper." And with that, she scurried belowdecks.

I stared blankly after her.

Harland shook his head with a small smile. "She's like that." He quickly sobered. "He was going to kill her. The only way to distract him was to turn you in as a heretic."

"I guessed as much. But you saved my life . . . again. Thank you."

"I didn't save Art." He glanced away. "I warned him I was working for the maker."

I smiled coyly. "We have a *lot* to talk about," I repeated.

"*Oui, mon cœur,*" Aunt Emma said, jumping in to hug me from behind. "You must tell me everything that happened while we were in the kitchens. I see you found the jacket I left for you."

Her long hair was tied in a colorful scarf, and she wore a white apron beneath her flight harness and blouson. She seemed so full of life —happier than I'd seen her in years. I wondered at the change until Mr.

Jolly joined us at the railing and whispered something to her in Gallia. She giggled and blushed a deep rosy pink which, in turn, caused him to blush and rub the back of his bald head.

Mr. Jolly angled a shout over his shoulder. "Mae!"

"Whatcha want now, Da?" she hollered from the helm.

"Fly the ship home faster, will yeh? We haven't had any supper."

"Yeh order me in the kitchen, but I won't take yer orders on my ship!"

"Yer ship?" he challenged. "Yeh take orders from Miss Robin Renegade now!"

Mae sulked but didn't argue.

Mr. Jolly turned to me and winked. "At least until Art is above suspicion again. But I'm guessing he'll have to find his own ship now, won't he?"

I bit my lip and massaged my aching hands. I'd always planned to join Mr. Keays on the *Courtship* and become a Robin Renegade. But when he was in danger, I didn't hesitate to conduct magic. Unfortunately, the only choice I'd taken was his. Even if he forgave me for stealing the name Robin Renegade, how could Mr. Keays ever forgive me for stealing his ship and crew?

Aunt Emma distracted me from my guilt by brushing my cheek. "What's next for the Renegade?"

I straightened my shoulders. "I think it's high time she reclaimed her inheritance, don't you? I may be a fugitive now, but Cecily needs another patron if she plans to put her make into the hands of as many cogs as possible. But we'll need a plan. I'm sure Grandmother left more of her schemes and traps in our path."

"The Magicstry won't like what happened to Citoyen," Harland said.

"True," I agreed. "And that man, Belwater, is going to be looking for revenge. I did what I thought was right to save Mr. Keays . . . but now I'm not so sure."

Mr. Keays had professed the honest truth. He'd given me his locket, but every worry and guilt pressed in on my thoughts until I felt as if I'd imagined the laughter in his voice and love in his gaze.

Aunt Emma strung her arm through mine. "You look troubled, *mon cœur*."

"I wonder if Mr. Keays will thank me for rescuing his reputation or curse me for stealing his ship."

"Well, you're right on time from when the letter arrived."

"What letter?"

Her lips quirked. "The letter was directed to me." But she released my arm, pulled a letter from the pocket of her kitchen apron, and handed it to me.

With shaking hands, I turned it over. The red wax seal was embossed with a gold crown.

I hastily unfolded the letter and read:

My Dearest Aunt Emma,

I write to inform you that you may expect your niece's arrival shortly.

I hope I've learned my lesson by now not to underestimate Audrey. Depending on how the events of tonight unfold, she may very well manage to steal my ship. But it should come as no surprise that the Courtship, my locket, everything I have was hers from the moment I stepped into her carriage. Her true character was never anything other than herself, the confident Robin Renegade.

On a second point, I ask that you kindly return my belongings (in particular, my favorite wool derby) to 344 Beryl Drive at your earliest convenience care of

Your Honest Servant,
Art Keays

P.S. It would be wise to remove all flammables before supplying Cecily with a workspace.

P.P.S. Audrey, my love. If you wanted a letter from me, you could've asked.

I LAUGHED AND CLUTCHED THE LETTER TO MY CHEST— letting the honest truth of his words sink into my heart.

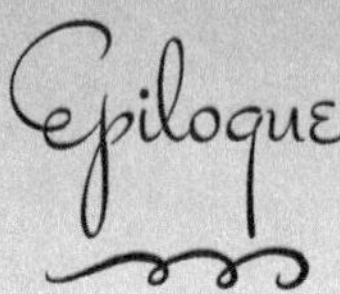

Epilogue

ART

THE ONLY SOUNDS IN THE FAMILY TEA ROOM WERE THE light ticking of the standing clock, the soft scrape as Mum turned a page of her novel, and the occasional snort from Sweetpea as he slept belly-up on a flowery cushion.

I covered my eyes with a doily—the patterned pink and yellow wallpaper against the pansy furniture fabrics was too bright after such a long night—but startled upright as a metal letter tray clanged loudly on the end table beside my head.

Sweetpea yipped, and I wrestled free of the padded chair and doily. I blinked against the sudden brightness.

"The morning paper, sir," said Daweson mildly.

"That's a bit louder than paper."

Daweson ignored me and gently placed a box tied with a thick ribbon on the coffee table beside Mum. "A delivery for you, ma'am."

She marked her page. "It must be my new order from the Glass District. Thank you, Daweson."

"Yes, *thank you*, Daweson."

"My pleasure . . . sir." He turned on his heel and left.

I rubbed my temples and opened the newspaper, flipping through the first few pages. Each story was more fantastical than the last. The rumors were flying faster than the Renegade herself. Robin Renegade had been spotted at a cog rally in the Accent Territory harbor of Eastport. That very same night, six mages escaped from a Gallia Magicstry over the border. The Renegade was impossibly in two places at once.

I grinned.

Robin Renegade was not only rescuer but champion of magic for the masses. The gems tried to produce their own make; however, ever since cogs went public with their—far superior—version of the make, magic and wealth had become more widely distributed. As a result, all parties—cogs, mages, gems, and makers—were keeping each other in check, and it was all thanks to Maker Cecily Keays and her partnership with the illusive Robin Renegade.

They certainly were wreaking havoc in every society and on every continent.

Mum leaned forward eagerly. "Is there news of Robin Renegade?" And by extension, Cecily. Mum had taken her departure with surprising equanimity, but the worry lingered over every conversation.

"You've had a letter from Cecily only yesterday. I expect you know more than the papers can tell us."

"I asked about *Robin*. Besides . . . I want to know what other people are saying."

I flipped to the next page and scoffed. "*The Diamond Daily* is turning into a penny dreadful," I answered. "This reporter says Robin Renegade was stalking a helpless mage in the dark with eyes that glowed like a fox."

"Miss Clune surely has made a name for herself."

"She was always meant to be Robin Renegade." I grinned again. "I much prefer to be useless."

Mum gave me one of her deadly serious looks. "I think we both know by now that's a lie. You cared enough for your sister to risk everything. Miss Clune cared for you the same way by claiming to be the Renegade." She sighed and pressed her novel to her chest. "The world is changing so fast. Thank the Maker there are two of you now."

I stared, dumbfounded.

"What? Miss Clune may have conducted magic, but that didn't alter my logic. You still travel to Gallia every other week. No suit coat, however fashionable, warrants a racing ship. Though I am relieved those agents finally stopped watching the house. Did you take my advice?" she asked.

"*Er*—which piece in particular?"

"Did you confess your feelings to Miss Clune before it was too late?"

I carefully folded the paper and returned it to the tray. "She knows the truth," I admitted quietly. But was that enough? Thanks to the magic of her song, I hadn't been able to find her. But she hadn't returned to me either.

Whatever her choice, my locket would always belong to her regardless.

Mum nodded sadly and frowned at the box on the table. "Come to think of it . . . my order isn't due to arrive for another two days." She untied the blue ribbon, lifted the lid, and removed an embossed card from the folds of patterned paper within.

"That's strange . . . the box is empty, and I don't recognize the label . . ." Her eyes widened, and she glanced between me and the card. "I think this is meant for you. *My Dear Hattie Keays*," she read aloud, a smile forming. "*I apologize for my delayed response. I would love nothing more than to accept your kind dinner invitation. On a second point, please inform your son that I am in possession of his missing belongings, and I would be most delighted to call in person to return said belongings at your earliest—* My dear boy, where are you going?"

I was already dashing from the room. "Daweson!"

"Sir?" He peered out from the end of the hallway and recoiled as I skidded to a halt in front of him and grabbed him by the shoulders.

"The box," I demanded. "Who delivered it?"

"I-I don't know. A girl . . . a cog girl. But she was well-dressed."

"What was she wearing?"

"Come to think of it, I thought it odd she was wearing a bowler hat similar to yours."

I left him blinking in confusion as I raced back down the hall.

"She's staying at the Duette Docks, East!" Mum shouted as I passed the tea room. "Bring the girls back for dinner tonight!"

Sweetpea had followed my mad dash into the hall. I leapt over the startled dog, flung open the front door, raced down the steps, and wildly searched the paved walkway.

Both directions were empty.

I jogged to the corner and hailed the first hackney. A sleek, black steam auto pulled up to the curb. The driver got out to assist me, but I'd already let myself inside. "Take me to the Eastern sky docks," I ordered and shut the door behind me.

When the driver didn't immediately return, I leaned forward and peered through the opposite window. A man in a floppy cap had stopped the driver outside.

A melodious voice shouted through the open window behind me. "Stand and deliver all your valuables!"

I finally put the pieces together—highwaymen had stopped me on the street.

I hid my smile and turned.

A beautiful renegade was watching me from the walkway. She leaned casually against the nearest lamppost and tipped her stylish bowler hat in my direction. A dark blue blouson matched her modern split skirt.

I ran a hand over my neck. "Have we been introduced?" I asked.

"We have met, yes."

"Then you should know, I already gave you my greatest treasure."

She kicked off the lamppost, opened the passenger door, and slid inside the auto beside me. I moved to make room, but our knees still touched. Her slender fingers hovered with hesitation before she tenderly combed back my hair and placed the hat onto my head. "I'm sorry I took so long to return this. And to tell you the honest truth. I wanted to make sure we both had a choice. Without the magic and without expectations."

"What honest truth is that?" I asked.

She met my gaze, and her eyes sparkled like sapphires. "Only that I love you, and I want more. I want to be together always."

"May I kiss you?" I whispered against her lips.

"Anytime."

"I'd like to right now."

Someone loudly rapped against the side of the car.

I groaned and buried my head against her shoulder.

"Yes, Ceci?" Audrey called.

Cecily popped her head in through the window. "Did you ask him yet?"

Audrey pinched her lips together, fighting a laugh. "Not yet. We had a couple of things to sort out first."

"Well, we really do need your help, Art. We think the Magicstry plans to infiltrate one of our main manufacturing partners to steal my new designs. You have more connections in Gallia. Oh, but you won't believe what I've come up with this time!"

I grinned. "First, you're coming to dinner. Mum will feed my bones to Sweetpea if I don't bring you home."

"All right, but hurry. We need to plan."

"We'd better listen to her," Audrey said. "You didn't tell me your sister would be so bossy. She and Mae can really get into it. Once Ceci gets an idea into her head, the only person who can convince her differently is Harland."

I frowned out the window. "Harland isn't invited home."

Audrey laughed. She took my hand and dragged me toward the door, but I snatched her around the waist and caught her mouth with mine. Her lips softly parted. She hummed with pleasure and pushed my back to the seat—resolutely pressing our bodies together.

It was useless to fight the honest truth.

I'd been caught by Robin Renegade.

THE END

Acknowledgments

The concept for this book originated from a magic system to explain chronic pain. I grew up on the stage. At the height of my dance career, I rehearsed hours a day and participated in 24-hour charity dance marathons. However, after several injuries, I inexplicably began to lose mobility. In the following years, I was often bedridden. I couldn't dance and was forced to quit every job I started because the intensity of my pain was too overwhelming.

I lived with chronic pain for nearly two decades, but the idea that the pain in my joints was simply excess magic provided a helpful visualization throughout my healing process. Ultimately, my health challenges helped me to stretch, grow, and reach for something higher—the dreams I once thought too fantastical to pursue. I've been ghostwriting and freelancing for years, but it took an embarrassingly long time for me to put my name on the cover of my original work.

In essence, this book marks the beginning of my dream to become a fantasy author. It took me a long time to write, with many changes to the overall structure, but I couldn't give up on Audrey and Art. Thank you to all my friends who supported me along the way.

Nothing in my life would be beautiful without Nat, my dashing airship pirate. Art has nothing on your optimism and romance. You moved across the country with me even before we knew I'd been accepted into my writing program—you believe in me that much. You and Bastien (my love and my joy) deserve all the recognition for your patience and countless sacrifices in support of my writing.

I'm forever grateful to Brandon, Isaac, and the Moth Group for being the first to read this book and for giving me the skills to pursue my dream of becoming a writer.

Thank you to my incredibly supportive beta readers: Nat, Brittany, Aubrey, Anna, Daniel, Dustin, and Emily. *Especially* you, Kiri!

I am so lucky to choose my own publishing team of incredible collaborators—people I genuinely enjoy working with. Thank you, Karen, for your focused and detailed edits. Many thanks to My Lan and Hannah for bringing this story to life. Your artistry is perfection!

And thank you to Nat (again), Brooke, and Martyn for providing a full strategy and business support team.

"I'd never considered that a dream might become a choice."

www.ingramcontent.com/pod-product-compliance
Lightning Source LLC
Chambersburg PA
CBHW030534310726
48979CB00010B/1908/J